**Cassid**

MW01611125

"I have neve

any other story I've read. I felt an ache when Cassidy was hurt, fear when her life was in jeopardy, and happiness when she made it through another day. A solid five star adventure."

— Lindsey Gray, Author of The Redemption Series

"I love classic superhero stories and I have to say – CASSIDY JONES ROCKS!!!"

—Erik, This Kid Reviews Books

"I loved this book so much! And I mean that I really, really love it...I'm a lifetime fan of Elise Stokes."

— Rachel, Rachel's Book Reviews

"Rarely ever have I come across a story that was such a complete and utter joy to read...Cassidy Jones Adventures is, hands down, the best series I've had the pleasure of absorbing."

— Javier A. Robayo, author of *The Gaze*

## Cassidy Jones and the Secret Formula

"Brimful of danger, secrets, a bit of romance and fun, this debut author's entertaining plot and well-drawn characters not only is all it promises to be, but will leave readers looking for more...Highly recommended!"

— Gail Welborn, Examiner

"I was hooked from the beginning...The plot was generally original, the climax was pretty epic, and the story had some complex concepts that were explained incredibly well. Not only that, but Stokes painted vivid pictures in my mind with her fantastic use of imagery..."

— Gabbi, Book Breather

"Everything about this book sucked me in completely… nail-biting action scenes kept the story flowing at a perfect pace, pulling me along on the roller-coaster ride that was Cassidy's life. She was a complete kick-butt heroine who pulled out an arsenal of moves and weapons…"
— Kristin, Better Read Than Dead

## Cassidy Jones and Vulcan's Gift

"Imaginative!—Modern!—Unpredictable! Riddled with delightful characters, magical adventure and a captivating plot, Stokes again captures young reader's attention with another dangerous, action-packed adventure…"
— Gail Welborn, Examiner

"As in her first book, Elise Stokes proves herself to be a master of suspense for tweens and teens with her ability to unfold a mystery with shocking twists and unexpected turns, all the while entertaining the reader with story lines of high school drama, relationships and pending romance…"
— Stephanie Laymon, Five Alarm Book Reviews

"Elise Stokes has done it again…This is by far turning out to be one of the most amazing and well-written, middle grade to young adult series I have ever read…This book has it all, wild adventure, non-stop action, hilarious banter, family value and love, teenage angst, and excitement at every turn…simply stunning and beyond superb!"
— Kitty Bullard, Great Minds Think Aloud

# ELISE STOKES

 AND THE THE SEVENTH ATTENDANT

---

## BOOK THREE

Јᴧᴄᴇ
Publishing LLC.

JACE Publishing LLC,
15600 NE 8th St., Suite B1, 287,
Bellevue, Washington 98008

Edited by William Greenleaf, Greenleaf Literary Services

Cover illustration by Kelly Carter, Mad Spider Studio
Cover design and layout by David C. Cassidy (c) 2013,
davidccassidy.com

ISBN: 978-0-9881851-1-1

Publishing LLC.

*Printed In The United States Of America*

*For my awesome father, Peter*

# Contents

# Prologue

Arthur King Jr. slouched against the concrete wall and tore another page from the Bible in his hand. It had been slipped through the tray slot in the steel door that morning, a gift from a well-meaning prison guard who hoped the message inside would reform Arthur.

"Fat chance of *that*!" Arthur announced loudly to no one in particular, since he was alone in the prison cell, which was a quarter of the size of the walk-in closet at his Seattle home. In fact, the dingy mattress on which his backside was now parked filled half the concrete floor.

"Okay, fellas," he addressed the prison guards who might be listening on the other side of the door. Or maybe they weren't—Arthur really didn't care. "Enough with the *hot box* already," he blathered as he carefully folded the thin paper into an airplane. "Learned my lesson real good. The décor alone is punishment."

He glanced up from his creation to look for a target. The tiny space boasted a stained white toilet, a wall sink, a barred window near the ceiling, and cream-painted walls. Arthur actually didn't mind the blandness of his surroundings. He liked being the only source of color, which he was, in his bright orange jumpsuit.

"Tell your *colleague* that I'm *sorry* for biting his hand," he rambled on, referring to the prison guard he had sunk his teeth into when the man had ordered him to stop griping about the food and move along in the cafeteria line. The assault had landed Arthur in solitary confinement for five days. He was on day two.

Arthur narrowed his eyes on the toilet bowl and took aim. "I promise to be a good boy and eat all of my peas." He launched the airplane, which hit the toilet rim and joined the other planes that had missed the mark on the floor.

Arthur spat a furious cuss word and savagely ripped another sheet from the Bible. "I'm bored, bored, bored, BORED!" he shouted like a petulant child, meticulously folding another plane. "Come on, this is prison! Where's the action?"

As if a prayer had been answered—not that Arthur King Jr. prayed—the alarm sounded.

Arthur straightened up on the mattress. Shouts, screams, and cheers could be heard under the blare of the alarm. When the unmistakable rapid pops from automatic weapons added to the commotion, Arthur eagerly jumped to his feet.

"Yeah, this is more like it," he whooped, pumping his small fist in the air. Gleeful, he listened as the violent ruckus came closer, feeling apprehension only when the screaming and gunfire entered his corridor.

Arthur backed up against the concrete wall and covered his ears, wishing he had been satisfied with *bored*.

The corridor fell silent. Arthur lowered his hands and listened. Footsteps echoed; heels clicked against the concrete. The commotion in the distance again sounded like a battlefield.

The clicking stopped outside his cell door.

"Arthur," a woman's voice sang from the other side, "stay clear of the door."

*BANG!*

Something struck the door with the force of a wrecking ball, denting the steel. Arthur flattened his back to the wall, his heart pounding with a mixture of excitement and fear.

*BANG! BANG!*

The door flew off the hinges and crashed into the wall inches from him. The thrill of nearly being crushed brought a twisted smile to his weasel-like face.

A petite woman stepped into the doorway. She looked like she was made of porcelain, with the palest complexion Arthur had ever seen. Sapphire eyes as cold as glass regarded him from a classically beautiful face framed by ivory curls. Her attire suggested that she was preparing to have tea with the queen of England: a perfectly fitted, high-collared dress in dusty rose, a matching hat rimmed with a two-inch veil, pearl earrings, and lacy white gloves.

Arthur's eyes slid down her delicately formed figure to her shapely calves, which appeared to be made of metal. Metal feet sported dusty rose pumps.

"My eyes are up here," she lightly reprimanded.

Grinning, Arthur looked up into her icy eyes. "Brrrr." He shivered playfully. "Where have you been all my life, gorgeous?"

"Behave," she scolded, peeling the glove off her left hand, which shone with a metallic gleam. "Time to go." She smiled at him sweetly. "Daddy wants you home for dinner."

Throwing back his head, Arthur exploded with laughter.

# One

# What Now?

I paced my bedroom floor as I listened to Emery Phillips shooting the breeze with my dad in our foyer downstairs. I was wringing my hands and sweating bullets—not that anyone can sweat bullets, but with me you never know.

"It isn't like this is a matter of life and death, Emery," I grumbled ironically, because what was headed our way was, indeed, a matter of life and death. Mine for sure, and maybe my family's and Emery's.

*Mom and Dad will freak when they find out, then take me to the hospital, and then some government agency will nab me—if I'm lucky.*

According to Professor Serena Phillips, Emery's mom and the geneticist indirectly responsible for my mutation, there were "depraved individuals who would stop at nothing" to acquire me if my secret were to get out. They might even use my family to get to me. One such individual was Arthur King Sr., Serena's former employer, who was richer than snot, and dead—or so the world believed. Serena said otherwise.

My pace quickened with each dire thought, back and forth like a caged lion—not an inaccurate comparison, considering the animal DNA fused into my cells. Since being infected with a strange retrovirus in Serena's former laboratory at Wallingford University a few months earlier, my changes had not been obvious—until now.

Before today, you would have looked at me and seen a perfectly average five-foot-five-inch redheaded fifteen-year-old girl, hardly anyone who would trigger alarm. Aside from Emery and Serena, no one knew that every living creature on the planet should feel alarmed by me, because if I wasn't careful, I could be downright lethal.

"Especially when you're not in control of your emotions," I sang to myself.

Side effects of the virus included ultra-enhanced senses, super speed and strength, and the ability to learn fight moves just by watching. I could also turn my skin rock-hard and heal rapidly from any injury, which might make me immortal—something I avoided thinking about. I suffered from extreme emotions and the urge to chase down fleeing objects—another thing I avoided thinking about and tried super hard to resist doing.

Needless to say, a red-hot temper and the ability to bend a crowbar with my bare hands did not make an ideal combination, and the fact that I was a teenager didn't help in the emotional department. It definitely made it harder to keep my cool.

*The beast doesn't help matters, either*, I added silently.

"The beast" was what I called the feral side of me—the part that was impulse-driven and acted upon pure animal instinct, the part of me I had to fight back with a mental stick when something set me off. It was exhausting, to say the least. Luckily, over the last couple of months, I'd gotten a better handle on keeping the beast leashed. Fear of exposure, hurting someone, and humiliating myself drove my determination not to go Hulk when I got angry, as did concern that if I released myself completely to savage impulses, Cassidy might be lost for good.

*Which I will never do*, I vowed, and complained at the door, "Oh, Emery, stop talking." Exasperated, I flung it open. "Emery!" I shouted, interrupting my dad midsentence.

He was updating Emery on some news about Stanford University, where the fifteen-year-old-college-graduate genius would have been advancing his degree in molecular biology if my accident hadn't upset his plans.

5

Because Emery tended to shoulder responsibility that wasn't his, he had opted out of California sun and college coeds to masquerade instead as a freshman of average intelligence at Queen Anne High School in perpetually gray Seattle, all to keep an eye on me. If that isn't the ultimate form of selflessness, I don't know what is.

With this in mind, I added more gently, "I'm in my room. Come on up."

Silence. Then Dad called back, "Cassidy, why don't you visit downstairs?"

"I can't," I answered, checking the panic rising in my voice. There wasn't a chance I was leaving my room. "I have to show Emery something—before the boys get here. Come up, Emery!"

"We'll talk more later," Dad told him with displeasure in his voice. I would surely get a talking to later, but maybe not. There would be more pressing matters to discuss once my family got a look at me.

"Excuse me, Mr. Jones," Emery said, sounding none too pleased either.

I shut the bedroom door.

Clasping the doorknob, I fine-tuned my hearing and listened to Emery casually climb the stairs until my dad left the foyer to rejoin Mom, Nate, and our six-year-old brother, Chazz, in the kitchen. Then he began skipping steps. I smiled with satisfaction at his sense of urgency, even though I knew he had felt it the entire time he was talking with my dad. Emery was a skilled actor and very good at hiding what he didn't want anyone to see. It was difficult to tell what was going on in his head most of the time, especially since his IQ was likely pretty high.

Before Emery could knock, I threw the door open, grabbed him by the collar, and yanked him into my room, slamming the door behind us.

"Your parents," he protested, catching his stumble.

6

"Too bad you don't worry more about *appearances* at school," I fired back, locking the door.

All was innocent between Emery and me, a fact he made abundantly clear to my mom and dad. Other than them, he couldn't care less about what anyone thought was or was not going on between us.

"Soon *everyone* will know the truth anyway, because there's no hiding these." I whipped around to give him the shock of his life.

Relief flooded Emery's face. "They haven't changed."

"*What?* Are you blind?"

"They haven't changed, Cassidy."

"Look!" I demanded, stomping my foot, something I swear I hadn't done since I was, like, six.

Emery's expression became stern. "Calm down," he ordered, enunciating each word as if this would make me behave. Usually when he tried to pull the parental stuff on me, it had the opposite effect. But since I was desperate for him to either acknowledge what was plain as day or tell me it was all my imagination—which I prayed like crazy it was—I obliged.

"Look," I requested. "Closely."

Humoring me, Emery clamped my jaw between his hands and wheeled us toward the window, tilting my face up to his utterly gorgeous one. He was six feet tall, solid build, with intelligent black eyes and black hair emphasized by a milky complexion and features on the edge of being described as "chiseled."

*He looks more like his dad every day,* I thought as he scrupulously studied my eyes in the natural light, shifting my head to different angles.

Emery's father was the handsomest and scariest man I had ever met. Lucky for me, the last time he had been home, I was conveniently at my Grandma and Grandpa Anthony's for Christmas. Good thing, because I had been preparing to leave the country when I heard he would be home for the holidays. Mr. Phillips handles finances for various corporations in China, or so he said. I said he was full of it, and dangerous. This was what my gut told me, anyway, and my gut is rarely wrong.

Pulling my face closer, Emery exhaled a warm, fragrant breath that swept up my nostrils, making me feel a little rummy. Smell affects me in crazy ways, and Emery smelled the way he looked: good.

"Every girl I know would be envious right now," I told him.

"Look left," he instructed.

"Of course, being looked at like I'm under a microscope sort of kills the romance."

"What I observe under a microscope usually isn't so chatty. Now look right. And if I were being romantic, this isn't the way I would go about it."

"And if I wasn't so stressed, I'd ask exactly how you'd go about it. Well? What's the verdict?"

"Now look at me."

My stomach sank. Emery was avoiding my question.

I met his serious gaze, silently confirming what I already knew. My eye color had changed. "No!"

Emery reached out to grab me, but got an armful of air. Already at the dresser, I leaned toward the mirror and stared at the horror looking back at me: round, vibrant, *jade*-colored eyes.

"The color change is slight," Emery reassured me, catching up with me at the dresser.

"Slight? They're jade. Have you *ever* seen eyes this color? What am I going to do?"

"Your voice," Emery warned, gripping my shoulders. "There's nothing to do. *No one* will notice, other than you. Just like the freckles."

"Thanks for bringing that up!"

The morning after I was infected with the retrovirus, the faint spray of freckles on my nose had vanished, along with

8

a gash on my forehead—both healed due to "rapid cell regeneration." This phenomenon had also reformed my windpipe after Arthur King Jr.'s ninja had crushed it with nunchucks and then jumpstarted my dead heart. It might also have made me immortal.

"Look at my skin!" I manically motioned to my face, unable to peel my gaze from my freakish eyes. "Flawless! Every inch of me looks like plastic, like a mannequin."

"Calm down," Emery insisted, but I couldn't do that. How could I? Secretly being different was tolerable, but *looking* different—not even close.

"Emery, I don't look real. Look at me. It's like I'm airbrushed—or a drawing from a comic book. How appropriate!"

Emery spun me around to him. "Enough with the hysterics," he ordered, ducking his face toward mine, trying to force me to look at him.

I glared at his shoes, resisting his efforts, and bit my lip hard as I fought back tears. I hated crying. I hated my life.

"Cassidy, do you trust me?"

I jerked a nod. The motion sent hot tears streaming down my face. I did trust Emery, I truly did. How could I not trust my protector, confidant, and best friend? He had put his life on hold for me. I was just afraid this would prove to be one of those rare instances when he was wrong.

"No one will notice," he repeated.

"What if it gets worse?" I choked out. "What if my pupils change—into slits, like a cat's? You already said my eyes don't blink when I'm concentrating." Serena's Formula 10X, which had started this whole thing, had been heavy on feline DNA.

"It won't, and they won't," Emery assured me without a hint of doubt, something I could rarely accomplish, since doubt was my middle name.

"How do you know? You didn't see *this* coming." I concentrated on his Nikes and willed my armor to come up. I

9

felt the rippling sensation move over my body, then thickness and numbness. If one of Arthur King's ninjas were to punch me now, he'd break his hand.

"True," Emery admitted, not loosening his grip, or maybe he had. It was difficult to tell when my skin was hard like this.

"And imprinting. That was a shocker."

*Imprinting* was what Emery called my ability to perform a fight move after observing it. Even I had to admit, this was a very cool skill to have.

"Yes, it was," Emery agreed, and then feigned a suspicious look. "Are you *trying* to make me jealous? 'Cause ya know I think your armor and sick ninja skills are *da bomb*."

Despite myself, I smiled. Emery sounded ridiculous talking his age and knew it. As part of his average teenager act, he muddled his perfect diction with slang words for those unaware that he was a brainiac, which was everyone I knew except my family and Ben Johnson, Dad's cameraman for his news show, *In the Spotlight*. They thought Emery's decision to attend high school was an attempt to regain his lost childhood.

"Slanguage always works, especially the oldies but goodies," Emery teased, referring to the fact that when he really wanted to make me laugh, he used slang terms our parents or grandparents would have used when they were our age. He seemed to have an endless reserve, as if he had memorized the Urban Dictionary.

"Not always."

"*Au contraire, ma beauté*. You become putty in my hands." He hooked my chin with a finger and tried to nudge it up, which would have been impossible for even a crane to do if I so chose.

"Stop," I said, swatting his hand away. "This is serious."

"Absolutely. You wanted me to look at you, so let me. Scout's honor, I'll give you an honest opinion."

"Don't be lame." I looked up into his sparkling black orbs, smiling.

Pursing his lips, Emery pinched his chin between his thumb and forefinger and pretended to study me. "Honest opinion," he said. "I see a very attractive redhead with a too-cute nose, a *to-die-for* complexion, and big, beautiful *green* eyes." Swiping a finger across my cheek, he added, "Minus the black tears, of course." He flipped over his finger, now caked with gooey mascara.

Instantly, my woes were forgotten.

"You gotta be kidding me!" I huffed. "That's supposed to be waterproof."

Emery busted up. I spun to the mirror to a truly horrific sight. It looked like my eyelashes had melted and were running down my cheeks.

*And Jared will be here anytime.*

"Must we always have a crisis?" Emery sighed when he finished laughing. He kicked back on my bed and grinned at the sight of me scrubbing the mascara off my face with a sock I had swiped from the floor. It was probably clean.

"Make yourself comfortable," I retorted, barely resisting the urge to spit on the sock. The mascara clung stubbornly to my skin. "This is more like crisis diverted. Who's going to notice my eye color if I can't get this stupid stuff *off?*"

"Frankly, an even better diversion is what you're wearing. A birthday gift?"

I paused while scrubbing my skin raw to glance down and admire my new black yoga pants and tank top with a cool lavender stripe slashed across the front. I had even painted my toenails lavender to match.

"A birthday gift from me," I confirmed proudly before resuming my task. "I bought it with my mom last night. Good thing I have a *job*."

My job was a sham, like everything else in my life. Supposedly I cleaned house for Serena weekdays and Saturday afternoons. In actuality, she ran a battery of tests on me in her basement laboratory where she secretly studied my virus, fostering the slim hope of an eventual vaccine. Emery's role was lab technician. He drew my blood two to three times a week. So we weren't being totally deceptive, I did some housework for Serena, which she paid me for—generously—calculating in my lab rat duties, too, I supposed.

"Happy birthday, by the way," Emery offered, fiddling with his cell phone.

"Yeah, a real happy birthday. I'm a fifteen-year-old mutant with spooky eyes."

"Beautiful eyes," he corrected, scrolling through email. "Just remember to blink."

I barked a cynical laugh. "Thanks for reminding me that I'm a freak and my eyes are already cat-ish. So what do you think? Do you like it?"

"Your latest purchase?"

"Yep." I watched him in the mirror as he looked me over.

"Very much."

I beamed.

"Now change into sweats and a T-shirt."

My smile flipped. "What? Why?"

"Because I won't be the only one who likes your outfit," he said, returning to his email.

I got what he was driving at and turned back to the mirror to see my cheeks burning crimson. To cover my embarrassment, I began scrubbing the mascara again.

"You really don't understand the inner workings of the teenage male mind, do you?" Emery continued. He didn't embarrass easily, unlike me.

"I assume you're going to enlighten me?"

"No, you've been traumatized enough for one day. Just take my word on it. We're a reprehensible lot. If you understood to what degree, you'd grab your baggiest sweat clothes and run to the bathroom to change."

"*Or* I could kick you out of my room."

"That's always an option."

"You're not serious, are you? Yoga pants and a tank top? Yeah, real risqué—" I stopped short, my ears picking up what I had subconsciously been waiting for: Jared Wells. By the frequency of his voice, I guessed he was coming up our front walk.

My heart shifted into high gear, which would be a normal heart rate for the average human. An extremely healthy heart meant one that didn't have to work so hard.

"Oh, man!" I said, forgetting decorum and spitting on the sock. I had to get the mascara off.

"I'll pretend I didn't see that," Emery said. "I'm assuming my students have arrived."

His students were boys from school who met Saturday or Sunday mornings for Fight Club, as they called it. It had been Nate's inspiration after their soccer games got rained out in the beginning of January a few weeks ago. Emery had become their natural instructor, since he was the most skilled in martial arts—or so they all thought. I was more Chuck Norris than Emery. Heck, I was more Chuck Norris than Chuck Norris.

"Yes, Sensei," I answered, finally getting my face clean. I dropped the sock on the floor and grabbed the mascara tube to reapply.

"You always were one to tempt fate," Emery teased.

The doorbell rang. Anxiously, I swiped mascara on my lashes.

"Isn't that the part of your face you *don't* want to bring attention to?"

"Are you now saying my eyes are spooky?" I challenged, painstakingly brushing the wand over my lower lashes. Those were always so hard to get.

"Dudes!" Nate, my twin brother, answered the door. Their voices were like a crashing wave—in other words, loud.

"No, I stand by beautiful," said Emery. "But either way, it won't be your eyes they're looking at."

"My friend," I said, moving the wand to my other eye as the boys clambered up the stairs, "if I wasn't trying to beautify myself, I'd kick your butt."

Nate drummed my door. "Cass! Em! Fight Club!" he shouted.

"No duh!" I yelled back, my stomach twisted into knots. Knowing Jared was just on the other side of my door made me feel like hurling. My nerves calm down after talking to him a bit—usually.

"I'll meet you up there," Emery told me as he rose from the bed. "Up there" was our attic, the perfect place for some friendly sparring.

"'Kay," I replied, tapping bubblegum-scented gloss on my lips. I hated the taste and smell, but it looked nice.

"Don't take too long beautifying—" Emery's cell rang. He glanced at the screen and answered the call. "Hi, Riley."

I rubbed my well-glossed lips together and smiled. Bail bond agent Riley was Emery's former college mate, current employer, and a redhead—a very hot one, I suspected. I didn't know for sure, since I hadn't met her yet. Every time I queried Emery about her looks, he just laughed, confirming that his boss was, indeed, hot. Why else would he avoid answering the question?

"Say hi to Riley for me," I sang softly, opening my door.

Emery nodded, but didn't comply. Instead he pointed at my hoodie on the floor, wanting me to cover up. I really wished he would give it a break.

"You're like my dad," I whispered.

He shrugged, his finger on the hoodie.

I rolled my eyes, which reminded me of my new problem. *Are you sure?* I mouthed, pointing at my eyes.

Emery gave me the *A-OK* sign, saying to Riley, "Employment records should turn that up."

14

*They're discussing a client who didn't show for court*, I deduced, which meant the client was now a fugitive. Emery did skip tracing for Riley, which meant he located possible places where a fugitive might be holing up by searching credit card reports, phone records, and whatever else he could dig up—or *hack into*—online. Once he located the fugitive's whereabouts, Riley sent her bounty hunters— Mickey, Marky, and Marty—to track down her delinquent client. I had never met them, either, though I did glimpse Mickey once—burly, red Mohawk, leather and tats, thin scar across the right side of his freckled face like a slash from a knife blade . . .

Emery cleared his throat to get my attention. He tapped his ear, signaling me to stop eavesdropping on his conversation.

I smirked, because he was so wrong. My ears weren't nosing around his business—this time.

"Have fun." I winked at him to throw him off and then left him to continue his conversation with his hottie.

## Two

# Boys Will Be Boys

*D*arn it, *Emery*. I hesitantly climbed the attic stairs, listening to the boys hassle one another, breathing in their scents, and feeling very self-conscious about what I was wearing. *Yoga pants and a tank. Big deal. Why'd you have to make me all insecure about something so stupid?*

Part of me suspected Emery had intentionally undermined my confidence. He hadn't been exactly thrilled about my reconciliation with Jared, viewing him as a potential threat in regard to my secret.

Jared was smart, but not *that* smart. In a million years it wouldn't have crossed his mind to think, *Ah-ha! Cassidy Jones is a mutant.* Despite Emery's qualms, I owed Jared an apology, so an apology is what he had gotten. Rekindling our friendship was the natural result, and we were *just* friends—frustratingly. Whatever romantic feelings he'd had for me prior to the horrendous 210 days that we weren't speaking had definitely evaporated. But I had my friend back, so I should be happy. Right?

Before going up the last few steps, I smoothed out my ponytail and my lip gloss with a finger, while rolling my eyes at Bobby Neigh's bragging about his latest romantic conquest. The guy was so full of himself. Taking a deep breath, I dismissed the idea that my outfit was anything other than totally cute and patted my stomach to calm the butterflies fluttering about. I continued up the stairs, sporting a manufactured smirk.

"Hey, gossips," I said in greeting. The boys congregating on the sofa side of the attic looked at me. "You're like a bunch of old women."

The cut received much approval. Amid the "oohs," the laughter, and "takes one to know one," Bobby demanded, "Dude, what did you hear?"

"Everything, *dude*," I quipped, my eyes avoiding Jared. "But nothing worth repeating."

Nate grinned with pride at the slam.

"Burn!" a few boys shouted as I strode toward them. I worked up the nerve to peek at Jared. Tousled, dirty-blond hair; perfect nose; rounded jaw; expressive, soulful, chocolate-brown eyes fringed with thick black lashes; sculpted lips; and a smile that started real slow at the corners of his scrumptious mouth. *Heavenly,* I sighed inwardly, careful to mask my succulent eyeful of Jared.

"Birthday noogies!" Bobby shouted, and before I knew what was happening, the big oaf had me in a headlock. If Jared's beauty hadn't enraptured me, there's no way I would have missed Bobby launching his stringy body off the sofa.

"Bobby," I growled. I fought the urge to sink my fingers into his mop of brown curls and flip him—a move Nate's wannabe-Kung-Fu-master-twin-who-could-hardly-throw-a-punch wouldn't know, let alone be able to perform.

"One," Bobby jovially counted, scraping knuckles across my scalp and messing up my hair.

"What are you, five?" I snarled through my teeth, mentally beating down the beast. "You were even a pain back then."

"I love you, *tooooo*." His knuckles grated again.

"Okay, Bobby," Jared said while the other boys snickered, deepening my humiliation. I could only imagine how ridiculous this looked.

*Enough!* I jammed my heel into Bobby's foot.

"Dang!" he yelped, letting me go.

I whipped around and shoved him, though not as hard as I wanted to.

Laughing like an imbecile, he lost balance and fell on top of Nate on the sofa. Nate enveloped Bobby in his arms and made loud kissing noises. My brother wasn't one to pass up on an opportunity to harass anyone.

"You wish!" Bobby shouted, flipping over on Nate and yelling the next genius inspiration to strike his pubescent mind: "Twin noogy!" Within a second, ten boys were piled on the sofa, noogying my brother.

"Animals," I shouted and dropped down on my backside, yanking the scrunchie from my disheveled hair—and I'd had it *perfect*!

"Just so you know," Jared said, scooting up next to me, "I was about to rescue you."

"Why are my heroes always *almost*?" I combed frustrated fingers through my hair. Being placed in a headlock by an overgrown child had embarrassed the nervousness right out of me.

Jared chuckled.

I shot him a sidelong glance and recognized another reason why I shouldn't feel embarrassed. *Buddy* was practically written on his face. *No secret crush, no unrequited love, just friends*. I sighed and gave up on my hair. What did it matter anyway? Friends don't care how your hair looks.

"Maybe I should get a hose?" Jared suggested, grinning as his friends made complete idiots of themselves.

"Tell me, why is it the more of you there are in a room, the more your IQs plummet?" I asked as I gathered tangled locks to the back of my head.

Jared forced a vacant expression. "Huh?"

"Funny." I turned to him, smiling, my hair in a messy ponytail. He smiled back, looking me fully in the face. I recalled my jade-green freakazoids and quickly looked away. *Better not let anyone get a close look at these babies*, I

18

thought, directing my eyes to the boys, who were pushing, shoving, and laughing their heads off. You would think they had mutant in them, too.

Emery appeared at the top of the stairs. No surprise to me, since I had heard and smelled him coming.

"Dudes," he said to the boys, palms up. "Do I need to get a hose?"

"Ha!" I punched the lean muscle of Jared's upper arm. You didn't have to see him play sports to know he was a stellar athlete. "That's what you said."

A hose turned out to be unnecessary. With sensei present, the boys disengaged on their own and migrated to the workout side of the attic, which featured an extra large gymnastic mat, treadmill, and exercise balls that they couldn't resist kicking at one another.

Nate strolled across the attic, his dark red hair sticking up every which way after having been properly noogied, apparently pleased with the good licks he had gotten in, too. He, Chazz, and I shared the hair color of our mom, Elizabeth, as well as her wide-set eyes and fair complexion. We all had the same eye color, too—up until about ten hours ago, that is. Our dad, Drake, was the odd one out, with golden blond hair, crystal blue eyes, and a million-dollar smile. He looked every bit the successful newscaster he was.

Emery led us through warm-ups. As we were wrapping them up, the attic door at the bottom of the stairs opened.

I heard Chazz running up the stairs. "Guys, more friends are here."

My little brother appeared, decked out in his Captain America costume. Trevor Young and Chad Dunham followed him. Trevor definitely qualified as a friend, but Chad was a friend only to himself, and a fair-weather one to his stuck-up friends at best. I hadn't actually talked to him before, being neither conceited nor popular nor mean enough to register on his radar. In other words, I wasn't Robin Newton or one of her remoras.

19

*How to describe Chad?* I mused, observing his deep dimples and brown hair that I suspected he had put as much time into styling that morning as I had mine. He and Trevor approached us. Captain America went back downstairs.

*Chad Dunham... Looks like a god but as shallow as a mud puddle. Oh wait, even better: Looks like a god but as shallow as the mirror he spends hours gazing into.*

I smiled to myself. That was a good one.

"Dudes." Trevor gave Nate a high five. "Hope it's cool Chad came with."

Chad shot Trevor a look that said, *Need you ask?* His haughty baby blues cut to Emery. "What form are you doing?" he asked, crossing his arms all superior like. His muscles flexed. I caught a snicker and heard Nate call Chad a name under his breath that also adequately described him.

"Nothing specific," Emery replied, looking bored, which likely wasn't an act. Chad was a yawn a minute. "What form are you into?"

"Taekwondo," Chad said, too full of himself to have picked up on the fact that Emery didn't give a rip. He strutted to the center of the mat and bent his hand back in a *come* gesture. "Who's first?"

A laugh shot up my throat. I masked it with a cough.

There were no volunteers, partially because Chad was too lame for words, and partially because some of the boys were afraid of him.

"Not how we do things, Chad." Nate said his name like it had a bad taste.

Disregarding my brother, Chad looked smugly at Emery. "Phillips?"

*Yes*, I thought, rubbing my palms together. *A much-needed humbling will be delivered shortly.*

"I'll pass," Emery replied dryly.

Chad had the nerve to make a chicken sound.

"I'll do it," I spoke up. Humiliating Chad might not be worth Emery's time, but it was worth mine. Who did he think he was, waltzing in here and ruining our fun?

Surprise crossed Chad's face, followed by laughter.

From the corner of my eye, I saw Jared push past Zach Guzman, probably lowering himself and volunteering to fight Chad now that I had. I jumped to my feet and ran for the mat, skidded to a stop in front of Chad, and bowed.

He laughed harder.

"Cassidy," Emery cautioned.

I gave him the *A-OK* sign to show it was cool. My temper was in check. I was totally in control. The jerk would be perfectly safe, once I knocked him on his rear.

"Don't worry, Phillips," Chad said, grinning at me. "I'll go easy on your girlfriend."

"I am *not* his girlfriend," I corrected.

At the same time, Nate said, "See that you do, Dunham, or I'll kick your ass."

Chad smirked at us both.

I smirked back at him. *Just desserts are on their way.*

"I'll go easy on you," Chad promised, giving me the dimples. *Translation: I'm taking you out swiftly, silly girl.*

No sooner had we bowed than Chad swung his leg at me in a roundhouse kick. Instantly, my vision adjusted, and I saw his foot coming at me in slow motion. My skin hardened as my brain registered a potential threat. If his foot connected with me, it would be like kicking a block of cement.

*How predictable,* I thought, and swept Chad's other foot out from underneath him. He hit the mat hard, knocking the wind out of him.

After a moment of stunned silence, cheers erupted, hands slapped in high fives, and Chad was mercilessly razzed. He appeared to hear none of it as he lay on the mat, blinking up at the ceiling.

*A bruised ego is a tragic thing*, I thought smugly, bending over him. Ponytail dangling, I smiled down at him and offered my hand. "Want some help?"

Chad stared at me as if he had never seen me before.

*Three*

# Daddy's Home

---

After Fight Club, Emery and I went across the street to his house. I was going to do housework for Serena.

"Does Chad think he's God's gift or what?" I remarked at the Phillipses' front door, watching Chad strut down the street. "Just look at him."

"I think I'll pass," Emery replied as he unlocked the door. "I must admit, Dunham handled defeat better than I had anticipated." In other words, Chad had kept his mouth shut and played nicely, stealing occasional glances at me, the girl who had proven he wasn't all that.

Emery pushed the door open and stepped aside so I could go in first. We headed down the hall of his Victorian home to the basement where Serena had created a makeshift laboratory.

"Hey, Serena," I said as we descended the stairs.

Her doe-brown eyes glanced up from the microscope. Surrounding the microscope was a variety of glass vessels, some containing liquid substances; scattered lab equipment and glass slides smeared with who-knows-what; dirty coffee mugs, wadded paper napkins, and food-encrusted plates that were a science experiment in and of themselves. There were probably all kinds of microscopic nasties crawling on them.

Bottom line, Serena was the messiest person I knew, and her appearance reflected her untidiness. Wrinkled lab coat, straight brown hair pulled back in a sloppy bun, and an ink smudge on the tip of her nose, which was actually sort of cute. Her perpetually disheveled appearance, heart-shaped face, fair skin, and petite figure gave her an elfin look.

23

"Happy birthday, my dear," she returned, smiling. Her expression was warm, which wasn't always the case. Serena had a Dr. Jekyll and Mr. Hyde personality. Jekyll was caring, consoling, and motherly, where clinical Hyde gave me a strong desire to take inventory of her scalpels.

"Thank you." I approached Serena. The slide under the microscope screen was dotted with blood—my blood, or some animal's. In addition to studying my virus and developing a vaccine to combat it, Serena was also trying to recreate her experimental gene therapy, Formula 10X.

Arthur King Jr.'s henchman, Raul Diaz, had set fire to her previous laboratory, destroying the data for her secret formula. Being a little old-fashioned, Serena had stubbornly not kept backups on her computer—something she regretted dearly, as did I. If she had saved her files, I might be cured today.

Formula 10X had been comprised of animal DNA and a biological weapon called Assassin, which Serena had been developing for the military sixteen years ago before she closed the program down, having decided it was too dangerous.

The Assassin "catalyst," as Serena called it, had birthed the virus that I was infected with—an unnerving thought, considering what it had been designed to do: spread rapidly from person to person, without displaying symptoms, until it made contact with its target's DNA. Upon exposure, the target would have less than an hour to live before the virus liquefied his or her organs.

*Guess that's one thing to be thankful for*, I thought. *The virus likes me and plans to keep me around for a long, long time . . .*

To Serena, I hinted, "So are you giving me the ultimate birthday gift?"

Serena took the question literally. "I wouldn't call it the *ultimate*. However, it is a gift a girl your age will appreciate, according to the saleswoman—"

My face heated up over the misunderstanding. I would never ask someone if they had gotten me a present.

"I didn't sense she was deceiving me," Serena went on, oblivious. Emery grinned to himself as he opened a drawer on the steel cart that held syringes. "But one never knows with these salesgirls—"

"S-Serena," I fumbled, embarrassed beyond belief.

She stopped and waited for me to continue. Emery chuckled as he prepared a syringe.

"I was asking if you found a *cure*, not if you bought me a present—but thank you. I'm very, uh, touched that you thought of me."

"You're welcome." She stared at my red-stained cheeks with fascination as she always does when I blush. "But what an odd question. No, I have not found a cure. As I have told you, the likelihood of success is abysmal—"

"I know, I know. It's like finding a needle in a haystack high as Mount Rainier."

"Mom, look at Cassidy's eyes," Emery chimed in. I supposed this was his way of changing the subject, though it was a topic I would have preferred to avoid. If anything was going to make Serena go all Hyde, it was a new mutant anomaly.

However, just like a Phillips, Serena did the opposite of what I had anticipated.

She pulled my face down to hers and studied my eyes. "Interesting," was her only comment. Releasing my face, she made a beeline for her desk.

"What's interesting?" I asked. Emery hadn't even hinted at what to look for. "The color? Did you notice the green is, like, jade now?"

"Jade is an adequate description," she said by way of reply as she wrote in her Mutant Girl journal. No problems with interpretation, though. She had noticed the color change.

But what did it mean?

25

"Serena, is this something I should worry about?"

"No," Emery answered for her. "Come on, Cassidy. Let's get on with this. Your mom will be taking you and your friends to have your nails done soon." He grinned. "Believe it or not, that is the first time I have said that in my entire life."

"Having your nails done?" I said absently, distracted by Serena. "What do you think she's writing?" I asked Emery as I slipped off my coat and sat on the exam table.

"Your guess is as good as mine," he said lightly. He tied the tourniquet on my arm.

I frowned, because that so wasn't the case. Emery had a very good guess about what his mom had written. He just didn't want to tell me.

"After I transcribe her notes tonight, I'll text you relevant details," he whispered.

My scowl deepened, because he would do no such thing. I was on a need-to-know-basis about the microbes that had invaded my body, and as far as Emery and Serena were concerned, I needed to know very little.

Emery removed the tourniquet. I concentrated on keeping my skin from reacting and hardening as he slid the hypodermic needle into a bulging vein. I hated needles.

Hunched over, I watched the tube fill with blood and fumed about being treated like a child. *Don't I have a right to know everything? It is my body—*

My senses abruptly sharpened. I heard footsteps on the front porch and straightened with alarm.

"Someone's here," I said. "On your porch, I mean."

"Mom, will you answer—"

"The door is opening!"

Emery and Serena's heads snapped to one another like the ends of a rubber band.

"Dad," Emery said at the same time Serena said, "Your father."

My blood ran cold. *Mr. Phillips cannot be here!*

Emery pulled the needle from my arm, and he and Serena kicked into high gear, hiding evidence wherever they could cover or stash it. Problem was, where were they going to stash me?

"Cassidy, get up," Emery ordered in a whisper. Terrified, I hopped down from the most incriminating piece of evidence in the room: a medical exam table.

*It's not totally inconceivable that a geneticist would have an exam table in her lab*, I assured myself as I listened to Mr. Phillips walk past the stairs to the kitchen. "He's in the kitchen," I warned, apparently too loudly, because Emery and Serena shushed me.

"Dishes," Emery commanded, motioning to Serena's lab table.

I hustled to the table and swiftly stacked the dirty dishes. *Good cover. I am being paid to keep things tidy*, I thought. The basement door opened, and I almost dropped the stack of dishes I was in the midst of picking up.

"Serena, Emery," Mr. Phillips called.

My stomach plunged. Man, he scared the bejeezus out of me.

Serena stared at me. "Gavin?" Her next reaction was completely unexpected. Her face lit with unadulterated joy, and she sang—yes, sang, "You're home!"

Mr. Phillips came bounding down the stairs, and Serena ran to meet him. He swept her off her feet and turned her in a full circle, kissing her. It was the hottest, most romantic thing I had ever witnessed.

"Dad," Emery said, beaming.

My throat tightened as I watched Emery join them. I had never seen him or Serena so happy before, and this made me happy. The six-foot-four-inch mountain of a man placed his tiny wife on her feet and gathered his son into his hulking arms.

"How are ya, Tiger?" Mr. Phillips said to Emery, squeezing him in a big hug.

A laugh escaped me, and I covered my smile with my free hand, soaking in the scene. Emery had a nickname. How sweet was that?

Mr. Phillips looked over Emery's shoulder at me. The grin disappeared from my face.

"Hello, Cassidy," he greeted with a friendly smile, releasing Emery from the embrace. He seemed genuinely pleased to see me.

I drummed up another smile, wrestling with my memory of him and the man before me now. "I'm fine, Mr. Phillips, thanks. Welcome home."

I truly meant it in that moment. Emery and Serena were so happy. How could anyone who made them this happy be all bad?

"Thank you, Cassidy." Mr. Phillips pulled his family to him, one on each side. "It's good to be home."

"Well," I said brightly, "I'll let you all visit then. I've got dishes to do upstairs. See you later." With that, I made my retreat.

~~~

While rinsing and stacking dishes in the dishwasher, I ruminated over what had terrified me about Mr. Phillips the last time I'd seen him. He was totally intense and watched me like he thought I was going to steal something. *Well, duh,* I reasoned. *His wife and son decide to move to this rental the same day they're rescued from Junior. Who wouldn't be suspicious?* Then Serena had left her cushy Wallingford University position to do research in her basement, and Emery turned down Stanford University to go to high school. His excuse? "I have a crush on the girl across the street." Yeah, that made sense. Mr. Phillips must have thought his family was taking crazy pills. No wonder he acted crazy himself . . .

*But what about his appearance when he finally did make it home last time?* another part of my mind countered. He had looked beaten up, and he had lied that he had fallen down airplane steps. Obviously he had escaped from someone, someone who probably worked for Junior. Then Junior had talked about Mr. Phillips like he knew him, and the thought that Emery's dad was coming for him terrified him.

*Of course they know one another.* I palmed my forehead, feeling like I was seeing the situation clearly for the first time. When the military had contracted Serena to develop Assassin, she was working for Arthur King Sr. She hadn't met Junior prior to his kidnapping her, but that didn't mean her husband didn't know him—

I froze, hearing someone coming up the basement stairs. I knew the sound of Emery and Serena's footsteps, and these weren't theirs. My stomach knotted, and I started scrubbing the chili-encrusted saucepan harder, regretting my polite decision not to listen in. Due to that decision, I was clueless about why Emery's father had come home. Last I had heard, he wasn't due back until early spring.

The door creaked open. My sponge moved faster over the pan, and I whistled to give the impression that I was unaware of Mr. Phillips's presence. Why I felt the need to deceive him, I can't say.

He cleared his throat. I feigned being startled and splashed water over the front of my shirt.

"Oh, sorry about that," he said good-naturedly. "Usually people hear a big lug like me coming from a mile away."

I swallowed the lump in my throat and croaked out a laugh, casting a cautious glance over my shoulder. His expression was as amicable as his tone.

"No worries. You just startled me," I fibbed as he came closer. Another fib slipped out before I could stop it. "Plus, I'm a total klutz."

"You and me both," he lied.

Mr. Phillips opened the pantry and frowned, probably at how empty it was.

"Um, I didn't know you were coming home," I ventured, trying to sound easygoing. I think it worked.

"That's because Emery and his mom didn't know." He moved to the refrigerator. "I wanted to surprise them." He pulled the door open and groaned, "Serena."

"I know," I commiserated. The shelves were occupied by a few straggling condiments, a carton of milk, and a couple of take-out containers that probably contained more mold than food. They had been in there for a while. "They have the worst diets. You'd think a couple of geneticists would take the food pyramid more seriously. Emery won't eat anything fresh. I have to force him to eat an apple."

Mr. Phillips laughed. "You managed to get him to eat an apple? I'm impressed and humbled. Never could get that kid to do anything he didn't want to do."

"He is stubborn," I agreed, causing Mr. Phillips to laugh again. "If you're hungry, there are TV dinners in the freezer."

"Don't I know," he replied with distaste. He shut the refrigerator door. "Looks like I'm off to the grocery store. I'll pick up a few apples now that I know Emery has met his match."

He winked at me and turned to go, and I had to wonder why I had never noticed how cool he was before.

I sighed. *I'm ridiculous. Why did I get wigged out about him last time? He's a nice guy.* Shaking my head at my overactive imagination, I put some real force into scrubbing the pan.

*Four*

# Like Father, Like Son

Mom treated Miriam Cohen, Bren Dawson, Carli Cooper, and me to manicures, while Dad and Ben took Nate, Jared, Emery, Bobby, and Chazz to play laser tag. The plan was to meet at our house for pizza and cake afterward.

If my mom had suggested doing manicures on my last birthday, I doubt I would have been very enthused. I'd just gotten into the girlie stuff lately, but the manicure was a blast, and I couldn't stop grinning as the nail technician pressed glittery star decals onto my perfectly filed, aqua-blue fingertips. My nails had never looked so smashing.

My friends chose color combinations that suited their personalities. Miriam went with hot pink polish and red lip decals. Carli chose bright yellow polish and rainbow smiley faces. And Bren couldn't resist the snarling bulldogs, which looked awesome against gunmetal gray.

The guys arrived home before us. As we came through the front door, talking a million miles a minute, I instinctively took a scent inventory: pizza, Dad, Ben, the boys, Serena, and Mr. Phillips were all here. Laughing and chatting, we entered the kitchen, running into Emery first. The others were helping themselves to pizza and salad at the island in our very white kitchen that my mom was a slave to. She spent countless hours keeping it perfectly clean.

"Emery, check it out." I showed off my nails, wiggling my fingers so the decals caught the light.

He studied them and remarked, "They're very . . . reflective."

"Reflective?" I laughed. Emery sure knew how to give a compliment.

"You should've heard the lady complain about them," Bren said. She pushed her straightened, espresso-colored hair back from her dark face and cleared her throat. "Li'l gul," she said, imitating the woman who had done my nails, "you dwink *too* mush meelk. Deez nalls ah like dwagonz—"

"You're so mean!" Carli cut her off, giving tiny Bren a good-natured bop on the head. Bren yanked Carli's long blond hair in return. Everything about Carli was long—hair, arms, legs, fingers, feet. Only now were the boys in our class finally catching up to her in height.

"Well, that's what she said!" Bren insisted. "Cass has 'dwagonz' nails."

Emery looked at me, chuckling. Though his expression was carefree, his eyes were assessing. I smiled to let him know all was well. So my nails had become rather thick? Minor compared to my other mutant anomalies. I was just relieved no one had noticed my eyes today, not even my mom, who was the only person who had noticed when my freckles had vanished. She had chalked up the disappearing act to getting older.

Miriam, who had been uncharacteristically quiet, bulldozed in, shoving her hands in Emery's face. "I thought of you when I chose these," she said flirtatiously, fluttering her fingers and eyelashes.

"Thank you," he said with his easy grin. The grin masked discomfort. Emery didn't know how to take Miriam. Most boys didn't.

"Anytime." She winked a sparkling cobalt-blue eye and gave her silky black curls a calculated shake.

Emery laughed, not knowing what else to do. Miriam laughed, too, delighting in the knowledge that she had made the boy she was enamored with feel awkward. Miriam was a complex creature.

32

"Let's eat," Carli suggested cheerfully, shoving me toward the island. "Birthday girl first."

I noticed a free chair next to Jared at the table and didn't protest. I slapped a slice of pepperoni pizza onto a paper plate and got a spoonful of salad, then hustled to the vacant chair next to Jared like someone was racing me.

"Hi," I greeted everyone as I sat down. Whipping my head to Jared, I flashed a big smile, startling him. "How was laser tag?" I blurted, two decibels too loud.

Before he had a chance to answer, Bobby said, "Real fun—for Jared and Em. They dominated! Totally shamed me with all the points they scored off me."

"You wore white," Jared pointed out with a shrug.

"The little girl scored off you, Bobby," Ben teased.

With mocha-colored skin, happy amber eyes, and an infectious smile, twenty-three-year-old Ben was one of my most favorite people in the world. "Your arms glowed, dude, like targets." He shook his head and laughed. The movement brought his corkscrew hair to life. "Black, Bobby—*always* wear black." Which every male at the table was wearing, with the exception of Bobby, of course. Even Emery's dad wore a black knit shirt.

*Black suits him,* I decided, shifting my gaze to Serena on his right. I blinked as if I was hallucinating. Curled hair, floral dress, blush, and lipstick, Serena was—"Beautiful. Serena, you're gorgeous!"

She and Mom stopped talking. Serena stared at me as if I spoke an alien language, while Mom raised her eyebrows in disapproval.

"I mean, Mrs. Phillips," I quickly amended. My mom didn't know Serena and I were on a first-name basis. "You look so beautiful tonight."

"Oh, you do, Mrs. Phillips," Miriam quickly agreed. Carli and Bren complimented her, too.

"Thank you," Serena said, more baffled than embarrassed.

33

"When is she not?" Mr. Phillips chimed in, dreamy eyes drinking in his wife. Leaning in, he nuzzled her neck.

Miriam dug her nails into my forearm, ogling. I bobbed my head in silent agreement. Their chemistry was almost palpable.

"Break it up," Emery joked, plopping his plate on the table. He squeezed a chair between his parents. "What will the neighbors say?"

Miriam pouted.

"Party pooper." Mr. Phillips sported a devilish grin as he entwined his fingers and stretched his arms over his head.

Miriam's nails dug into my forearm again. Together we watched Mr. Phillips's short sleeves ride up ripped biceps, revealing a tattoo on his upper left arm.

"Gavin," Ben said, noticing the tattoo, "you're a SEAL."

Nate stopped talking to his friends. His eyes shot to Mr. Phillips.

Bringing his arms down, Mr. Phillips looked at the tattoo thoughtfully. It was an eagle with one talon wrapped around an anchor and the other clutching a pistol.

"I was, another lifetime ago," he replied, running a hand over the tattoo. "This isn't government issue. Goes without saying, having a SEAL's trident on your arm is risky, personally and to a combat mission." He smiled wryly at the tattoo, as if reliving a memory. "This is the result of a night of stupidity and too much tequila."

My jaw dropped. Tequila and stupidity were not things usually discussed at our dinner table.

"No way!" Nate exclaimed. "You were Special Forces?"

"Special Forces!" Chazz cheered, having no idea what Special Forces was.

From this point on, the boys and my friends fired questions at Mr. Phillips, who barely had time to answer before the next question was blurted at him. I noted that Jared didn't ask any, though. He concentrated silently on Mr. Phillips, digesting information. I was quiet, as well, but not because I was interested in Mr. Phillips's military experiences. Emery had hurt my feelings. Why hadn't he told me his dad was a Navy SEAL? This was sort of a big deal and the type of information friends share with friends, especially close friends.

"Dude, why didn't you tell us about your dad?" Bobby said, verbalizing the question that had been bothering me. "All I can say is, like father, like son—right down to the tat."

"Tat?" I jerked forward, shooting Bobby an inquiring look. He wore an *oops* expression.

My brother palmed his forehead.

"What are you talking about?" I demanded. "Emery doesn't have a tattoo."

Nate let out a low whistle.

"Uh . . . maybe I shouldn't have said anything." Bobby glanced sheepishly at Serena.

Her lips flattened in a thin line of disapproval, confirming that Emery did, indeed, have a tattoo. This knowledge ignited an array of emotions in me. Why hadn't Emery told me?

Mr. Phillips patted his son's shoulder good-naturedly. "We'll call it Emery's night of stupidity."

"I want to see!" Miriam squealed, clapping her hands.

"Where is it?" I blurted. *How could Emery not tell me when he knows everything about me? Even Bobby Neigh knows.*

Peripherally, I caught Dad's smile. Obviously, my ignorance of the tattoo's location on Emery's physique pleased him immensely.

"Oh, dude," laughed Nate, shaking his head.

"Well? Show us!" I demanded.

"Cass," Dad lightly chided.

Even Bren advised in a whisper, "Chill, Cass."

"Whatever," I snapped, glaring at Mr. Cool-Calm-Collected-and-Totally-Unremorseful. *Why would he hide this from me?*

35

"I want to see it, too," Chazz said, oblivious to the tension I had caused.

"I'll show you later," Emery promised, smiling. To everyone else, he said, "Now if we could get back to the SEALs before my mom decides to ground me again."

I snorted, arms crossed. As if Emery had ever been grounded in his entire life.

At least, I didn't think so.

"So, Mr. Phillips," Bobby said, honoring Emery's request Bobby-style, with foot inserted in mouth, "how many people have you killed?"

~~~

Eventually the feverish SEALs Q&A ran its course, and Mom brought out a beautiful birthday cake. She lit candles, and everyone broke out into a jubilant round of "Happy Birthday."

I was having a difficult time shaking Emery's nondisclosure about the tattoo. To him, not sharing that he had a tattoo might have seemed like no big deal and none of my business—which it wouldn't be, if I was just the girl who lived across the street, but this wasn't the case. I wondered if I should trust him as implicitly as I had, and I didn't like having doubts about the person I had entrusted my life to.

We moved to the living room to open presents and had just settled in when Mr. Phillips's cell phone rang. He excused himself and left the room.

"I'm in charge of presents," Chazz announced, shoving Carli's gift at me.

Nate and I switched off opening the gifts Chazz handed us. Feigning joy and gushing thank-yous, I forgot what I had unwrapped as soon as my moment was done. I was too unsettled to pay close attention.

"Here, Cassidy." Chazz placed a pretty little package in my hand, wrapped in silver paper. It was from the Phillipses.

With a pasted-on smile, I unwrapped the gift: a stainless-steel charm bracelet.

"It's beautiful!" I exclaimed with genuine pleasure and looked up at Serena in the wingback chair. Mr. Phillips sat on the floor in front of her with his arm slung over her knees. I hadn't noticed he'd returned. "Thank you so much," I said to her and Mr. Phillips, not looking at Emery.

"You're welcome, my dear," said Serena, while her finger played absently with her husband's hair. "I thought we could add a new charm each year."

"How wonderful, Serena," raved Mom. The girls agreed.

All I could picture was a bracelet loaded with charms as I lived on and on, long after everyone I'd ever known and loved was gone.

*Don't even go there*, I advised myself, and passed the bracelet to Miriam. If anything would spiral me deeper into despair, it was the thought of immortality and knowing everyone in this room would eventually leave me. *Now stop!*

Chazz approached me, a wide grin plastered on his cute, round face, and handed me a tiny gift he had clearly wrapped himself. Scotch tape covered the entire surface of what I guessed to be one of his toys, wrapped in leftover Christmas paper.

"Well, what do we have here?" I winked at Chazz. Surprise crossed his face, and he gave me a big wink back, as if we shared a secret. He could hardly sit still as I went to work on the tape.

"I can't wait to see," I told him, and meant it. His joy was contagious.

Dad's cell phone rang. He looked at the screen.

I tore the first strip of tape away.

"Excuse me," Dad said. He answered the call as he briskly left the room. "Hello, Drake Jones here."

I managed to get another piece of tape off. "Chazzy, you wrap so well!" I wormed my fingers through paper and encountered hard plastic.

Chazz giggled into his hands.

I freed a plastic action figure from the confines of the candy-cane-striped wrapping paper and felt an unnatural smile stretch across my face. *Oh, crud.*

"Oh, look!" I announced as I held up the action figure. "It's Dash, from *The Incredibles*."

"He has super speed." Chazz beamed.

I waited for a wink, but it didn't come.

"*Super speed*," I enunciated, looking at Emery. He was kicked back on the floor, his face sporting an easy grin. Beneath the veneer, I knew he was thinking what I was thinking: *We're doomed.*

In my mind, I called forth the image of the picture Chazz had drawn recently, captioned "The Amazing Cassidy," depicting me in a purple spandex costume and cape. There had been other clues that Chazz suspected my secret, but there wasn't "conclusive evidence," as Emery had put it, so we decided to keep our eyes open, but not to tip our hand until there was no question about what Chazz knew.

"Dash is my favorite superhero of all," I told Chazz, hugging him.

"Spiderman is mine," he shared, and I hugged him tighter, figuring this was a good sign. *Maybe Chazz doesn't know.* Over his shoulder, I saw Dad enter the room. He looked troubled.

*What now?* I thought.

Dad forced his million-dollar smile. "Oh, I missed Chazz's present."

Chazz broke free from the hug to look at him.

"He was so excited to give you Dash," Dad told me, his smile clashing with the worry lines creasing his forehead.

Emery straightened up to scrutinize my dad. From the corner of my eye, I saw Mr. Phillips watching him, too.

"Is everything all right, Drake?" Mom asked.

"We'll talk later," he told her quickly, shifting his smile to Chazz. "Are there any more gifts?"

"Nope, they're all opened," Chazz said, scooping up wrapping paper and tossing it in the air.

"Well, in that case—kids, if you don't mind, I need to talk with the adults, in my office," Dad said, cluing everyone in that something was amiss—everyone but Chazz, who threw more wrapping paper, since no one was stopping him.

Mom, Serena, Mr. Phillips, and Ben promptly got to their feet. As they did, Dad added, "Emery, you too."

*What the . . . ?* Nate mouthed to me.

Sick to my stomach, I shrugged. I had every intention of finding out what was going on.

When the adults and Emery left the room, whispers broke out among those remaining. But the only discussion I cared about was the one happening in my dad's office.

I curled forward on the sofa, elbows on knees, and concentrated on the stars sparkling on my thumbs until they blurred. The voices in the room faded, and the voices down the hall, behind a closed door, became distinguishable.

"This is nuts," Ben said. "No, he's nuts. I can't believe it."

"Drake, did they tell you how?" Mom's voice was fraught with worry. "How did he escape?"

Ben's statement and Mom's question provided all the information I needed. Arthur King Jr. had escaped from prison.

~~~

Everyone was still in Dad's office when the girls and Bobby went home. Jared was spending the night, since his mom was gone on a business trip overnight. He had spent the night most weekends before my blunder had estranged us. Needless to say, it was nice having things back to normal.

Nate, Jared, and Chazz went into the family room to play Xbox while I remained in the living room, eavesdropping.

To sum it up, Arthur King Jr. had escaped from prison during a riot and was presently at large. My mom was concerned he would seek revenge, since the testimonies of Dad, Serena, and Emery had put him behind bars. Serena kept silent while the men and Emery reassured my mom that there was no need to worry. I took Serena's silence to mean she was worried about Junior, too. Finally, she spoke up.

"It is not the son we need to concern ourselves with," she warned.

*It's the father*, I finished, a chill scurrying up my spine.

"Serena," Mr. Phillips said, but at the same time I heard my name spoken, which yanked my attention from the office.

"Cassy?"

I practically jumped out of my skin. Jared stood in front of me.

"Oh, geez." I placed my hand over my heart. "Where'd you come from?"

His mouth turned up in the corners the way I loved.

"Question is, where were you?" He plopped down on the sofa next to me, so close our thighs touched. For some crazy reason, I inched away. He didn't seem to notice, though. "I don't think I've ever seen anyone thinking that hard before," he remarked, grinning. All at once, the smile disappeared, and he asked intently, "Are you worried about the top-secret meeting?"

I nodded and gulped a breath, pulling in his intoxicating scent. His fragrance danced across my tongue and clung deliciously to the back of my throat. *I'd die if he knew I could smell his scent like a bloodhound.* Blushing at the thought, I averted my gaze to the Elliot Bay Bookstore bag on his lap. "What's in the bag?"

"For you." He handed me the bag. "Sorry it isn't wrapped."

I stared at it, computing. "It's a gift?" I deduced.

"What else?" His eyes glided over my burning cheeks. He seemed pleased. "Take a look."

"Why didn't you give it to me earlier?" I rubbed my forehead. The blush was even hot to the touch. I probably looked like a lobster.

"Will you just open it? Never mind, I'll do it for you." He made a grab for the bag, which I easily dodged. Jamming my hand inside, I pulled out a book: *The Tenant of Wildfell Hall*.

My throat tightened with emotion. This was perhaps the kindest gesture anyone had ever made toward me.

"You didn't mention that Brontë sister," Jared explained quickly.

A few weeks back, I had rambled on and on to him about *Wuthering Heights* and *Jane Eyre* and felt like a complete imbecile afterward. I was sure he thought I was the lamest girl on the planet, and now he'd done this.

"Th-this," I groped for words. "This—" My arms were around his neck before I had time to think better of it. "Thank you," I whispered, breathing in his wonderful smell.

Tentatively, his hands touched my back. He cleared his throat. "Glad you like it," he said, his voice strained. He cleared his throat again. "Um, don't take this wrong, but I can't breathe."

"What?" I gasped, and realized I was choking him. Letting go, I asked anxiously, "Did I hurt you?" *How could I be so irresponsible?*

"Man—" Jared tilted his head from side to side to stretch muscles. "You've got quite a grip. Love you to death, huh?" he teased.

Despite myself, I laughed, and he laughed, and then we were both laughing so hard we could barely catch our breath. Though honestly I don't know what was so funny about nearly smothering him to death. "I'm glad we're friends again," I told him between laughs.

"Me, too, crazy girl," he said, relaxing into the sofa. He ran a finger along the rim of his eye to wipe away the moisture laughter had produced. "It's on the back of his right shoulder."

"Huh?"

"Emery's tat."

"His shoulder?" I turned to Jared eagerly.

"Yeah. Don't ask me what the big deal is. With all the secrecy, you'd think it was on a lower region."

"Emery is all about secrecy." I knew I sounded bitter.

Jared didn't comment, though he was no doubt mulling over my statement, examining it from all angles, theorizing different meanings, and then stashing it away in some compartment in his brain to study again later. I knew how Jared processed. Curling forward, I did some processing of my own.

"Of course. The locker room," I said a moment later. "That's how you all know about Emery's tattoo." The realization made me feel a little better. Emery was not showing off his tattoo to everybody but me, like I had originally thought. "What's it of?"

"I don't know. It's a blue circle."

"A knotwork circle?"

"Yeah."

"Huh." I visualized the tattoo on Mickey the bounty hunter's arm: an aqua knotwork circle with a dragon blasting fire at it. *Why does Emery have the same tattoo?*

"What does Emery's dad do for a living?" Jared asked out of the blue.

"He's an accountant," I said, repeating what I had been told. I didn't see the harm in doing so, since it was probably a lie anyway.

"An accountant?" Jared laughed. "Don't think so. Look at the dude. He's a mercenary or something."

Excitement swirled in my chest, and it really shouldn't have. I needed to get Jared off of this train of thought, but not until I found out . . . "What exactly is a mercenary?"

"You know, a soldier for hire, working for a foreign government, or—"

"A hit man!"

He looked at me hard. "Do you think Emery's dad is a hit man?"

I shook my head, though that was exactly what I had thought, until today that is. "No. No, I don't," I said with genuine conviction. "I'm just agreeing with you. Emery's dad is hardly the stereotypical accountant. You just don't think of an accountant being—"

"A brute?" Jared offered with a devilish smile.

"A brute? No, not a brute. Though he does *look* like one. But that doesn't mean anything. Looks can be deceiving. Okay, I admit, I had my doubts about the accountant thing, too, which was totally judgmental of me. So he doesn't fit the accountant *image*. But who says accountants can only crunch numbers? It's not like a law or something. Furthermore—"

"I'm going to keep talking in circles," Jared interrupted, mimicking my voice with a grin, "until I convince myself Emery's dad wouldn't hurt a fly."

Impulsively, I swatted him with his gift, surprising him as much as I surprised myself. That would have been my reaction to Nate or Emery.

Jared busted up. "Guess we really are friends again."

"You doubted it?" I whacked him with the book a second time, in case there were any lingering doubts.

*Five*

# Betrayal

When the "inner circle" finally emerged from Dad's office, my parents brought us kids up to speed about Arthur King Jr.'s escape, reiterating over and over that there was nothing to worry about. Having had firsthand experience with the maniac, I begged to differ, but refrained from doing so until later that night with Emery.

At the stroke of midnight, I slipped my pathetic attempt of a poem about Jared into my nightstand drawer. The opening line: *Your eyes are like pools of chocolate*—in case there were any doubts about it being bad. *Well, his eyes are like pools of chocolate*, I defended myself to myself, as I yanked on the black ski mask. *When I look into them, I feel like I'm drowning in a fondue pot.*

I made a mental note to add that line to my pathetic poem later on.

I pushed the window up, leapt out, and was crawling through Emery's bedroom window within seconds. He didn't tell me much more than I had overheard, but he did tell me he had come across an alarming detail on a law enforcement website he had hacked into. Prison guards and prisoners had reported that a woman led the small army of armed men who had stormed the prison. Her description: petite, approximately five feet four inches, curly white-blond hair, unnaturally pale skin, and wearing a pink dress, hat, high heels, and metallic nylons.

I stated the obvious. "Those weren't nylons. Lily broke Junior out."

Lily White had kept a low profile since "the magical suit of armor" she'd worn had melded into her skin when I had kicked her into a fire. Inexplicably, it had made her fantastically strong, fast, and impenetrable from the collarbone down.

Basically, Lily had turned into metal.

Since her escape, Emery and I had scoured the Internet for clues to where she might be. We chalked up a string of armored truck robberies to Lily, though it was difficult to know for sure if she was the perpetrator, since media and police reports stated the robbers had been masked. But the steel doors that had been ripped off of the trucks were a pretty good indicator.

"Why would Lily show her face now?" I thought out loud. "And how weird is it that she, Junior, and I'm guessing his *dad* have teamed up? What are the chances?"

"In answer to your first question, Lily may be getting too big for her britches. She is a power-hungry narcissist—"

"And a murderer," I added.

"Yes, that too. About the only thing she isn't is discreet. She'll hang herself eventually. We'll help her do that if given the opportunity. Regarding your second question, it is weird, but it's also a small world, especially in the criminal community. The odds of Lily being hired by Arthur King are better than you would think."

"So what do we do about Lily and the Kings?"

"We wait for an opportunity."

~~~

After leaving Emery, I went on my nightly run through the dark alleys and streets of Seattle and came up with a whole slew of other worries. Since Nate and Miriam walked to school with us in the morning, I didn't have an opportunity to share my concerns with Emery until we entered Queen Anne High School later that morning, where the noise could mask our whispers.

"Why would King break his son out of prison now?" I whispered to Emery. I had concluded that Junior's dad had hired Lily. Otherwise, how could Junior have contacted her from prison?

When Emery didn't respond, I glanced up at him. He had switched back into his black-framed glasses, which he had switched out for contacts during Fight Club and laser tag yesterday. Now he exchanged smiles with Anna Slater as she passed, as was their morning ritual. Looking at him, you would think he didn't have a care in the world.

"Will you stop flirting and answer me? Your mother could be in big trouble."

"I don't think King is sending Lily after my mom, if that's what you're worried about," Emery replied, now smiling at Grace Fletcher.

Grace giggled.

"Well, why not? He kidnapped her for Assassin data before."

"He also discovered that she doesn't have what he wants."

"How do you know?" I grumbled, but Emery didn't hear me. He was too immersed in flirting with pretty Kaitlyn Littleton.

~~~

Emery had managed to get into five of my seven classes when he registered for school last October. However, he couldn't charm his way into my Spanish and world history classes, which was really too bad for him today. My world history teacher, Mr. Loescher, was taking his classes to the traveling Egyptian Queen Kiya exhibit on display at the Arthur A. Denny Museum of Art and History, or the Denny, as we locals called it.

Queen Kiya's tomb had been unearthed in the 1970s. Aside from mummies and artifacts, a curse had been discovered etched over the entrance to her tomb: *Death will come swiftly at the hands of the seven attendants to those who disturb the sacred headdress of the queen*—or something along those lines. Apparently the queen had been rather attached to her crown, and upon her death it was laid to rest with her, as were seven guardsmen.

Goose bumps had cropped up on my arms when Mr. Loescher shared that seven men were put to death in order to guard their queen in the afterlife. Morbid, to say the least. He also told us that when the tomb was uncovered hundreds of years later, one of the attendants was missing.

"Maybe the seventh attendant went after some grave robbers and got lost," Nina Puskara had suggested. Her joke received much laughter, but I thought it was an interesting theory. If mutants were possible, why not an embalmed man coming back to life?

~~~

After lunch period, Mr. Loescher's students piled into two school buses. Shana Carlos slid into a seat, and Carli sat next to her. Lucretia Burns and I sat behind them.

A slow, steady stream of bodies brushed past us as we four girls chatted. The stream paused, and I felt fingers comb into my hair.

"Hey," Chad said, giving my hair a tug.

Lucretia's eyes widened.

Taken aback and mad as a hornet that Chad would *dare* touch my hair, I yanked my head around to glare at him.

The jerk smiled.

"Hey, yourself," I spat. "Get your hand out of my hair."

Behind him, bleach-blond Mindy Ames stared at me like I was a piece of gum stuck to the bottom of her shoe. She hated me, as did all of Robin Newton's remoras. I can understand why Robin didn't care for me. I had broken her nose, which made her face not so perfect anymore. It was an accident, of course, but tell Robin that. Her minions despised me simply because she did.

"How did that happen?" Chad asked. He was still feigning surprise over my hair being entwined around his gross fingers.

I'd had enough, so I reached behind my head and secured his wrist. Chad smiled like he thought I was playing along. Once I started squeezing his wrist, forcing his fingers to flex, he would change his assessment.

While this was going on, Mindy complained, "You're holding everyone up, Chad." She pushed against him.

He exaggerated a sigh and extracted his hand from my hair. "Later, Red," he said, grazing my cheek with the back of his hand.

Stunned by his brazenness, all I could do was watch him and Mindy move to the back of the bus to sit with the other elitists. *Good thing for you and your nasty fingers I was too appalled to react*, I thought as he plopped down in a seat, grinning at me. Apparently he thought he had won me over.

"Tell me . . ." Carli hooked my face and pulled it around to her. "What was *that* about?"

"Cassidy kicked Chad's butt," Shana eagerly answered for me.

I laughed. *Geez, talk about embellishing.*

Carli's mouth hung open, revealing the blue bands on her lower braces. "You did not tell me this," she protested. "When? Where? *How?*"

I didn't need to tell her. Shana did.

"Why didn't you tell me?" Carli complained again after Shana had given her the scoop.

I shrugged. Frankly, I hadn't thought about Chad since Fight Club, not with everything else occupying my mind.

"I can't believe you didn't know," Lucretia said to Carli. "Everyone's talking about it."

48

"Makes sense," I contributed. "Boys are big blabbermouths."

"I wish you were," Carli bellyached. "Well, here's something I bet you don't know." She leaned toward me with a smug expression. Lucretia, Shana, and I leaned toward her in turn. "Chad and Robin Newton are going out."

~~~

The Queen Kiya exhibit was super cool. Next to a life-size replica of an Egyptian tomb, the exhibit showcased artifacts recovered from the queen's tomb: ornate gold necklaces and armlets encrusted with precious stones, a shrine box with figurines depicting the queen, a carved wooden head coming out of a blue lotus representing her divine birth. There were alabaster jars for perfume, beetle rings symbolizing the afterlife, a model of the solar boat transporting her to the afterlife, a slew of shawabty helper statues that looked like mini-mummies, and of course, real mummies, too.

The queen lay in a gilded gold mummy case carved with hieroglyphics. A golden death mask covered her face, and her crown rested on her chest. The crown was stunning, with inlaid emeralds that showcased a large amber stone centered in the golden circlet. Over her coffin hung a translation of the curse.

It said, *They that shall remove the crown will meet a swift death by the hands of seven.*

Seven coffins that looked like packing crates were lined up on the other side of Queen Kiya. Each held a mummy, save for the seventh coffin. These mummies were disgusting, obviously not having been wrapped with the care that their queen had been. Ashy-looking decay peeked out from strips of tattered linen, and what had once been flesh was piled around each body like gray sand. It seriously made me want to hurl.

"This is so gross," I said to my friends.

"They look like something from a horror movie," remarked Carli.

"Totally," Lucretia agreed. "You expect them to leap up or something."

"And grab one of those." Shana pointed to machetes in a display case.

"Or those." I aimed my finger at hooks that were used to remove innards.

"Ewww," the girls said.

Carli announced, "I'm going to the restroom, anyone wanna come with?"

Lucretia and Shana did. I opted out. When my friends left, I moved closer to the case to take a look at the other items. I was examining limestone jars that guts and brains were once stored in when a familiar face caught my attention in the display's glass. Because it was such a surprise to see him there, it took me a second to place him.

"Mr. Phil–" I started to call out, stepping out into the open. A split-second evaluation of Emery's dad, and I quickly ducked back behind the display case, squatting down.

I peeked between the falcon and jackal head jars and observed Mr. Phillips through the glass. Dressed in a black leather jacket over a turtleneck and slacks, he leaned casually against the wall near the tomb, his sharp eyes surveying the room. His expression was stony, not friendly in the least. He hardly looked like the same person from yesterday. This Mr. Phillips looked dangerous.

He moved to the tomb's entrance, unhooked the chain across the closed exhibit, and stepped to the other side. Refastening the chain, he went into the tomb.

To avoid drawing attention, I forced myself to stroll to the tomb's entrance. Whistling, I glanced around to ensure no one was watching. No one was. Quickly, I ducked under the chain and slipped in behind him. The soles of Mr.

50

Phillips's dress shoes echoed through the dimly lit tomb; voices droned farther down. I was too stressed to tune them in. Plastering my back against the hieroglyphic-laden wall, I slid down the corridor after Mr. Phillips. At the end was a narrow doorway, giving passage into the Treasure Room. I stopped here.

"Everything secure, Meyer?" asked a man with a French accent.

"Yes," Mr. Phillips responded.

*Meyer?* I thought. *An alias? This can't be good.*

"Now, my friend, if you please," said the Frenchman.

I ducked through the doorway, crawled behind a long, painted chest, and peered around the edge.

Mr. Phillips, a robust museum guard, and a lithe blond man with the build of a dancer stood in the burial chamber at the back of the room. The security guard handed a thumb drive to the blond man, who slipped it into his overcoat pocket and produced a cell phone. He struck an elegant finger against the keypad and brought the phone to his ear.

"This is Moreau," he said, then spoke in French. He spun his finger at the security guard. "Your account number, please."

The security guard recited a string of numbers that Moreau repeated into the phone. While doing this, the security guard glanced uneasily at "Meyer." It was understandable, considering how menacing Emery's dad looked.

"*Je vous remercie, Monsieur,*" the Frenchman said, ending the call. He placed the phone back in his pocket and told the security guard, "Your new bank account balance will satisfy you."

The security guard grinned. "Nice doin' business with ya."

Moreau returned the smile, the sort of highbrow smile that said, *I tolerate you because I must.* Mr. Phillips's face held no expression.

"Good of Queen Kiya to visit the Emerald City," said the security guard, and swept a ridiculous bow. "Good for me."

"Good for us all," agreed Moreau in a pleasant tone. "That is, *if* the security schematics that I have paid handsomely for are what you have guaranteed—"

The guard ceased his celebrating and glanced at the Frenchman.

Moreau added to the threat: "If they are not, then we have a problem. To be precise, you become Mr. Meyer's problem."

The security guard stared with fear at the man he knew as Meyer. Mr. Phillips's mouth turned up into a slow, chilling half-smile. His eyes were heartless.

"It's all there and up to date," the guard assured them hastily. In his nervousness, he repeated, "Nice doin' business with ya, Mr. Moreau."

"Yes, my friend. It has been a pleasure."

The guard couldn't get away fast enough.

As he walked past the chest where I hid, Moreau muttered something in French that I was sure was an insult about the security guard. Then he asked Mr. Phillips, "Have arrangements been made?"

"Assassin data recovery is set for oh-one-hundred hours Wednesday. Drop-off has been confirmed for zero hours on Sunday."

I caught a gasp. *Assassin? Serena's Assassin?*

"Excellent, Meyer. Shall we?"

The men came out of the burial room. I shrank behind the chest.

"If that cretin has sold me a blank thumb drive, you will put a bullet in his head for me, won't you, Meyer?"

"With pleasure."

Moreau chuckled. "And I am not one to deny another man his pleasure, especially—" Moreau abruptly stopped speaking. Their feet stopped moving, too.

52

I held my breath. I judged them to be on the other side of the chest.

"Did you hear some—" Moreau began, cutting himself short again. I imagined Mr. Phillips flipping a hand up for Moreau to stay silent so he could listen. If he had my hearing, he would have heard my heart crashing into my ribcage.

"Lohan, Brinkley, and Sanchez are assembling," said Mr. Phillips. The men began walking again. I waited until it sounded like they were halfway down the corridor before releasing my breath.

By the time they exited the tomb, I had a pretty good idea what was going down. Mr. Phillips and Moreau planned to rob the Queen Kiya exhibit on Wednesday at 1:00 a.m., if I was calculating military time correctly. What I couldn't figure out was what Assassin had to do with the exhibit. And I wasn't sure whether or not to tell Emery about his dad. The thought made me sick. Was it necessary for him to know that his dad was involved in orchestrating a heist in order to come up with a plan to thwart it? And why was Mr. Phillips after a biological weapon's data—data that had been destroyed?

Or had it?

*What do I do? What do I do?*

Emery needed to know about the robbery ASAP, especially since it had something to do with Assassin.

*But he doesn't need to know his dad is in on it just yet,* I decided. *And he doesn't need to know his dad is a cold-blooded killer.* Moreau had said as much, and Mr. Phillips's "with pleasure" confirmed it. Jared and my gut had been right: Mr. Phillips was bad to the bone.

My heart sank at the thought of Emery's pending devastation. Although he had never come out and said it, I knew he believed his mysterious father was a decent human being. What son wouldn't?

*I can't think about this right now. I have to figure out what's going on. Lives could be at stake.*

Resolving to keep Emery in the dark about his father for the time being, I texted him about what had transpired, mentioning Moreau and the security guard and what I had gleaned.

He texted back: *Examine the exhibit. Report anything unusual.*

Without a moment to lose, I was on my feet and on my way.

~~~

I peered around the corner of the tomb's exit and didn't see Mr. Phillips or Moreau in the vicinity. Nor did I see my friends.

*Good, they've moved on to another exhibit,* I thought, making a beeline for the nearest case displaying Queen Kiya artifacts. I adjusted my vision and slowly scanned the items lining the shelves, but saw nothing more than dust particles, fingerprint smudges, and stray hairs. The next display case didn't reveal anything either. I wasn't having much luck on the third display case when Chad's scent wafted up my nose.

"What do you want?" I said, not bothering to turn around.

"Hi to you, too." He pressed his back against the case and looked at me. I studied artifacts. "How'd you know I was there?" he asked, all grin and dimples.

"Spidey sense," I smart-mouthed. I sidestepped left so I could see around him into the case. He slid between me and the glass.

I glared at him. I didn't have time for stupid games.

"Why are you so interested in this stuff?" he asked.

"I'm an interesting person."

"You're funny."

"You're not. Go away." I stepped right. So did he.

"What were you doing in the tomb?" He smiled like he thought he had me.

*Chad was watching me? Did he see Emery's dad?*

I willed my rising panic not to show on my face and looked Chad square in the eye. "What's it to you?"

"I don't care." He smirked. "But Mr. Loescher might."

"Well, why don't you run off and tell him, then," I said, waving for him to go. I turned to an ornate throne carved of wood.

Chad stepped ahead of me and parked his backside in it.

"Get up," I ordered.

"Why?"

"Because it's *priceless,* and your butt isn't."

He lifted an eyebrow. "Are you sure about that?"

"Pig," I muttered, and turned my back to him again, walking toward Queen Kiya. Chad jumped to his feet and blocked my progress.

"*What* do you *want?*" I demanded, throwing my hands up in exasperation.

"I want you to go out with me."

I laughed, incredulous. The guy was a fool. I moved around him and continued on to Queen Kiya's coffin.

"I'm being serious," he insisted, catching up with me.

"You didn't even know I existed until I knocked you down yesterday."

"That's not true. I always thought you were hot."

"I'd be bad for your rep." I examined the golden death mask made in the queen's likeness. Kiya had been very beautiful. "Plus, your girlfriend might object."

"Oh, you're worried about Robin?" he said, as if the rejection finally made sense. "I can solve that issue in about a minute."

"You'd be doing her a favor," I retorted, my eyes traveling down the neck of the mask. So far I hadn't seen anything out of the ordinary.

"Robin's right about you," he spat. "You are a—" And he called me a name that Robin had certainly called me on several occasions.

"Sweep me off my feet, why don't you?" I called after him as he stormed away. I wasn't usually this antagonistic. Chad just brought out the worst in me.

My eyes shifted to the crown perched on the queen's chest.

A voice came over the loudspeaker: "Queen Anne High School students, please return to the lobby."

I let out an exasperated breath and prayed Mr. Phillips was long gone and hadn't heard the unfortunate announcement.

"It would be just my luck if he had," I grumbled, and made haste for the lobby with the rest of my schoolmates who had been lingering in the exhibit.

*Six*

# Riley and Her Bounty Hunters

We arrived back at school fifteen minutes before dismissal. Emery was out front, waiting for me.

"See ya," I said to my friends after we had gotten off the bus. I made my way to Emery, who was leaning against the flagpole, wearing his "mission" face. "What are you doing here?" I scolded. Emery abided by school rules—when they suited him.

"Skippin' class," teased David Hsu as he passed by. He patted Emery's shoulder and moseyed along.

"Let's go," Emery ordered.

I tossed my arms. "The bell hasn't even rung yet!"

"We'll miss the bus if we don't go now." Emery caught me by the coat.

"Where are we going?" I asked as he pulled me along. I really hated getting detention.

"On a field trip."

"But you know I didn't find anything." I assumed his field trip meant going back to the museum.

"We're not looking for clues. You're meeting my employer."

"Well, why didn't you say so?"

Emery practically had to race me to the bus depot.

~~~

From my seat at the back of the bus, I called my mom to let her know I was running an errand with Emery. Then Emery explained exactly what that entailed.

57

"Riley is an expert on security systems," he whispered. "Let's just say she *specializes* in them."

I nodded, assuming he meant she had worked for ADT Home Security or something. His next statement proved me wrong. Emery meant bigger security systems, much bigger, like for a bank.

"I need to draw on her expertise to break into the museum."

"Okay," I said, not taken aback in the least. Considering Emery's other shenanigans, breaking into the Denny was somehow predictable. I even had a good idea what my role would be. "So I dress up like a mummy and stop the heist?"

Emery looked crestfallen. "Well, that's a letdown," he admitted. "No shock? No outrage? No protests?"

"None."

He frowned. "You take all the fun out of it."

"Oh, I'm sure there will be plenty of *fun*." His dad's face flashed into my mind's eye. Quickly, I blotted it out. This was not the time to tell Emery about Mr. Phillips's involvement, or so my gut said.

"You have something to share," Emery's voice broke into my mental deliberation.

I met his scrutiny. His stare was intense, as if trying to penetrate my skull to see what was tumbling around in there.

*Thank heavens he can't.*

"What do you think Assassin has to do with this?" I misdirected.

"You read my mind," Emery teased. "There are details about the Assassin Project that will shed light on what's likely going on. As you know, my mom decided to shut down the project when she got wind of corruption. What you don't know is that Arthur King Sr. was at the heart of the nefarious doings. For security reasons, she created five research teams to develop different components of Assassin. Her reasoning was that one person should not have complete access to data for a weapon that could be used to assassinate key world leaders, topple governments, and wreak global havoc, other than herself.

"Her decision met much criticism, especially from her employer, Arthur King. The acting secretary of defense at the time supported her and mandated that all Assassin research be destroyed when she advised it. My mom learned, after these orders had presumably been executed, that King had paid a scientist from each of the five teams to copy data onto a microchip. Individually, the microchips hold little threat. Put them together, and the Assassin development can be resumed. King was in the process of collecting microchips when his private jet crashed—"

"The crash he was killed in?"

"The crash he somehow survived and used to throw the government off his trail, according to my mom."

"How does she know this?"

"This may come as a shock to you, but she was not 'at liberty' to disclose how she knew." Emery smiled wryly. I tried to smile, but couldn't manage it. The Phillipses were a strange bunch.

"However, she did reveal that three of the scientists had double-crossed King. They hid their microchip and demanded more money. Subsequently, all three scientists died under suspicious circumstances, including the two who did hold up their end of the bargain with King. Obviously, King doesn't like leaving loose ends."

"You mean he murdered them?"

"That would be my guess."

I nodded. This was a lot to take in. "So King has two microchips—"

"Four, presumably. When King Jr. held my mom captive, he revealed they had four microchips and were in the process of acquiring the fifth, which I'm guessing is hidden somewhere in the Queen Kiya exhibit."

"But how would King know?"

"I doubt he would have killed anyone without knowing the microchips' locations first."

"You mean he tortured the scientists?"

"The condition of the bodies made it difficult for coroners to determine the cause of death."

I sank back into my seat, processing. Torture. Murder. A top-secret biological weapon in the hands of a madman . . .

What was Emery's dad's role in all of this? Did he work for King? What would his motivation be?

*Money,* I concluded. There was no other explanation.

In that moment, everything fell into place. Mr. Phillips's long absences, Junior being acquainted with him, Mr. Phillips showing up with perfect timing for Junior's prison break, the conversation in the tomb, the danger he exuded like radioactive energy . . . Mr. Phillips had been rounding up microchips all these years. Maybe he had them, and not King.

Maybe he had even murdered those scientists.

"I have to stop him," I said out loud.

"*We* have to stop King," Emery corrected, misunderstanding—thank goodness.

"Why did King kidnap your mom?" I forced my mind away from Emery's dad. King knew Serena didn't have the microchip, so what further use would she be to him?

"He needs someone to create Assassin after he has acquired the recipe. Who better than chief scientist of the program?"

It made sense. "So this means King is close?" I surmised, glancing around at the other passengers. How would their lives be affected if King gained possession of the fifth microchip?

Or if Emery's father gained it?

"King believes he is," Emery said. "Here's our stop." He reached across me to yank the cord.

As the bus eased toward the curb, he gave me a rundown of vital information I needed before we met Riley and her bounty hunters. "You know that I'm a college graduate, that I do skip tracing for Riley, which you think is extremely cool, by the way." The bus halted, and we stood up. He stepped into the aisle and added, "Oh, and you're my girlfriend."

"Your *what*?" I blurted.

The woman who had slid in behind Emery smiled at me. "You're his girlfriend, dear," she said loudly, causing heads to turn.

Emery's shoulders shook with laughter.

~~~

We entered an older brick building that stood only blocks from the museum. Opting for stairs over the ancient elevator, we wound up three flights, entered a corridor, and walked to the door at the end of the hall.

O'SHEA BAIL BONDS was painted in bold, no-nonsense letters across the obscure glass.

"Ready?" Emery clasped the doorknob.

I nodded, suddenly not feeling very ready at all.

"Shall we hold hands?" Emery winked, obviously trying to settle my nerves, but that just wasn't going to happen. Being struck with shyness wasn't unusual for me when meeting someone new.

"Why did you tell them I'm your girlfriend?" I whispered.

"I didn't. I told them about the beautiful girl I live across the street from. They drew their own conclusions." He began turning the knob. I placed my hand over his hand to stop him.

"So you didn't lie and tell them I'm your girlfriend?"

"Of course not. Only a fool would lie to Riley."

"Whoever's out there, grow some cojones and come in!" a man shouted from inside. He had an Irish accent.

My eyes widened on Emery.

"You'll love them," he assured me and pushed the door open. "Nice first impression, Mickey."

I peeked around Emery. Mickey's hands were folded behind his head, feet propped up on a desk stacked with files. He wore jeans, a fitted black T-shirt, a pewter Celtic cross around his neck, cowboy boots with steel tips, and the same devilish grin I remembered glimpsing from my window.

"Well, well, well, look who the cat dragged in," he teased.

I noted he had grown his Mohawk out. His bright red hair was clipped close to his scalp. "Long time no see, little brother." He flipped his feet to the floor and was on them in a second flat, pulling Emery into a bear hug.

I watched them in shock. This type of familiarity was totally unexpected.

Mickey gave Emery a solid smack on the back and directed his roguish grin at me. "And you must be the reason Emery has made himself so scarce. Nice to make your acquaintance, Miss Cassidy." He extended his hand to me. "Mickey O'Shea."

I shook his hand, surprised that he knew my name. "Thank you," I said, charmed. "It's nice to meet you, too. Emery has told me a lot of great things about you."

Mickey laughed heartily. "If that be the case, he hasn't told you everything." He winked at Emery. "The Slave Driver's going to love meeting you." He turned his head away and yelled, "Mom!"

"Michael Seamus O'Shea," an Irish woman bellowed from behind a closed door at the back of the room. "How many times have I told you not to yell?"

The door flew open to an amply endowed, stout woman whom I guessed to be in her late forties. Her flaming red hair was teased into a frenzy. She wore a leopard-print blouse, black leggings, stilettos, and a square ton of makeup. Shrewd green eyes peered at me between false eyelashes, her candy-red lips curving into a wide smile.

"My boy," she exclaimed, walking toward us, arms out, "you've grown inches! You're as tall as this lug." She smacked Mickey's chest with the back of her hand and threw her arms around Emery's neck, forcing him to bend over awkwardly to hug her. He didn't seem to mind, though. "Looks *and* brains, always a dangerous combination." She mussed his hair and patted his cheek affectionately.

"Riley," Emery said, gesturing to me and grinning at the shock on my face. I hadn't been positive until that very moment that this vibrant, wild woman was, indeed, Riley. It was a lot to absorb, especially after picturing her young, hot, and not a mother—especially Mickey's mother. "This is Cassidy Jones."

"As if I need an introduction with the way you *rave* about her. Let's have a look at you, girl." Riley clutched my face between long red fingernails that could almost qualify as lethal weapons and studied me. For some reason this didn't bother me.

"Hmmmmm . . . With that hair I'd say you have a bit of Irish in you, but not a freckle on your face, beautiful child, and those *eyes*!" Riley inspected them, while I willed my expression to remain calm. I had forgotten about my freaky eyes. "I've never seen such a color. Magnificent, lucky girl . . . and you!" Releasing my face, she turned her attention to Emery. "You're a lucky boy."

I took a deep breath, collecting myself. The woman was like a whirling dervish, or a cartoon come to life.

"What brings you in?" Riley cut to the chase. Obviously, she knew Emery wasn't there to introduce me.

"Can we talk in your office?" Emery asked.

"By all means." Riley smiled, suspicious. "Cassidy, would you like a pop? Mickey, get her a pop. Have a seat, sweetie. Mickey will keep you company. Mickey, where are your brothers?"

I nodded to myself. *Mickey, Marky, and Marty. Of course they're brothers.*

"Bringing in Rusty. I rescheduled his court date."

Riley growled, "That one has caused me nothing but grief. He'll make that court date if I have to drag him there by the hair." Riley and Emery went into her office. He closed the door behind them.

Mickey grinned at me. "She would, you know," he said.

"I wouldn't cross her," I admitted.

Mickey busted up. "Very few have and lived to tell the tale," he said with a wink. "Take a load off, and I'll get you that pop, unless you'd prefer something else?"

"Do you have bottled water?" I asked, sitting down in the chair in front of his desk.

"We shall see."

As Mickey crossed the office to a refrigerator, I took the opportunity to look around. Marky and Marty's desks were behind me, piled with files. Alongside the door we had entered, there was a vinyl sofa and a coffee table with magazines fanned across the top, and pictures hanging on the walls of a green landscape that I guessed to be Ireland. I assumed this was Riley's decorative touch. The wall behind Mickey's desk was devoted to police-wanted bulletins. Inspecting the mean faces of fugitives, I listened in on Emery and Riley.

"I received a tip that an exhibit at the Denny is somehow connected to a top-secret military project my mom headed," Emery explained. "I need to examine the exhibit more closely—"

"You want me to get you in," Riley interrupted.

"I want to pick your brain about the security system the museum uses. I'll get myself in—"

"Here you are, Cassidy." A water bottle appeared before my face. The distraction resulted in an auditory disconnect with the next room.

"Thank you." I took the water.

Mickey swung his leg over his chair and sat down. He caught me eyeballing the long, thin scar under his right eye. "A souvenir from my rough and tumble days," he explained, relaxing in the chair. "Before my mom forced us boys to reform and become respectable bounty hunters."

"A knife fight?"

"He had a knife. I had these." Mickey made fists.

I chuckled, surprisingly at ease. It almost felt like I had known Mickey my entire life. *Because he reminds me of Nate*, I realized. Both were good-natured and rascally.

"Your tattoos are cool," I said, examining the dragon blowing fire at the knotwork circle. "They look symbolic."

"Indeed." Mickey pointed to the knotwork circle on his freckled bicep. "Brotherhood, friendship, loyalty," he explained. "The fire represents indestructibility."

"Your brothers have the circle, too?"

"They do."

"So does Emery?"

"Emery is like our little brother. He surprised us with the tat about a year ago." Mickey smiled at the memory. "Surprised his little Irish mama, too."

"Serena's Irish?"

"Through and through. Her maiden name is Connolly. From bloodline to character, Emery has every right to bear that tat. You'll never meet a more loyal person."

"No one could ask for a better friend," I agreed, thinking of Emery's father. *I'm keeping the truth about his dad from him,* I thought, watching the water swirl in the water bottle. *What kind of friend does that make me?*

I looked at Mickey. Elbows on the desk, he nestled his chin on folded hands and stared at me intently. "I can see how much you care about Emery," he observed. "I like that."

"Thank you," I whispered, feeling the threat of tears. Suddenly it occurred to me that I was being rude. Mickey had a hand in finding out who had kidnapped my dad and Serena. "By the way, thank you for helping Emery stake out

Selma Heart and find my dad." Selma Heart was Junior's right-hand man—er, woman.

"I'm amazed." Mickey leaned back in his chair, shaking his head. "Emery told you about that? That's not like him."

"I saw you pick him up at my house that night," I explained, pressing a finger under my eye to head off a tear. I had good reason to be emotional, in light of everything going on, but Mickey didn't know that. Last thing I wanted was to start bawling for no apparent reason.

"Hold on," Mickey said, jumping up.

"Otherwise Emery would have never said anything," I added as Mickey briskly walked to the table next to the refrigerator. He swiped a napkin and came back.

"Now that *is* like Emery," Mickey remarked, handing me the napkin.

"Thank you," I said thickly, dabbing my eyes. *He probably thinks I'm a total weirdo.*

"You're welcome on both accounts." Mickey sat down and leaned toward me, grinning. "Think Emery's ears are burning yet?" he asked, mischief twinkling in his eyes. "What do you say we set them on fire? Tell me all about him in high school. I've had a hard time wrapping my head around that one."

"It's pretty funny," I admitted, smiling. "You'd die laughing if you heard him dumbing himself down, using slang. He always sounds strange to me, since I know how he really talks, but he fools everyone else. No one suspects a thing— well, except for maybe one person," I amended, thinking about Jared. Emery thought Jared was suspicious, anyway. "Emery's super popular, almost a legend because of what happened at King Pharmaceutical and on Catamount Mountain when he tranked those men who set the tiger loose. He also humbled our school bully, Dixon Pilchowski, by putting him in an elbow lock when Dixon was giving my friend Miriam a bad time. Emery totally won her over. She's crushing on him big time, like half the girls in school are—"

I stopped talking, suddenly remembering who I was talking to. A grown man—who was a bounty hunter, no less. *Yeah, like Mickey really wants to hear a bunch of stupid school drama*, I thought, blushing.

"Well, don't stop now," Mickey protested. "It was just gettin' good."

I laughed. Mickey was fast becoming one of my favorite people. "Okay, like I was saying, half the girls at school are crushing on him. No one can figure out what he's doing with me, which has caused me some grief. Before Emery, I basically blended in with the woodwork."

"Now you listen here," Mickey chided, wagging a finger. "Don't sell yourself short. You're something special, no doubt about that. Emery certainly thinks so. I've never seen him so taken with anyone."

Before I could respond—not that I had a clue what to say anyway—loud male voices filled the hallway. I figured the elevator doors had just opened.

"That'd be my bros," Mickey told me, rolling his eyes.

Two identical redheaded men burst through the door, talking over one another and dragging a man with them. Marky and Marty, obviously twins, were tall and burly like their big brother, with identical faces full of freckles and enough energy between them to light a building.

"Rusteeeeeee," Mickey shouted over his brothers, throwing his arms out as if welcoming the man. "Appears we need to go over the rules again."

Slack-jawed, Rusty blinked his bulging eyes, as if trying to decipher what Mickey had said. Clearly he didn't have a lot going on upstairs, but he projected creepiness like a neon sign. "What'd *she* do?" he demanded, nodding in my direction as one of the O'Shea twins stuck him in a chair.

"This here is the infamous Little Red Riding Hood," Mickey replied. "Don't let that angel face fool you. She's a big-time carjacker."

Marky and Marty howled with laughter.

"Bull," Rusty said.

"Look at her. She's a carjacker if I ever saw one. Okay, enough lookin'." Mickey threw a paper cup at Rusty, nailing his forehead.

"Ow," Rusty complained, rubbing where the cup had hit him.

"Always happy to make the acquaintance of a carjacker. Marky O'Shea." Marky shot his hand at me, grinning.

I shook it. "Nice to meet you. I'm Cassidy J—"

"Bssdbssdbssd," Mickey interrupted, making gestures with his fingers for me to stop talking. He motioned to Rusty with his eyes.

I nodded.

"She's Emery's girl," he explained to his brothers.

"Hi, Cassidy," Rusty called over.

Marky whipped around and pointed at him. "Eyes forward, and mind your own business."

Rusty pouted. "Jus' bein' friendly."

"Ah-hem." Marty cleared his throat and made crazy eyes to warn Rusty to take heed. Then he offered me his hand, and a big, toothy smile took over his freckled face. "Marty O'Shea at your service."

I shook it, taken with all of the O'Shea boys. They were totally charming.

"Rusty Blagojeviche!" Riley hollered. Her office door flew open.

Rusty quivered.

"I have a bone to pick with *you*." Riley pointed at him and gave him the eye. Emery followed her out, assessing me. He smiled, seeing that I felt right at home.

"Whoa-ho-ho! Look who's here." Marty put his hand out as if to shake Emery's hand and dope-slapped him instead.

"Good to see you, too, Marty." Emery gave him a sinister grin.

"Don't antagonize him," Marky advised his twin, slinging an arm around Emery's shoulders. "You know payback's a-comin'."

Marty shook a finger at Emery. "Don't even think about hacking me again."

During this playful exchange, Riley approached Rusty in measured steps, her expression stern.

Rusty shrank in his chair.

"You're going to listen, Rusty Blagojeviche, and you're going to listen good." She bent forward, hands on hips, sticking her face in his.

Fidgeting, Rusty averted his eyes to her enormous chest, before catching himself and forcing his gaze to the floor.

"Look me in the eye," she ordered.

His eyes bounced up to hers, wide with terror.

"I haven't always been lawful."

"Here we go," Mickey sighed.

"My dear, sweet husband, Seamus O'Shea, God rest his soul"—Riley reverently made a quick sign of the cross over her chest, as did her sons—"and I were master thieves back in Ireland. There wasn't a lock or security system that could stop us. Even churches weren't immune to our thievery, I am deeply ashamed to admit. Good offerings went straight from the safe and into our sacks. I tell you this to give you a taste of what we were. Stealing benevolence." Riley shook her head regretfully, clucking her tongue. "And we continued our crooked ways here in America, until fate caught up with us. Our criminal reign came to an end that night, as did Seamus." Riley compressed her lips, fighting to control strong emotion.

My throat tightened with sympathy.

"New York State gave me plenty of time to think over my wicked ways," Riley continued when she'd regained her composure. "While I was incarcerated, my boys lived with my brother and his wife back home. I had two options: to change or not to change. I chose change.

69

"I took college courses in prison, passed them with flying colors, and was accepted into Wallingford University while still behind bars. On the day of my release, the first faces I saw walking through those prison gates were those of my beloved sons, and they saw a new woman. We flew to Seattle the following morning, where I attended the prestigious Wallingford. Me—Riley Bryne O'Shea, poor Irish girl, safecracker, and convicted criminal! Now if that isn't a story of inspiration, I don't know what is. Are you making your next court date, Rusty?"

Rusty bobbed his head, gulping.

"My ears need to hear it."

"Yes, Riley. No more problems from me."

"Be a man of your word, like these four behind me."

"Yes, ma'am."

"I'll hold you to it." Riley straightened up. "Lass," she addressed me, "did Emery tell you how we met?"

"He said you met in college."

She nodded, looking impressed that I knew this much. "We were the odd ones out, so to speak. Someone had to take the little tyke under their wing." She walked over to Emery and drew him into her arms. "Be wise," she whispered in his ear. "You're not infallible."

"Thank you, Riley," he said, his tone revealing his affection for her. Riley and her sons were very special to him.

Riley released him from the hug. "We should all get back to it," she announced. "You and your lass run along." She avoided saying my name in front of Rusty. She turned to me. "On your feet. I want a hug good-bye."

I got up and hugged her and exchanged handshakes with the O'Shea boys, bidding them all good-bye.

"Bye, Cassidy," Rusty called as Emery opened the door for me.

"None o' that," Marky reprimanded, boxing Rusty's ears.

We closed the office door to Rusty's whiny protests.

A couple office doors down, I halted and smacked the back of my hand against Emery's chest. "Who do you think you are, keeping them all to yourself? They're awesome. I love them. Why didn't you tell me about Riley?"

"Because I wanted to see your face when you finally met the girl I'm smitten with." Emery gave me a gooey look.

"Well, of course I was going to think she was some hot young thing. You met her in college. What was I supposed to think?"

"That Riley is some hot young thing." He flashed a smile.

"Well, yeah, but are you disappointed?"

Emery raised his eyebrows questioningly. "About what?"

"You know—that Riley didn't give you any advice"—I lowered my voice to a whisper—"about breaking into the museum."

"What makes you think she didn't?"

"You mean she did?" I said, flabbergasted. "So what was the whole 'I'm reformed' speech, then?"

"Riley knows I'm trustworthy and wouldn't go to such extremes unless it was necessary." Emery was great at replying without really answering my question. "She also knows I'm capable of handling an undertaking of this magnitude."

"How would she know that?"

"She just does," Emery said mysteriously. He started walking, while I stood there, staring in amazement at the boy who I knew but didn't know.

"For your costume," he said over his shoulder, "should we go with ready-made or custom?"

*Seven*

# The Mummy

As luck would have it, we found a used mummy costume from a movie that had been filmed locally, or so the price tag claimed. The quality of the costume certainly suggested this to be true, and best of all, the costume appeared to be my size. Not wanting to draw attention, Emery wouldn't let me try it on, so after he purchased the costume and face paints, we crossed the street to a boutique where we pretended to browse for a couple of minutes before I snapped up a dress.

"Can I try this on?" I asked the girl at the register.

She kept her nose in her romance novel as she waved for me to go ahead.

In the fitting room, I wiggled into the costume and smiled, pleased at my reflection. I looked just like a mummy from a B-rated horror flick.

"Mendel," I said, calling Emery by his middle name, "come tell me what you think."

Emery slipped through the curtain. A grin expanded across his face.

"Fetching," he said. "*All* the girls will be jealous."

I rolled my eyes. "Don't think it's me, though. Thanks anyway." I shoved him back through the curtain and took the costume off.

The salesgirl didn't even look up when I placed the dress on the counter and left.

*Eight*

# Ambush

The next day, Emery skipped a couple classes at school to scope out the museum for our break-in later that night. I wasn't clear on what Riley had advised him to do there, but according to Emery, her tips would help him hijack the security system and cameras via his laptop.

The plan went as follows: After Emery took over the security system at midnight, he would pick the locks on the museum's loading dock entrance and let me in, dressed as the mummy. Connected with Emery by phone, I would wait for the thieves in the seventh attendant's coffin—ick. But I could do it. When the thieves showed at 1:00 a.m., I would play dead until Emery, watching security feed on his laptop, told me what the thieves were after, which we both believed was an artifact from the exhibit that the microchip had been hidden in. This would be my signal to spring from the coffin and take the thieves by surprise. Once I knocked them out cold, I would grab the artifact and hightail it out of the museum. Emery would then trip the alarm, and the police would show up to find the thieves unconscious. I prayed like crazy Emery's dad wouldn't be among them.

As Emery had given me the rundown, I struggled with whether or not to tell him about his father's involvement, but concluded it still wasn't the right time. For better or worse, we had to get the microchip before revealing what I'd heard in the tomb—or before Mr. Phillips exposed his involvement by being arrested. We'd deal with any repercussions then. However, my resolve didn't do a thing to alleviate the tremendous guilt I felt about keeping Emery and Serena in the dark. My only morsel of consolation was that this was *exactly* what they would do if they were in my shoes.

~~~

At 10:59 p.m., I zipped my black jacket over my new yoga outfit, yanked on a black ski mask, pushed my window open, and leapt out, landing in a crouch in our grassy side yard.

Masked, Emery waited for me on the sidewalk. We walked briskly to the end of our block before removing our masks and continuing on to the bus stop at the bottom of Queen Anne Hill.

Fifteen minutes later, we exited the metro bus in front of the museum. Circling the large building, we made our way down a dimly lit alley and stepped into the alcove of a dark doorway next to the museum's loading dock. After ensuring no one was watching, Emery flipped on a flashlight so he could see. With my feline night vision, I had no problem, of course.

"Is your earpiece in?" Emery lowered into a squat.

"Check."

He placed the flashlight on the ground and slid his laptop bag and backpack off his shoulder. I realized then that I hadn't offered to carry one of the bags, having been consumed with fretting and thinking of everything that could possibly go wrong.

"Where's your phone?" Emery pulled the mummy costume from the backpack.

"Oh, right. Thanks for reminding me." I took the phone from my coat pocket and had a *duh* moment. My yoga pants didn't have pockets.

"We'll establish a phone connection when you're in the coffin," Emery said, while I tried to figure out where to put my dang phone. There was only one option that would work.

Checking to make sure Emery wasn't watching, I quickly slid the phone into my sports bra.

"Sheezzzz," I gasped when the cold plastic touched my skin.

"What?" Emery asked without looking up.

"Nothing." I unzipped my jacket and slid it off. The icy air bit into my bare skin, producing another gasp. "It's freezing."

"This will warm you up." He handed me the costume. While I put it on, he prepared white and gray face paint. "Just like old times." He smeared white paint on my face.

"At least it's not purple." I aimed the flashlight beam upward so he could see what he was doing. Before we stormed King Pharmaceutical, he'd had me dress in a ninja costume and had painted my face purple.

"Now for some decay." Emery daubed gray paint over the white base, rubbing more over my lips with his index finger. "You look like death itself."

"Charming," I replied.

"Not my best work." Emery patted a bit more gray along my cheekbone. "But it will do for our purposes."

After fussing with the mummy hood and arranging the gauzy fabric over my face just so, Emery took out his cell phone. He struck a few keys and announced, "The alarm is off, and the camera feed is looping."

"That's my cue." I forced a brave expression, not that it mattered with my face all covered in gauze, anyway.

Emery riffled through his laptop bag while I directed the flashlight beam at it.

"This won't help your nerves," he warned, taking a small blue case out of the bag. "But it's necessary for the guard's safety."

My confidence took a nosedive. "Guard?"

"Yes, there's a security guard. I thought it would be better not to tell you beforehand."

Suddenly I felt a tad less guilty about the secret I was keeping from him.

Emery flipped the top of the case open, revealing a syringe. My head swam as he instructed, "Remove the cover of the needle, sneak up behind him, and administer the sedative in his upper arm, the deltoid muscle. Here." Emery indicated the spot on his own arm.

"Stick the needle in his *arm*?" I croaked.

"His deltoid muscle." Emery showed me on my arm. "He'll be out within seconds. Then hide him."

"Hide him?" I bent over and clasped my knees. As the instructions sank in, I felt myself begin to hyperventilate. *People will get hurt tonight—by me.*

"Deep breaths." Emery rubbed the base of my neck. "You can do this, Cassidy. We're protecting the guard. Moreau could get him out of the way permanently."

That was all the encouragement I needed. "Give me the shot." I straightened up and flipped my hand out. Emery placed the syringe in my gauzed palm. The hypodermic needle was ultra thin, not much wider than thread. But geez, was it long!

"So I push this whole needle in his arm?"

"Into his deltoid muscle. You won't hurt him. If you can't get his arm, inject the sedative in his midthigh, front or side." He patted my leg to show me where.

"And I push this thingy down to get the sedative into him?"

"Yes, push the plunger all the way down."

I nodded. "I can do that."

"Of course you can." Emery went to work on the first of three deadbolts with his lock picks.

Studying the syringe, I envisioned removing the plastic cap from the tip, the needle going into the upper arm of a faceless man, my finger pushing the plunger down, and the man collapsing into my arms. *Wait, what about the syringe?*

"Replace the cap and dispose of the syringe in a trash can," Emery said, answering my private thought. I hated it when he did that. It was downright eerie.

The door's hinges squealed as Emery opened it.

"You did that fast." I peered into a vast storage room filled with wax United States presidents. Apparently the museum had a special exhibit planned for Presidents Day.

Emery couldn't see the wax sculptures. To mere human eyes, the doorway looked like a black hole.

"You should be glad you can't see what's in there," I whispered.

Without replying, Emery pulled me into a hug. My fingers curled around the syringe.

"This will go smoothly," he assured me. "I'll be at the coffeehouse across the street, monitoring everything on my laptop." He needed Wi-Fi for the Internet, and the coffeehouse was the closest source. "Remember—"

"Don't make a move until you tell me to. Then meet you in Post Alley, at Gum Wall." Post Alley was secluded and blocks from the museum. Gum Wall was self-explanatory. Seattle residents had been decorating it for years.

Releasing me, Emery hefted the laptop bag and backpack onto one shoulder and glanced at his phone. "You have twenty-seven minutes and thirty-three seconds. See you soon." With that, he swung away and headed toward the street.

My heart pounded like a jackhammer. I wanted to run after him, but I couldn't. I had to save the world.

"Everything will be fine," Emery assured me again in a whisper as he walked briskly. He knew I could hear him. "Twenty-six minutes, fifty-seven seconds. Go."

I took a deep breath and entered the storage room, pulling the door shut behind me.

Darkness swallowed the room, although darkness didn't really exist for me. My eyes required a very small amount of light in order to see. I felt my pupils expand and was sure they looked every bit as freaky as my surroundings. Who had thought of making wax statues of people, anyway?

Weaving around Lincoln, Truman, Kennedy, Clinton, and a slew of other former presidents, I adjusted my hearing, searching airwaves for the security guard. I picked up the echo of footsteps on the second floor.

With the syringe gripped tightly in my fist, I sped lightly on the balls of my feet through the various exhibits, tracking the security guard by sound and smell. At the main entrance, I flew up the marble stairs, skipping three steps at a time, and glimpsed him in the modern art section when I reached the top.

The portly man in a navy blue uniform made faces in a mirrored sculpture, clearly bored.

*He won't be bored for long*, I thought, removing the cap from the hypodermic needle. Gulping down nerves, I stuck the cap between my teeth and slithered up behind him. His eyes widened when my reflection appeared like an apparition in the small mirrors.

As the guard's mouth formed into a scream, I jammed the needle into his right upper arm and injected the sedative into his muscle. This didn't stop the scream.

"H-h-help!" He flopped onto his belly and squirmed across the floor like a salamander. I capped the needle, resisting the urge to tell him he was safe. Letting him hear my voice would be unwise.

He crawled on the floor with great effort. "The crrrrreeeeeture's real. Yer aliiiiivve—" he slurred, and went limp. He had escaped a whole ten feet. Knowing he would wake up safe and sound eased my conscience a tad.

"I'm so sorry . . ." I turned him over. Drool trickled from the side of his mouth. I read the badge around his neck. "Jeremiah Kagan, I'd better hide you before the real fun begins."

I tossed the syringe away into a trash can positioned next to the women's restroom and scanned for a place to hide Jeremiah. I decided the safest spot would be the restroom.

I gathered him in my arms, a task that proved awkward due to his size, and carried him to the women's restroom, only to discover that the door was locked. Luckily, the keys clipped to his belt had jiggled the entire way over.

I set him down and huffed with frustration over the ring packed with keys. There had to be, like, fifty keys.

"Of course," I grumbled, selecting a key at random and jamming it at the keyhole. It slid right in, amazingly. That was the last thing I had expected. "Yes!" I pushed the door open. "Jeremiah—the first key! Can you believe it? Looks like someone is watching over you."

Once I had situated him as comfortably as I could on the tiled floor, I locked him inside, placed the keys in a big ceramic urn just outside the restroom, and sped to Queen Kiya's exhibit, reclining inside the seventh attendant's coffin a beat later.

The *real deals* in their coffins, alongside mine, would have freaked me out if this weren't a life-and-death situation. Lying in a coffin next to mummies in a dark, deserted museum was the stuff horror films were made of.

"The thieves will certainly think so." My voice echoed. Shivering at the sound, I quickly wormed my phone from my bra and struck the speed dial.

Emery picked up after the first ring. A mishmash of neighboring conversations flowed from the receiver. Apparently the coffeehouse was a popular hangout in the middle of the night.

"Nice job with the guard," was his greeting. "All is quiet so far . . . Thank you. Can I have the check, please?"

"What?" I said. "You ordered coffee, at a time like this?"

"For appearances' sake only." I could hear Emery sip his coffee. Black, I knew. "I retract my previous statement. Someone just tapped into the security system."

"How do you know?" My voice wobbled more than I would have liked. Not that it mattered. Emery already knew I was scared stiff.

"I'll explain later. Get prepared. Put your phone away."

"Okay," I tried to say, but the word stuck in my throat. I hated this stuff. "But don't look, you know, on your laptop." As I fumbled the phone into my bra, Emery's voice flowed through the earpiece.

"Thank you," he said with a smile in his voice. "Keep the change."

"Thanks, handsome," a woman's voice replied.

I arranged gauze to hide the costume's collar with trembling fingers, muttering, "I'm in a coffin surrounded by dead people, about to attack crooks, and *you're* drinking coffee and flirting with waitresses."

"Baristas," Emery corrected. "One barista, to be precise, and she was doing the flirting."

"Could she see your laptop screen?"

"I'm not an amateur. I have my back to the wall. Cassidy . . ." Emery's voice lost its playfulness. My breath caught. "Six men wearing ski masks entered through the loading dock. Five are armed with semiautomatic weapons. I hadn't anticipated this type of firepower. Abort now."

"You mean leave? No! What kind of weapons?"

"Saiga Twelves, a twelve-gauge combat rifle often referred to as 'the zombie killer.' It's a big, ugly gun that can rip a hole in the side of an elephant in seconds. Abort. Now."

"No. We can't let them get the microchip. Think of what that would mean. We can do this."

A frustrated pause, then, "The new plan is 'snatch and dash.' You are to follow my exact instructions. They're armed with nine-millimeter Glocks. They have the Saiga Twelves in slings. I want you to be long gone before they can get them off their shoulders. Once I see how they're configuring and have identified the item they're after, I will tell you who to take out and how to escape with the item. Is that clear?"

"Crystal," I replied, relieved the new plan didn't include leaving behind a room full of unconscious thieves for the police. *Maybe Emery will never have to know about his dad, or that he's possibly working for King.*

"They're moving west down the main corridor on the first floor. No more talking. Close your eyes, listen, and don't move a muscle. I will be your eyes. Do *exactly* what I tell you."

I crossed my arms over my chest, shut my eyes, and concentrated, searching for the sound of their movements.

"Where's the guard?" I heard a male whisper.

There was no response. I pictured Mr. Phillips making a slashing motion across his throat, warning the man to keep quiet. *Maybe he isn't with them,* I thought, but my heart fell with my next breath. Mr. Phillips's scent mingled with the other smells I inhaled. I recognized Moreau's scent, too.

"Four are coming up the main entrance stairs," Emery said. "Three are armed, one is not. Two armed men remain on the first floor. What—?" He sounded surprised. "One is posted at the bottom of the stairs," he continued a split second later. "He's stationed near the gift shop where there's good visual. The other man is moving south, probably to secure the exits."

A scent curled up my nose, stirring the beast.

I inhaled deeply, suppressing a growl, trying to identify the unusual odor triggering all of my alarms. I couldn't, although it did remind me of the reptile house at Catamount Mountain Zoo. There was definitely something snake-ish about the scent.

Emery gave me a couple more updates, which we both knew were unnecessary. I could hear every shoe sole scrape against marble, every intake of breath, and even hearts beating, if I listened carefully. None beat as wildly as mine, though. The men's scents burned in my nostrils, as if branding me so I would never forget the event that was about to take place. I also smelled the distinct scent of Bazooka bubble gum, while trying to ignore the reptilian odor drifting from somewhere within the museum, beckoning my full attention.

"Do not move, do not breathe," Emery whispered. "All four men are entering the exhibit."

He whispered the positions they took as I listened to the men move into place. One was posted at the entrance they had come through, while another crossed the floor to secure the other entrance, and two men walked toward me. I knew, by scent, that Moreau was one of them.

"Two men are approaching you on your left. They're approximately twenty feet away. One is armed."

The men passed the seventh attendant's coffin without a pause, not noticing there was an additional mummy.

Emery barely whispered, "They're heading for Queen Kiya's coffin—"

*They're after the crown*, I guessed, since that was the only item I hadn't gotten a good look at—of course.

"When I tell you, take out the man closest to you, on your left—he's armed—then take out the man at the south entrance, also armed. The man at the north entrance has to move into position to get a clear shot, so the south entrance is your best escape."

I sent up a prayer that Mr. Phillips would not be one of the two men Emery had instructed me to attack.

"What a pleasure to make your acquaintance, Your Majesty," Moreau cooed. "What a magnificent crown."

Emery instructed, "When I say 'now,' grab the crown, go through the south entrance, and run straight through the exhibits to the stairs. At the bottom, go out the emergency exit on the right. Don't worry about the man on the south side. He is not in a position that poses a threat. You'll be on Fifth Avenue, so hide quickly."

"Ah, it's lovely," Moreau said. I assumed he had the crown in his hands.

"Now," Emery ordered.

I sprung out of the coffin and dove for the floor, catching marble with my palms. Immediately, I pushed off into a back flip, landed on my feet, and swung my leg in a roundhouse kick at the armed, masked man. My foot connected with his chest. His body curled around my foot, and he flew backward, his Glock skidding across the floor. I could tell by his build that he wasn't Emery's dad.

The thief at the south entrance whirled around to see me coming at him, and his eyes widened with disbelief. A wad of pink bubble gum dropped from his gaping mouth.

Moreau screamed.

Simultaneously, I grabbed the gum-chewer by his shirt collar with one hand and seized his weapon with the other, then flung him through the air like he was a feather pillow. From the corner of my eye, I saw Mr. Phillips barrel forward, yanking back the slide on his Glock, as the man I had thrown crashed into the third attendant's coffin. Both coffin and mummy flipped on top of him.

"Abort!" Emery ordered.

I ignored his command. No way could King, Mr. Phillips, Moreau, or anyone else get that last microchip.

Pivoting, I faced Moreau.

His legs shook as he clutched the crown to his chest, looking as if he wanted to run but was prevented from doing so by an invisible force.

"No!" Moreau cried, hugging the crown to his chest. In a moment, it would be ripped from his hands, and I would be gone before he even knew what had happened.

I let the gun fall to the floor and launched forward into a spray of bullets. Mr. Phillips had gotten his clear shot.

With the first puncture of burning metal, my skin hardened, stopping the progression of the bullet into vital organs and numbing the pain. The impact caused me to stumble backward. One after another, bullets struck my midsection, ripping holes into the gauze and into me. Swaying and stumbling with the percussion of each bullet, I didn't go down but pressed forward to Moreau. Then there was silence, almost as deafening as the gunfire had been. Mr. Phillips had emptied his gun into me. I looked up at him, stunned.

Undeterred, he dropped the Glock and yanked the zombie killer up to his eye.

"Get out now!" Emery thundered.

An alarm wailed and lights flashed.

Confused and overwhelmed, I swung away and bolted toward the south entrance, hurdling over the thief I had kicked to the ground. I ran into the adjoining room as the wall next to me seemed to explode, chunks of painted canvases and drywall flying everywhere. I stayed just ahead of the onslaught of bullets that lay waste to the museum and the precious works of art adorning its walls.

As I jetted into the next exhibit, the gunfire ceased. Mr. Phillips had likely emptied the weapon's magazine. I tore around the corner to the balcony where I remembered the stairs were located and came to a screeching halt.

Before me stood a hooded figure that appeared as equally startled as I was. Around five foot eleven, the man wore a Grim Reaper's black cape, his face hidden deep beneath the hood. I say *a man*, but his snake-ish scent told me otherwise. He was definitely not human.

Wary, we each took a slow step away from one another. Cold seemed to emanate from him, as if he were the walking dead. As he took another sliding step, something yellow flickered from the hood and disappeared back into the folds of fabric.

*Was that a tongue?* I wondered, feeling a growl rumble deep in my throat.

A bullet whizzed between us, sending us our separate ways. Mr. Phillips had reloaded and was coming after me.

The hooded figure went over the rail of the balcony in a fluid movement as if he were flying.

I ran for the floor-to-ceiling plate-glass windows that overlooked Fifth Avenue, tucking my face to my shoulder. There was no time to mess with stairs. The glass shattered around me as I plunged through the window and fell to the sidewalk, landing in a catlike crouch. Car tires squealed as drivers slammed on their brakes, and shards of glass rained around me, erupting into particles against the cement.

I lurched to my feet and ran blindly down the street with a belly full of bullets.

# Nine

# Failed Mission

A police car screamed past me as I veered off Fifth Avenue and into an alley. Sirens came from every direction on their way to the museum. I ran until I was sure no one was pursuing me and slid into the shadows of a doorway to assess the damage. A small cry of panic tore from my throat when I saw the ravaged costume, spotted with blood. I had been shot so many times, it was a miracle I hadn't been cut in half.

"No, no, no, no," I chanted, worming a trembling finger into a bullet hole. Due to the hardness of my skin, I couldn't feel anything through my numbed fingertips, so I ripped away the costume and lifted the black tank underneath, exposing my stomach, which was peppered with bullets. They reminded me of corks lodged in wine bottles. Small amounts of blood burbled up around the bullets, as if they plugged a dam.

Tears of relief smarted my eyes. This was one of those rare occasions when I was grateful to be a mutant.

"It's going to be okay. These can be removed. I'll heal." I dried my eyes with my forearm and suddenly realized I couldn't hear Emery in the earpiece, nor the background noise of the coffeehouse. We had somehow lost our phone connection. I retrieved my phone and punched the speed dial.

"Are you all right?" Emery answered. The sounds of sirens, the museum's alarm, talking, shouting, and a police officer on a megaphone flowed through the receiver along with his voice. "Cassidy," he said again when I didn't answer.

"I don't know what to do." I wiped back a sudden flood of tears with the tattered sleeve of my mummy costume. "My head's scrambled. I can't think straight."

"Do you know where you are?"

"Yeah." I glanced around. "No. I'm not sure. It's weird that I can't feel any pain. I should feel pain."

"Cassidy, listen carefully," Emery said slowly and calmly, which meant he wasn't calm at all. "You're only four blocks from Riley's office—"

"How do you know—" I began to ask, then remembered GPS. I struck my forehead with my palm in an attempt to clear the haze.

"You'll be fine," Emery soothed. "I'll take care of you. Please concentrate."

He explained how to get to the back of Riley's building through alleys, avoiding the main streets. I would have known this if I could think properly.

"There are a lot of people on the streets now, so take care not to be seen. I'm only two blocks away from Riley's office. I'll let you in through the emergency exit in back. Everything will be fine, Cassidy. This is almost over. Repeat back to me everything I just told you."

I tried but couldn't. The bullets felt heavy in my stomach. A horrifying thought struck me: *What if my skin suddenly softens and the bullets get swallowed up in my flesh?*

"Hurry, Emery." I disconnected the call and shot toward the street. *We need to get these bullets out of me!*

At the street, I looked around, recognizing where I was— or believing I did. Spying an alley, I ran across the street toward it, leaping over a parked car. I saw two men and a woman in the alley ahead. One man held a switchblade to the other man's throat while the woman riffled through his pockets. I moved so fast, none of them saw me until the mugger with the switchblade was yanked off his feet by the back of his jacket collar.

"Help!" he screamed as I dragged him behind me, arms flailing, boot heels bumping along the asphalt.

I emerged from the alley into a street bustling with activity and flung the mugger toward an oncoming police car. Lights flashing, siren blaring, the police car screeched to a halt and the mugger hit the hood, tumbling over it with the switchblade still gripped in his hand.

I jammed the cell phone between my teeth and took a flying leap at the nearest building, catching a windowsill on the second floor. I scaled the protruding bricks as swiftly as a spider scurrying up a wall and heaved myself over the ledge and onto the roof. Pausing to catch my breath, I spat the phone into my hand and looked down. A small crowd had gathered below to gape at me.

The dazed mugger, sprawled atop the police car, dropped his switchblade, which clattered across the hood and onto the asphalt. The officer in the passenger's seat stared up at me with a radio microphone to his mouth, but his lips weren't moving, as if he were at a loss about how to call in what he had just witnessed.

Turning away from the street, I grabbed my head and demanded it to *think*. I had to get hold of myself. I forced air into my lungs and released my breath slowly while I looked around. It occurred to me that I was only a few buildings away from O'Shea Bail Bonds.

I hit speed dial on my phone.

"Where are you?" Emery answered, sounding breathless. The silence and echo in the background suggested he was now indoors.

"Good—you're in Riley's building," I deduced, oddly proud that I had control over myself again. My voice even sounded calm. "Change of plans. Go to her office and open the window. I'll be coming in from the roof."

Emery didn't ask questions or disconnect the call. I listened to him as he hoofed it up the stairs while I sped across rooftops, leapt over an alley, and landed on the roof of O'Shea Bail Bonds. Amazingly, being shot hadn't affected my strength and speed. The adrenaline coursing through my veins likely didn't hurt, either.

A window opened, and I hung my head over the edge of the roof. Emery's head poked out. He craned his neck to peer up, and boy, did he ever look stressed.

"I'm coming down the drainpipe," I said, tapping the drainpipe conveniently located alongside the window.

Emery gripped it and shook. "It's safe. Come down," he called up.

I lowered myself over the edge of the roof and shimmied down the drainpipe four floors. Emery grabbed my waist and hauled me in.

"I'm so sorry," he whispered, embracing me quickly before pushing me out at arm's length so he could survey the damage. He had a difficult time mastering his expression.

Finally he cleared his throat. "I have an idea how to remove these," he said, sounding calmer than he looked. "Lie down on the sofa."

As I did this, he headed to the storage closet. "Take the costume off. Do you need help?"

"No, I can do it." I was beginning to feel uncomfortable. His clinical tone bothered me, as did the fact that he hadn't made eye contact with me since seeing my stomach. *He's just overwhelmed,* I surmised. I wiggled out of the costume, which came off easily enough, being all shot up and torn.

I rested my head on the sofa's arm and lifted the torn tank top from my midsection.

"What a mess," I declared so Emery could hear me in the storage room. I felt strangely detached, as if observing someone else's stomach. The lack of pain probably contributed to my emotional disconnect. My skin was still rock-hard and almost completely numb. "Weird that my skin is still hard. Maybe it will be until the bullets are out. I counted eighteen."

"His magazine held twenty rounds." Emery emerged from the closet, holding a toolbox. "He didn't miss."

The bitterness in his voice took me aback. What would Emery do if he knew his father had shot me?

*He can't know, for now.*

"You've been struck in the collarbone and the chest, over your heart." Emery spoke through his teeth, not even attempting to mask his anger any longer.

I glanced down to see that he was right. A bullet stuck out an eighth of an inch from my collarbone, and there was another bloody hole over my right breast. Odd that I hadn't noticed, especially a bullet imbedded in bone. The area throbbed mildly, but other than that, I didn't feel a thing.

Emery shoved the coffee table aside, pulled up a chair, and sat down to evaluate the task before him. With a heavy sigh, he flipped open the toolbox lid and selected pliers.

I gulped.

"Cassidy, I'm going to poke you with the pliers. Tell me what you feel."

"Not really much of anything. It'll be fine. Go for it." I reassured him with a smile. This appeared to bother him.

With some effort and continual sidelong glances to make sure he didn't detect pain on my face, he managed to remove the first bullet. The sensation was similar to having a tooth extracted from gums numbed with Novocain. I felt a slight pulling and discomfort, but nothing more.

"One down." Emery released the bullet into a mug on the coffee table. It made a rattling sound as it hit the ceramic bottom. "Nineteen more to go."

Now that he knew he wasn't causing me pain, Emery got into a rhythm, using necessary force when need be to extract the bullets. Watching him, one would think he was pulling nails from a board. As he worked, he explained what had happened after he'd tripped the alarm.

"The alarm caught the gunman off guard," Emery explained, not realizing he was talking about his dad. "If it hadn't, this would be much worse than what we're dealing with now. Unfortunately, everything in the Queen Kiya exhibit, after you were shot, is on film. The looping feed stopped when the alarm came on. But the footage will be limited in the rest of the museum. I didn't want to tell you this at the time, but the cameras lost visual—"

"You mean they turned off?" I asked, recalling the hooded man. Our brief encounter had been so surreal that I would have chalked him up to a figment of my imagination if it hadn't been for his distinct scent. The memory of it was so strong I could smell him all over again.

"They lost visual," Emery repeated. "I don't know if they were turned off."

"Maybe the cameras were torn down?"

Emery stopped working to scrutinize me. "Who else was there?"

"Good question," I said and shared what had happened.

"You say he leapt off the balcony?"

"Yes, very gracefully. Almost like he flew."

"Hmm," was Emery's unsatisfactory response before he went back to removing bullets.

I scowled, wondering if he thought I'd hallucinated the hooded man, but I didn't feel like talking about it anymore, so I changed the subject. "What happened when the police got to the museum?"

"Nothing. There was no one to arrest." Emery dropped another bullet in the mug. "The thieves escaped."

"That sucks." I carefully suppressed my mixed feelings. Mr. Phillips *should* be behind bars, but for Emery's sake, I was glad he wasn't. "And they have the crown?"

"They do."

I *so* wanted to kick myself. How could I have let them get away? "I'm a failure. A complete and utter failure."

"You are noble and courageous," Emery countered, grimacing. By the sensation, I guessed he was digging at another bullet. "Your only fault is unquestioning trust. I failed *you*, with arrogance and short-sightedness."

I hated it when Emery was hard on himself. "How were you supposed to know a commando team would break into the Denny?" I challenged, and rushed on before he could rip on himself some more. "We need to find Moreau and the microchip."

"First I need to find out *who* Moreau is, which I should have done before putting a flimsy plan into action and risking my friend's life." He produced the bullet he'd been after, covered in fresh blood. Sweat beaded on his forehead.

"Whose life was at risk? Obviously not mine." I motioned to my midsection, glancing down at my stomach. The wound from the bullet Emery had just extracted was already closing up, healing. The only evidence of the other bullets were small, red rings of blood. The flesh in the center of each ring was healthy and whole. "Holy cow, I'm a freak!"

"You are not, and stop trying to make me feel better." Emery frowned as he clamped onto the next bullet.

The extractions went smoothly until bullet 19, the one in my collarbone, and removing it was not without pain. Who would have thought bones had so many nerve endings? By the time Emery finally worked it out, sweat was dripping down his face, soaking his shirt collar and the hair on the back of his neck.

"That was challenging," he admitted, adding the bullet to his collection. He deflated in his chair.

I huffed out the breath I'd been holding. "That hurt like— you know what."

"I'm sorry," Emery said, and I knew he meant for more than the pain. He stared wearily at the hand I held over my heart. "Let's get it over with. Take off your shirt."

"Excuse me?"

"I have to remove the last bullet. Take off your shirt."

"No!"

"Cassidy, this is not a big deal. I don't care."

"Well, I do." I flipped out my hand. "Pliers."

"As you wish." Emery placed the pliers in my hand and turned around in the chair to give me privacy.

The only thing to be said about bullet 20 was that bullet 19 lost its title of Most Challenging.

The moment I dislodged bullet 20, my skin relaxed, returning to normal, and I dissolved into tears.

"Can I turn around?" Emery sounded distressed.

"No," I sobbed, resituating my sports bra and tank. "O-k-kay. I-I'm d-decent."

Emery moved to the sofa and pulled me into his arms. "Let it out," he soothed, rubbing my heaving back. "You've experienced a lot of trauma. Plus, there's the adrenaline. You know how these crashes go."

I knew exactly what to expect from an adrenaline crash, but this was more than adrenaline. This was overwhelming guilt produced by an accumulation of lies and my failure to get the microchip. Why had I let a few bullets stop me, even from the zombie killer?

"I-I'm-m-m s-sorry." I wept into Emery's shirt. My apology encompassed all of my failures and deceptions.

"What on earth do you have to apologize for?" he chided. "Don't worry. We'll find the microchip."

This made me cry even harder.

~~~

Once the waterworks had ended, Emery handed me my shoes and coat and assigned me the task of putting them on while he cleaned up after us. When everything was as we had found it, we caught a bus home.

On the bus, we kept to ourselves, coming down from our traumatizing evening and meditating on what had happened—or at least, that's what I was doing. My thoughts had moved beyond being shot, because what was there to think about? I had been shot, the bullets had been removed, and I had healed—end of story. What I couldn't get past was who had shot me and how I was going to deal with the situation at hand. Emery's father was a thief and a killer, and he now had possession of biological weapon data. Put plainly, Mr. Phillips was the enemy.

*How am I going to get that microchip back?* I asked myself for the millionth time while staring listlessly out the window. *When I do find it, then what? Turn Emery's dad over to the authorities?* That would be the responsible thing to do. Question was, could I do the right thing at the risk of losing Emery?

Emery slipped his hand into mine, which had been flopped on my thigh like a wet noodle. Tears welled in my eyes. Keeping my face to the window, I squeezed his hand. *How am I going to tell him? How can I hurt him like that?* A homeless man curled up in a doorway caught my attention. Recognizing him, I sat straight up, horrified.

"What's wrong?" Emery asked. He leaned forward so he could see out the window, too.

"It's Joe." I pressed my nose to the glass.

Salt-and-pepper dreadlocks peeked out from the dingy blanket that Joe wrapped around himself, his hands clutching the edge. The blanket didn't quite make it around his lanky frame. Joe's face looked miserable. A quick vision adjustment revealed that his brown skin had a purplish hue, indicating he was very cold. A violent shiver shook his body. "He's freezing."

"Joe has lived on the streets for a long time," Emery said of my friend, whom he had never met.

I'd met Joe when he'd witnessed me scaling the Space Needle, and we'd been friends ever since, even though he didn't know my name and had never seen my face.

"He's fine," Emery added.

94

"He is *not* fine," I fired back, losing sight of Joe.

Joe had been wandering since being released from prison for manslaughter nearly twenty years ago. Denying himself the comfort of family, friends, and a home was a self-inflicted penance for the single punch that had killed his friend Theo. The fistfight that had ended in tragedy had been over a girl. Joe couldn't even remember her name anymore.

"Joe is in his sixties and should not be out here," I protested. "Why isn't he at the shelter?"

Joe had promised me when I last saw him—on a cold, blustery night in early January—that he would spend nights in a local homeless shelter until spring.

"This is Joe's choice," Emery pointed out. "You can't help someone who doesn't want help."

"We'll see about that." I glared at the street. This was another situation I would resolve.

I *would* find the microchip, and Joe *would* accept my help.

*Ten*

# It's Alive!

---

At 2:39 a.m., I dove through my bedroom window in my typical fashion, catching carpet and somersaulting. As I came to my feet, it didn't surprise me to find Chazz sleeping in my bed, all snuggled up with my pillow decoy. He had gotten into a bad habit of crawling into my bed at night. Thankfully, he appeared to be quite unaware of the difference between me and a couple of pillows formed under the covers to look like me.

*What am I going to do with you, Chazz?* I winced when the window squeaked on its tracks as I pulled it shut. *It's freezing in here.*

I took off my shoes and unzipped my jacket, shivering when cold air touched my exposed stomach. Discarding the jacket, I swiped a T-shirt off the floor and pulled it over the torn tank top, frowning. I had really liked that tank.

With a series of gentle tugs, I wriggled the pillow from my brother's hold and slid under the blankets to cuddle up with him. The room might be cold, but he was warm like a little radiator. He hadn't even stirred.

*Good thing you sleep like a rock, Chazzy.* I closed my eyes and yawned. It felt as if I had just fallen sleep when I became aware of being jostled.

"Wake up, sleepyhead," Chazz sang, shaking me. "Time for school."

"Stop," I complained, swatting blindly at his hands. I couldn't peel my eyelids apart. *It can't be six fifteen yet.*

"Mommy said to get up." He yanked the covers back.

"Knock it off!" I groped for the blankets.

Chazz pulled them completely off my bed and ran.

"You'd better run!" I yelled after him, curling into a cold, coverless ball. A few seconds later, I gave up and threw myself out of bed. There's a reason my family calls me Sunshine in the morning.

~~~

Everyone was in the kitchen, including Ben. He, Dad, and Nate sat at the table, reading an article on Dad's laptop. Chazz, who sat on Dad's lap, glanced at me briefly as I entered the room, then looked back at the screen as he pretended to read along.

"Done," Ben said. Stretching, he noticed me standing at the island, about to pour Cheerios into a bowl. A huge grin stretched across his face. Only one thing would make a passionate conspiracy theorist and believer of all things mythical this happy. I had made the headlines.

"Cassy girl, weren't you just at the Denny?" Ben's amber eyes sparkled.

I willed my face into a mask of innocence. "Yeah, why?"

"The curse—it's aliiiiiiive!" Nate threw his head back, laughing maniacally like Dr. Frankenstein.

"Well, *something* is alive," Dad said, frowning at what I assumed to be an article about an ancient mummy on the loose. I wanted to be anywhere but there at that moment.

"What's going on?" I asked grudgingly. Deceiving my family was really getting old.

"A miracle!" Ben answered. He urged Dad, "Go back to the video. Wait till you see this, Cassy girl."

I moved to where I could see the laptop screen and avoided looking at Mom, who was preparing sack lunches at the counter. I especially hated lying to her.

With my arms crossed, I waited for the video of the museum's security footage to load with a mixture of excitement and dread. This would be the first time I saw myself in action.

"Yay!" Chazz clapped his hands when the video started to roll. He tossed me a smile.

I smiled back, crossing my fingers that none of the mummy's red hair had gotten loose.

A slender mummy with a bullet-torn midsection came onto the screen. Luckily, the black-and-white image was grainy and hard to make out. Not that there was anything to make out. Cool as a cucumber, Mr. Phillips robotically dropped the Glock and yanked the Saiga 12 to his eye, aiming steadily at me. Behind him, Moreau collapsed to his knees.

"Whoa!" Ben hollered. "Will you look at that?"

I cut my eyes back to the mummy, but I was no longer in the frame. Camera frames shifted to a white blur in the next exhibit and debris flying in my wake from bullets as they struck the walls. The video ended. I wondered if this was only the footage released to the public, or if this was all that had recorded. Emery did say camera connections had been lost.

"Is this all?" I asked, thinking about the hooded figure. Today, I questioned whether he had been real. Considering how traumatized I was, could I have cooked him up?

"That's all that's posted from *inside* the museum," Ben said, flying high. "But check this out. Drake, click the second tab—Nate, dude, you haven't seen this yet, either. Some guy caught this on his cell. The comments on YouTube say he started recording when the alarms went off in the Denny. He didn't expect to have his mind totally blown."

I frowned. I hadn't noticed anyone on the street when I jumped through the window. In fact, I hadn't thought of it until that very moment. The broken glass could have injured an innocent bystander. *You have to think, Cassidy*, I chided myself as we waited for the video to load. *You could have killed someone.*

The wobbly view of a quiet Fifth Avenue, lit by streetlights, came on. The man filming the scene obviously didn't have a steady hand. There were only a couple of cars on the street, which appeared to have slowed down while the drivers gawked at the museum, trying to figure out what was going on. Suddenly, there was an explosion of glass from the left, and a white figure with outstretched arms, straight legs, and pointed toes appeared in the air. The cars jerked to a halt. Incredibly, the man didn't drop his phone. How shocked he must have been!

"Holy crap!" Nate shouted.

Pride welled up in my chest. I looked so graceful—sleek, tough, and powerful, like an action heroine in a movie.

"Badass," Nate breathed as I landed in a crouch, shards of glass striking the cement around me.

I couldn't help it. I smiled.

"I can't fathom this," Mom said, leaning over Dad's shoulder and squinting at the laptop, as if squinting would help make sense of what didn't make sense.

On the screen, I shot off in a white streak. My smile grew. I was badass.

"Do you think it's some kind of special effect?" Mom asked.

Staring at the laptop, Dad rubbed his chin. "I don't know what this is, Lizzy."

"It's as plain as day," Ben said, beaming. "It's an honest-to-goodness miracle—a mummy from ancient Egypt. I talked to Leroy on my way over. He's already all over this."

Leroy Rays had been the host of a big-game hunting show. After a run-in with a certain Sasquatch, he'd become the host of a new cable show called *Monster Hunters*.

*Yet another person I've led astray,* I thought, discreetly observing Ben's shining face. I had single-handedly dismantled any doubts he'd had that the stuff of urban legends wasn't real. With supernatural ninjas rising from the dead, Sasquatches protecting old women from hungry tigers, and now ancient Egyptian mummies jumping through plate-glass windows, he'd become a true believer.

"That's a trip." My sour mood had returned. Then I noticed the number of views for the video, and my jaw practically slammed to the floor. "One hundred twelve thousand people have watched this already?"

"It'll be one hundred twelve million by the end of the week," Ben predicted.

You'd think this would cheer me up, but it had the opposite effect. *I'll be famous. Woo. Hoo.* How would being a YouTube star solve my problems, including Emery and Serena's imminent heartbreak? *It won't do squat. Nothing will.*

"Ten minutes before you have to leave," Mom's voice interjected into my angry thoughts. She squeezed my shoulders, and I stiffened, gritting my teeth with annoyance. "Get some breakfast."

I was only too happy to down some breakfast and then get the heck out of there.

~~~

Ten minutes later, Nate and I left the house. Emery waited for us at the end of our walk, as he did every weekday morning. His eyes scanned my face. He looked tired.

I attempted a smile. The result felt like a sneer. I was still fuming about all the things that I had no control over.

"Hey," Emery greeted Nate and me. His eyes remained locked on mine. Beyond him, his front door opened, and his dad walked out.

My heart jumped to my throat.

He saluted us, smiling. "Have a good day, kids."

"Bye, Dad," Emery returned.

"You, too, Mr. Phillips," Nate called back, waving.

I glared.

The lying, murdering snake headed to Serena's car. *What is he up to?* I wondered, panic rising in my chest.

"Where is he going?" I demanded of Emery.

Mr. Phillips climbed into the car.

"A meeting," Emery said.

"*What* meeting?"

Emery's gaze shot to my face. "I don't know. Why?"

"Don't bite my head off! I was only asking."

"Geez, Cass," Nate said, butting in. "Take a chill pill."

"Leave me alone!" I yelled in his face and stalked off.

Behind me, I heard my brother whisper to Emery, "Sorry, dude—"

My hands balled into fists. What made him think he had to apologize for me?

"Must be that time of the month."

Snapping up a pinecone at my feet, I whipped around and chucked it at my brother, pegging his left shoulder.

Shocked, Nate grabbed where I'd hit him. His eyes ignited. "Get a grip!" he shouted at me. "Stop being such a psycho."

Emery, watching me with a rare look of alarm, took a step forward so he walked ahead of Nate, as if to protect him from me.

*What does Emery think I'm going to do to my own flesh and blood?* Now I was really pissed.

"Leave me alone!" I pivoted on one heel and quickened my pace. Angry tears stung my eyes.

"Give her space," Emery advised Nate.

"See me running after her?" Nate snapped. "Dude, have you been teaching her how to pitch balls, too? At the risk of sounding like a wuss, that hurt!"

He and Emery busted up, Miriam's voice joining them. I had glimpsed her front door opening a moment earlier.

"What's happening?" she asked, out of breath from running to catch up with the boys.

"*Cassidy* is what's happening," Nate said.

I clenched my teeth.

"*You're* the jerk," she told my brother. "What did you do to her?"

"*Moi*?" Nate sounded amused. My eyes narrowed on the expanse of sidewalk before me as I pictured the waggish look I knew he'd have on his face. "Hey, now. Easy, girl."

I didn't need to look to know that Miriam had tried to hit him—playfully, of course. I knew Miriam and Nate through and through.

"*What* did you do to make her mad?" she demanded.

"Breathing makes her mad."

Miriam chuckled at Nate's joke—but not the object of his joke, mind you. "Cassidy, wait," she called.

I kept walking.

"She needs space, Miriam," Emery told her. "Give her a chance to cool down."

"From what?"

"Take your pick," Nate said. "Something is always setting her off."

*Let's see how you'd handle animal DNA being twisted into* your *cells,* I retorted in my head. *With your temper, you'd make the Hulk look like the Jolly Green Giant. Ha!*

But why was I angry? Nate wasn't the source of my anger. Helplessness was.

*How could I let Mr. Phillips drive away like that, knowing he might have the microchip with him? But what could I do, tackle him to the ground and frisk him?*

I recalled what he had said to Moreau in the tomb: *Drop-off has been confirmed for zero hours on Sunday.*

He had obviously been referring to the microchip. That meant I had four days to find the microchip before it exchanged hands. And just how was I going to do that?

102

I still hadn't come up with a solution when I entered Queen Anne High five minutes later, other than not letting Emery's dad out of my sight, which I had already failed at.

"There needs to be twenty of me," I muttered as I flung my locker door open.

Emery caught it. "We need to talk," he said in a low voice.

"There is nothing to talk about." I unzipped my backpack with a ferocious tug.

"On the contrary, we have *a lot* to talk about."

"No. We. Don't." I wrestled my overstuffed binder from the overstuffed backpack. "I can't believe how much work these teachers give us. Don't we have enough going on in our lives? Why—"

Emery grabbed the backpack. "We're leaving."

I yanked it back. "You leave."

"That's not happening." Emery flipped me around and gripped my shoulders, bringing his face inches from mine.

I glared into his eyes. No way was I letting him intimidate me.

"We need to discuss what you're experiencing."

"Currently—*embarrassment*," I retorted, referring to the attention that we were drawing. Whispers had kicked up around us when he'd spun me around. Ogling eyes watched us.

"Be straight up, and the *scene* ends," Emery said.

"Try to not be so predictable."

"Predictable?" His mouth curved into a grin. "I think not. I suggest you humor me and listen, or I'm liable to become very *unpredictable*."

Scowling, I jerked my head up and down, acquiescing with resentment. We had already provided enough entertainment for our fellow schoolmates, and I had no doubt Emery would follow through with his threat and give them more to gossip about later.

He pushed my hair back and brought his mouth to my ear, which didn't help in the not-being-a-public-spectacle department, but did prevent snoops from overhearing.

"The bullet wounds may have healed, but your mind hasn't," he whispered, his hot breath tickling my ear. "It will take time to recover from the emotional trauma of being shot, but you don't need to do that alone. I'm here for you."

My eyes misted, and I let my backpack drop heavily to the floor so I could wrap my arms around his neck. Let the gossips talk.

*My dearest friend, how am I going to tell you about your dad?*

Emery continued to whisper, listing possible symptoms of emotional trauma: confusion, anxiety, fear, anger, mood swings, guilt, sadness, and hopelessness—all of the symptoms I was experiencing, but not because I'd been shot.

"I'm so sorry, Emery," I whispered, apologizing for his dad being no good, something he would learn soon enough.

"No need to apologize. I understand why you were irritable."

No, he didn't.

"Get a room, kids," Bobby heckled behind Emery.

My arms flew from Emery's neck, and I shot a dagger glare at Bobby.

Bobby winked and went on his merry way, as he always did when he made a passing rude comment.

"He needs his butt kicked," I grumbled to Emery. Leave it to that oaf to make me feel even more like a moron than I normally did.

"Not by you," Emery teased, and yanked my hair to coax a smile out of me. It worked.

"Unwritten" sang from my coat pocket—the ringtone I had chosen for the cell phone my parents had given me. I'd picked that particular song because who knew what was going to happen in my life?

I fished the phone from my pocket and looked at the screen. It was a text message from Chad:

*Hi Red Hot! Wanna know how I got your number? <3 Chad*

"You've *got* to be kidding me."

"Who texted you?"

"A maggot." I punched out a response: *NO.*

"Well, don't reply to Dunham," Emery said, grinning. He had guessed correctly whom I was referring to. "You'll just encourage him."

"*No* will encourage him?"

"Yes. He'll eventually get bored if you ignore him."

"*Eventually* better be this very second." No sooner had I slipped the phone back in my pocket than it rang again.

"He must have a death wish," Emery remarked, amused. "Dunham knows you're taken."

"What does that mean?" I asked, even though I knew exactly what it meant. Who *didn't* think I had a thing for Emery, especially when I was hanging off his neck like a Christmas ornament.

"My life sucks," I grumbled, and returned to extracting my stupid books from my stupid backpack.

*Eleven*

# Worlds Colliding

The need to get the last piece of Assassin out of sinister hands weighed heavily on me—along with the growing list of lies I'd told—and by the end of the school day, depression swaddled me like a lead sheet. I couldn't shake it off or come up with a solution for locating the microchip—not without help, anyway. I needed a partner. I needed Emery, which wasn't going to happen.

If I had learned anything in these last several months, it was how to create a façade of cheer. The only person I usually couldn't fool was Emery. However, today turned out to be one of the rare times when his barometer was down. He didn't pick up on my troubled thoughts, perhaps because he had plenty of his own.

"You look exhausted," I told him at our locker after seventh period. We shared a locker because there hadn't been any available when he'd registered for school. There may have been now, but we sort of enjoyed being locker mates.

"I'm fine," Emery said. He pulled books off the upper shelf, frowning.

"So you say, but the bags under your eyes say otherwise." My cell rang again. Emery's mouth turned down even more. Chad's texting had been relentless, which had ceased to amuse Emery around fourth period.

"Being that this attention is for my benefit, I'll talk to him." Emery shoved a textbook in his backpack.

*Algebra*, I noted, a subject he'd probably mastered in kindergarten.

"What do you mean?" I asked.

"Chad is challenging me." Emery grabbed his biology textbook—an even bigger joke.

I bristled. It wasn't that I welcomed Chad's sudden interest in me, but I couldn't help being a little offended. "Maybe this isn't about you. Maybe he's genuinely attracted to me."

"No argument that you'd be a coveted trophy," Emery teased, forcing the zipper over the contents of his backpack. "But that doesn't change the fact this is about me."

"Looks like Chad isn't the only one around here who has a big ego."

Emery grinned. "And this surprises you?"

"Nothing surprises me anymore," I muttered.

We flowed down the hall in the river of bodies, migrating toward the double doors that would release us into the world. And what a world it was.

*Only two of us in this cattle corral are aware that the world is on the brink of change, and not for the better. I have to get the microchip back.* I continued to brood as Emery chatted with Daisy Hoffman, who had muscled her way between us. *Where are you right now, Mr. Phillips? What are you up to? How am I going to stop you from doing whatever you've set out to do, other than holding you captive and beating the location of the microchip out of you?*

I couldn't rule out any possibilities.

As I left the building, I caught sight of Mickey's flaming hair, and my stomach sank. With his burly arms crossed, his feet firmly planted, and his mouth flattened into a serious line, he scanned the crowd from behind dark shades, looking for Emery.

"Mickey's here," I said, giving Emery fair warning.

His head turned in the direction I was looking. Mickey spotted him at the same time, and a knowing smile curved Mickey's mouth. He shook his head.

Emery grinned back. "It appears I'm being summoned," he remarked. "Perfect. We need help."

"W-why? By *Riley*? Riley wants you? What's going on?"

"Cassidy, don't you watch the news?" Emery flashed a smile and took off. I followed, a sick feeling of dread gripping my stomach. Riley had told Emery how to break into the museum—the museum that had been robbed last night. It didn't take a rocket scientist to put two and two together.

"Li'l bro," Mickey greeted him, pulling Emery into a hug. In Emery's ear, he said, "Ran into some trouble last night, did we?"

"Not trouble," Emery clarified in a hushed voice. "Company."

Mickey gave Emery's back a firm pat. Releasing him, he turned his big grin to me. "Nice to see you again, Cassidy. How was school today?"

"Fine," I replied, not knowing what else to say. How much trouble was Emery in?

"Good to hear," Mickey said, enthused. He clasped Emery's shoulder. "If you don't mind, I need to borrow Emery for a while, but I'll return him, good as new." He pretended to brush lint off Emery's jacket.

"Okay," I answered, at a loss for an even halfway intelligent response.

"Shall we?" Mickey said to Emery and yanked him along by the shoulder.

Emery mouthed to me, *Don't worry.*

I gave him a pained look. Like *that* was going to happen.

As they walked toward a black SUV with tinted windows, I had every intention of listening in on their conversation, but couldn't focus enough to locate their voices among all of the other noise.

A group of friends said hello to me as they passed. Absently, I lifted a hand in response, keeping my eyes pinned on Emery and Mickey. The SUV's passenger-side window rolled down, and a stern-faced Riley peered out. Marty ducked his head from the driver's seat to eyeball Emery, too.

*What is Riley going to do?* I wrung my hands. She loved Emery, so I didn't think she would go to the police, but what did I know? *And why does he think she would help him now?*

Emery got into the back of the SUV with Marky, who had fought a grin when he and Emery made eye contact. Mickey climbed in after Emery and closed the door. The SUV drove off, and I thought I would go mad.

"I can't take any more!" I declared out loud. My world was spinning out of control. I had to get a handle on it.

My thoughts turned to Joe. I started walking with a sense of purpose toward the metro bus depot, which swarmed with kids waiting for a bus ride home. I couldn't fix everything, but I could make sure Joe would be warm tonight.

"Cassidy," Jared called.

I came to a reluctant halt and glanced in the direction the bus would be coming from before I swung around to him. I wasn't going to miss that bus.

"Later," Jared said to the boys he had been talking to. Turning his beautiful smile on me, he meandered in my direction. I resisted spinning my hand to urge him to get a move on it. The bus would pull up anytime.

"I gotta catch the bus," I shouted, walking backward.

Jared's eyes slid to the depot, analyzing the crowd. He wasn't one to walk blindly into any situation.

"Alone?" he asked, loud enough to be heard over the chitchat, and picked up his pace to a slow jog.

"Yes," I called back, wondering why he asked. *Doesn't he think I can take care of myself?*

The bus came around the corner.

"Bye, Jared!"

He caught up with me.

"Where are you going downtown?" he questioned, keeping my pace.

"I don't know." I flopped my palms up. "I have an errand."

"Would you like company?"

"That's nice of you, but I can take care of—"

"I know you can take care of yourself. I'd just like to hang out with you."

I stopped walking and stared at him. His mouth curled at the corners.

"It's rare that you're not with Emery," he explained.

I nodded, because it was true. I was usually with Emery.

"I'd like to hang out with you, too," I said. It was a complete understatement. Jared Wells pervaded my every thought—that is, when my thoughts weren't revolving around other dilemmas.

"Cool." Jared looked pleased. "We'd better hurry. The bus is pulling up."

~~~

Once settled in a seat, I inhaled deeply to relax my nerves, pulling in a variety of scents, Jared's being the most prevalent due to proximity. With a sidelong glance, I watched him run a hand through his bangs and take note of who was around us before he turned to me, releasing a long breath while doing so. His chocolate-brown eyes met mine. I stared into them like a deer caught in headlights.

"Soooooooo . . ." He dragged out the vowel. "What exactly are we doing?"

*Good question.* I rubbed my lips together, wishing they were glossed, and regretted not putting mascara on that morning. I had been neglecting my appearance since learning Emery's dad was a criminal.

*How do I explain my plan without saying too much, and without lying?*

"Cassy?" Jared raised his eyebrows. "Did you hear me?"

"I can't stop thinking about this homeless man I saw yesterday," I explained. "He was very cold, so I'm buying him gloves and wool socks."

While Jared processed this, I analyzed what I'd said and smiled when I realized I'd told him the truth, for the most part.

Jared opened his mouth to speak. I expected him to ask an obvious question, like, "How are we going to find the homeless man?" or "Where did you see him last?" Both were questions I was prepared to answer. But Jared didn't always ask the obvious questions.

"Why this guy?"

"Huh?"

"Why him? There are tons of homeless people downtown. What was it about him that caught your attention?"

"Ummmmm . . ." My mind scrambled for an answer. *Dang.* I fidgeted in my seat. "I—uh—I told you, he was cold. I just want him to know someone cares."

Out of nowhere, tears sprung into my eyes as the truth of what I'd said sank in. I *did* want Joe to know someone cared about him, cared very much.

Sympathetic, Jared nodded to let me know that he understood. He redirected his gaze to the window so I could compose myself in privacy. "How about we start at REI?"

"Sounds good," I agreed, dabbing my eyes.

"We might not be able to find him."

"We'll find him. I'd better call my mom and let her know where I am—" I paused as I heard "Unwritten" playing in my pocket. "Weird, if that's her." I reached for the phone.

Turning back to me, Jared watched as I looked at the phone screen. I felt my upper lip lift with distaste.

*Surprise, surprise,* I thought, reading Chad's text. His message: *Shame, shame. Give Wells a big kiss for me.* Obviously he had seen Jared and me get on the bus. Being the two-timer that he was, of course, he would come to the conclusion that I was cheating on Emery.

"Creep," I muttered, and erased the message before Jared saw it. How embarrassing would that be? Hitting *Home* on speed dial, I relaxed in my seat and tried to look cool. I couldn't wait to tell my mom that I was going downtown with Jared.

~~~

Jared and I had a fabulous time searching for warm things to give Joe. Being on a mission with the boy of my dreams kept my worries at bay. In fact, we had so much fun that I forgot from time to time that he was the boy of my dreams. It was as if we had teleported back to a simpler time, before our feelings had crossed the friendship boundary and gotten into a tangle. We were buddies again, laughing, joking, and enjoying each other's company. For lack of a better word, we were *comfortable* together, and it had been a long time since I had been completely comfortable around Jared.

We found a couple pairs of wool ski socks with really cool designs, warm gloves made out of this stretchy material that I thought Joe would like, since he could pick up things easily when wearing them, and a Seahawks scarf to go with his Seahawks jacket. I contemplated buying him a new coat, and then realized I didn't have enough money in my bank account—much to my chagrin. I had gone on a shopping spree two weeks before. Why hadn't I thought of Joe then?

As we headed toward checkout, Jared plucked an aviator's hat with faux fur and earflaps from a display.

"Check it out." He pulled the hat on and grinned. My heart fluttered. This was one of the moments when I remembered I was in love with him.

"It looks *fantastic* on you," I gushed.

Jared's smile faded. "Thanks." He quickly took the hat off, appearing embarrassed.

112

Embarrassing him embarrassed me. I blushed on the spot.

"I meant for the homeless guy," he clarified.

"Oh." Of course he'd meant for Joe. Jared wasn't one to fish for compliments. "It's great, but I can't afford—"

"No worries. My treat."

"But you don't even know him."

"Well, neither do you."

I gave a relenting nod. "You have a point."

"And these—" He snatched a pair of socks from the shopping basket.

"You are not buying those!"

"*Who's* going to stop me?"

"That would be me." I grabbed the socks, and a playful tug of war ensued.

"Dang, you're strong," he said, having no clue just how strong I was. "And stubborn."

"*I'm* stubborn? You're the one who won't let go. You're getting the hat. That's plenty."

"You can't always get what you want," he teased.

"Have it your way." I released the socks.

Not prepared for this move, Jared stumbled backward, almost falling on his backside.

I chuckled as he righted himself. "Good save."

"Victory!" He grinned, holding the socks up like a trophy.

I watched him, thinking how he was everything I wanted in a boy, and in life. *But will I ever have the life I want?*

As I often did, I visualized the feral part of me as a snarling, restless, formless beast, chained in the recesses of my mind, waiting for me to relinquish control. And I'd done just that, twice—once to save my dad and once to save myself from Lily White. Regaining control had been much more difficult the second time.

*What if I let go someday and can't get the reins back?* This worry always cropped up after one of my beastly transformations. My body was still evolving, changing, so it

113

stood to reason that my mind would, too. One day, *Cassidy* might be completely gone.

*If Serena doesn't find a cure . . .*

"What's wrong, Cassy?"

Coming out of my thoughts, I met Jared's gaze. I didn't even know at what point I had looked away from him as I ruminated. I stared into his concerned eyes, and a deep loneliness seized me. I was tired of hearing only my own voice answer my fears.

"Do you ever feel like there's something dangerous inside of you?" I asked. "That if you ever let go, you'll lose control over it?"

Jared didn't laugh at me like most boys would. He had really thought this through. "I think I understand," he said after a pause. "My music helps me cope."

I opened my mouth, and then realized that what I was about to say would stimulate questions that might lead into a conversation I couldn't have with him. I also realized I was intentionally sparking this conversation. I wanted to spill the beans. I wanted to reveal my secret and tell him precisely what I coped with.

*Just as Emery has been worried I would do.*

In that moment, I understood another reason why Emery wanted me to keep Jared at arm's length. He knew I would be tempted to blab. Obviously, he wasn't far off base.

"That's cool," I answered, hoping to cover the fact that I wasn't being upfront. I wouldn't let Emery down today. "I wish I could play an instrument."

Disappointment crossed Jared's face. He knew I was holding back, but didn't challenge me on this. "If you're interested, I'll teach you how to play guitar," he offered instead.

I wasn't, although I was mighty interested in spending as much time with him as possible.

"That would be great. Thanks." I smiled.

He smiled, too, and then snagged the other pair of socks from my basket and ran for the register.

"If you buy those, you are so dead!" I shouted, running after him.

~~~

Jared and I walked toward Occidental Park in Pioneer Square, the last place I had seen Joe during the daytime. His scent revealed that he was there now, too.

When I caught sight of him sitting at the foot of one of the four totem poles, I stopped dead in my tracks. Elbows on knees, he rubbed his dark-lined forehead wearily. A Seattle Mariners baseball cap had been forced firmly over his salt-and-pepper dreadlocks.

*The hat Jared bought him will keep his head warm*, I thought, pained to see Joe looking so tired and so old. He meant the world to me. He should have been in a warm house, surrounded by a loving family, not out in the cold.

"Is that him?" Jared asked.

I glanced sidelong to see him staring at Joe, too.

"Yes." I pushed down the lump in my throat.

From the corner of my eye, I saw Jared's gaze cut to me. I pretended not to notice him scrutinizing me.

"Let's go," he said a moment later, walking forward, then stopping to look back when I didn't move.

I hadn't thought this part through. I couldn't hand Joe the REI bags and let him see my face. He would know by my gesture that it was me, and if he had any doubts, one look at my eyes would confirm his suspicion. Eyes, mouth, and the skin exposed by my ski mask were the only parts of my face he had ever seen. He would recognize my eyes for sure.

"You do it." I shoved my REI bag at Jared. He looked at me with surprise. "I'll stay here."

After analyzing my strange demand, Jared surveyed the area, uneasily assessing two homeless men to our left. His concern was totally valid. I had crossed paths with those two on more than one occasion during my midnight jaunts. They were very seedy fellows, indeed.

"I'll be fine," I assured him, urging him forward with a little push. I figured he would chalk up my reluctance to shyness. Jared knew I could be bashful at times.

Frowning, he sized up the men again while they hit up pedestrians for money.

"Shout if you need me," he instructed, and took off toward Joe. When he was about thirty feet away, I remembered something.

"Psst, Jared."

Wheeling around as if ready for a fight, he glared at the two men. When he saw that they were panhandling and not bothering me, his fierce gaze jumped to my face. I couldn't help but smile. Jared was so cute.

"Tell him there's a shelter on Yesler," I said in a low voice, exaggerating the word formation so he would understand me at this distance. Joe was perfectly aware of this, of course. This was my sneaky way of letting him know that I knew he wasn't spending the night in the shelter and he really should. Joe was a smart man. He would read between the lines.

Jared nodded, but looked less than thrilled about doing so. I wouldn't blame him if he didn't follow through. I wouldn't want to tell a perfect stranger where the nearest homeless shelter was, either.

Turning, he continued on his way.

I watched Jared cross the brick square with a mixture of excitement and apprehension. Two of my most favorite people in the whole world were about to meet. Who wouldn't be excited? Not only that, but a person from my *normal* life and a person from my *mutant* life were about to meet—worlds colliding. Who wouldn't be stressed?

Jared stopped a few feet from Joe and opened his mouth to speak. I weeded out competing noise and dialed in his frequency.

"Excuse me, sir."

Joe lifted his head from his palms and looked up at him.

"My friend, the girl ov—"

*Oh, geez.* I whipped my back to them, yanking my hood over my head in the process. I hadn't expected Jared to point me out.

In my surprise, I'd lost the connection. With my eyes fixed on the red brick under my feet, I searched for Jared's voice again.

"The redhead—" He stopped.

I shoved some stray hairs into my hood, assuming he was looking at me and wondering why I had just turned my back to him and put my hood on. He probably thought I was nuts.

"I mean, in the blue coat," he went on a moment later, confusion edging his voice. "She asked me to give you these."

The plastic bags rustled while exchanging hands.

Joe cleared his throat. "Thank you kindly." His deep, melodic voice, thick with emotion, stirred my emotions as well. I missed talking to him. "Please tell your friend I'm grateful."

"Sir . . . do you know her?"

*What?* Alarm crashed through me like a tsunami. Why would Jared ask that?

*Because he doesn't believe me.* Jared thought I was lying, and he was right. My shoulders hunched in shame.

"I don't need to know her to know what kind of person she is," Joe said. The bags rustled from being shaken. "This tells me all I need to know. Treasure her friendship, young man. A good-hearted person doesn't come around every day."

Joe's kind words failed to penetrate. I was completely unworthy.

"I know," Jared agreed, solemn. "And I do. She's been a good friend to me for a long time."

I shook my head, even more disgusted with myself. I had not been a good friend. Then Jared's words sank in. *He treasures our friendship?*

"Very pleased to know that," Joe responded with empathy, as if sensing my happiness.

*Jared treasures our friendship!*

Joe made a grunting noise like he was getting to his feet. "And I'm always pleased to meet an upstanding young gentleman," he said.

I couldn't help myself. I had to look. Shielding my face with my shoulder, I peeked at Joe and Jared shaking hands. Words cannot describe what I felt.

Jared introduced himself.

"It's a pleasure, Jared. Joseph Jackson, but you can call me Joe."

My jaw dropped, and I jerked my head forward again. Joe had never shared his full name with me before.

"Nice firm handshake. You can tell a lot about a man by the way he shakes your hand, looks you in the eye. Take care of yourself, Jared."

"Thank you, Joe. You take care, too. Oh, and my friend wanted me to tell you there's a shelter on Yesler."

A smile erupted on my face. He'd done it. Jared had kept his word.

"Tell her thank you."

"I will. See ya, Joe."

When Jared was out of earshot, Joe said in a hushed voice, "Thank you, Green Eyes. You're too good to me. For you, I'll sleep in that shelter tonight, but I tell ya, they're not as safe as you think."

Joe had told me this before. He'd been robbed in a shelter in Oklahoma City a few years before, which had soured him to all homeless shelters. Even still, a shelter *had* to be less dangerous than the streets.

118

"Lookin' forward to when the weather improves and we can visit again," Joe continued. "I understand about you not wantin' me to see your face, so don't fret about that if you're tempted to. I like him, Green Eyes. Edgar, I suspect?"

Lacing my fingers, I stretched my arms in the air to let Joe know he had guessed right. "Edgar" was the pseudonym I had given Jared when raving about him.

Joe chuckled. "He's a fine-lookin' boy, a trustworthy one . . . I got a feelin' about him . . ."

"Mission accomplished," Jared announced, coming up behind me.

Without turning around, just in case Joe was looking, I gushed, "You are *the best*, Jared Wells."

"And you are *crazy*, Cassidy Jones," he teased. He appeared at my side, grinning, and yanked my hood over my face. "What's with the shyness?"

"You know how I am." I pushed the hood up to look at him.

"Awesome." He snagged my backpack. "I'm carrying this," he informed me and started walking.

I didn't argue.

## *Twelve*

# Duplicity

---

Jared and I parted ways at the stone steps leading to the park below my street.

"See ya, Cass." He flashed a smile that made every nerve in my body tingle before he descended the steps that led to Spinning Park below. From there, he would cut through the city woods to his mom's apartment. I spent a lot of time in those woods, in the dead of night, racing around and swinging from tree to tree like a monkey to expel excess energy that built throughout the day. There was no way I could have slept a wink if I hadn't.

After losing sight of Jared, I crossed the street to Emery's house. He had texted me to come over on the bus ride home. My stomach was already in knots over what had happened with Riley. Mr. Phillips answering the door didn't help any.

"Hi, Cassidy," he greeted with a friendly smile.

*Act normal, Cassidy.* "Hi!" My tone was painfully loud, defeating "normal." "I'm here to work."

"Yes, I know." The scumbag seemed amused. "*S'il vous plaît entrer, ma belle fille.*" He pulled the door open, making a sweeping motion with his arm for me to enter.

I didn't know he could speak French.

Weak in the knees, I entered the foyer, wondering if this deplorable man was a multilinguist like his son. Emery knew seven languages.

"Um, I'm going to the lab to see if Mrs. Phillips needs help," I told him, not waiting for a response or even looking at him again as I went on my way.

120

"Sure, thank you," he called after me, sounding befuddled by my quick retreat.

I felt his eyes on my back as I hurried down the hall to the kitchen. Turning the corner, I paused at the basement door and regained my composure. I realized then that the television was on in the living room. I had been so stressed that I hadn't heard it right away.

Leroy Ray's voice boomed through the television: "Mummies, murder, mystery, and mayhem."

*Of course Mr. Phillips is watching Monster Hunters.* A disgusted sneer curved my mouth as I opened the basement door. *I'd want to learn more about what I'd shot, too.*

Closing the door behind me, I rested my forehead against the exposed drywall and shut my eyes, breathing deeply. Against my eyelids, I saw Mr. Phillips's heartless eyes targeting me, bullets shooting from the Glock's barrel, shells spitting into the air. Moving my hand to my gut, I recalled the first excruciating impact. It burned, as if a flaming arrow had struck my stomach. If my body hadn't released a natural analgesic, the pain alone might have done me in.

*I hate him. I hate him for hurting me and for betraying his wife and son, for betraying all of humankind. He deserves to rot in prison.* My fist pounded the wall.

Emery and Serena stopped talking. I had no idea what they'd been talking about and frankly didn't care.

"Cassidy?" Emery asked.

Pulling my face off the wall, I plastered on a smile that surely looked as fake as it was and descended the steps.

Emery regarded me with suspicion.

"Have you found a cure?" I asked Serena, simply because it was the first thing to come into my head. Of course she hadn't found a cure. She probably never would.

Serena was leaning over the lab table, jotting notes in her Mutant Girl journal. I avoided looking at Emery, who was perched on the stool next to her, but I could feel him watching me.

"We've discussed this, Cassidy," she lectured, continuing to write and not bothering to look up. Emery couldn't seem to get enough of my face.

"I'm kidding. How's Formula 10X coming along?" I inquired, just to make small talk.

Serena cut to the chase. "My dear, you have no interest in my progress with Formula 10X. You want to know what happened with Riley O'Shea. Emery will brief you." She slid off the stool, brushing some strands of hair off her face. "Emery, I'll keep your father occupied so you can get Cassidy up to speed. The man is exasperating. He watches us like a wolf. It wouldn't surprise me if he has my lab bugged." With that, she walked away.

I glanced around the room nervously.

"She's pulling your leg," Emery assured me. "I swept the house for listening devices early this morning. It's clear."

"Looking for bugs in your own home? You're kidding, right?"

Emery grinned. "We're talking about my dad."

I nodded, not pursuing the subject further. My conversation with Jared at REI proved how eager I was to spew secrets.

*Let spying on the family be the worst of Emery's concerns in regard to his dad,* I thought, easing onto the stool next to him. *His world will be rocked soon enough.*

"What were you doing downtown?"

"Let the interrogation begin." I let my backpack fall to the floor. "What would you do without GPS?"

"I'd have to use my other talents to keep tabs on you." Emery wiggled his eyebrows. "I'll demonstrate. Look into my eyes."

Emery stared into my eyes like he was concentrating very hard. I couldn't help smiling.

"Mm-hmm," he said, nodding. "Just as I thought."

"What do you see, besides freaky jade eyes?" I loved it when Emery was playful like this.

122

"Everything." He gave me a mysterious look. "Shall I tell you about your excursion?"

"Please do."

"Note: before I reveal all, I'm not pleased that you took a risk."

"Noted."

"You bought gloves and wool socks for Joe."

Okay, this was creepy. "How did you know that?"

"I can read your mind." He tapped his temple with that mysterious look. "All right, I admit it—I can't read your mind. I employed simple deductive skills. Here, I'll show you. Big-hearted redhead can't get her cold, homeless friend off her mind. Since she has no power to change his circumstances, she does what she has the means to do: buy him warm clothes. However, her coffer is running low after a shopping spree the weekend before last—thank you again for the T-shirt—and much to her disappointment, she realizes she can only afford a pair of socks and gloves. This realization floods her with soul-racking guilt, because why hadn't she thought about buying a coat and boots for him when she had the money—"

"You're giving me chills," I interjected. "You are seriously eerie. Right so far, and I still feel guilty."

"That's my girl." Emery chucked my chin. "After selecting socks and gloves in the most cheerful colors and patterns she can find, she hunts down her friend—literally—and charms a trustworthy-looking stranger into giving her friend the gifts while she hides and listens in on the conversation."

"Almost. I did find someone trustworthy to do my bidding, but he isn't a stranger."

Emery's expression darkened. "I wish you hadn't done that," he said in a controlled tone, making another spot-on deduction. "I can't fathom what would induce you to put Jared and Joe face-to-face. That was foolish, Cassidy. Let's hope there won't be repercussions. Use your head next time,

123

and don't let a childhood crush cloud your judgment. Your life and your family's lives depend on it."

My face burned with resentment, and I resisted a strong urge to slap him. His degrading my feelings for Jared and speaking to me like I was a toddler infuriated me beyond belief. But my own stupidity was even more maddening. Emery was right. I was a reckless fool.

"I'm sorry." My response came out frostier than I had intended. Was it Emery's fault that I was my own worst enemy? "Now that we've established the fact that I'm a complete idiot, tell me what happened with Riley."

Emery didn't refute the "idiot" remark. "I told her a third party tapped into the security system when I did, and since I suspected they were after the same thing I was, I decided to monitor them to see if they would reveal the item. After doing so, I planned on tripping the alarm to thwart the robbery. All true, more or less."

"What about me, the mummy? What did you tell her about that?"

"I gave her an accurate account of everything I witnessed on my laptop, though I did play down the shooting. Riley drew her own conclusion from there. She assumes another interested party broke into the museum first with the intention of ambushing Moreau. That would have been my conclusion, too, if I didn't know about you."

I nodded, uncomfortable. My parents had taught us kids that silence was as bad as bold-faced lying. But then, who was I to judge?

"I know," Emery said. "A lie of omission. Guilty as charged." He raised his hand.

"What?"

"A lie of omission is failing to correct a misconception, which—needless to say—I'm very good at doing. I don't take pride in duplicity, nor do I feel proud of holding back vital information from Riley, but both were necessary considering the circumstances. I'm not only protecting you,

I'm protecting the O'Sheas. The less Riley knows, and the less she's involved, the better. She's served enough time in prison."

"Agreed." The last thing I wanted was for Riley to become our accomplice and pay the price for our illegal activity, even though we had broken the law in the name of public safety.

"When consulting with Riley on Monday, I held back Moreau's name." Emery picked up his phone from the table. "I didn't want her aware of more information than she had to be, but that's changed now that Moreau has the microchip. It turns out Riley has heard of him. They ran in the same criminal circles in Europe. Is this the man you saw?" He brought up a picture of an elegant man wearing sunglasses while crossing a street, unaware someone was taking surveillance photos of him. He was definitely Moreau.

"That's him. What do you know about him?"

"Born on June 18, 1981, in Marseille, France, Julian Anton Moreau is an international art thief and on Interpol's Most Wanted list. He has been connected with some fairly notorious thefts, his latest being the most lucrative, potentially. Imagine the payday he'll have if we don't get the microchip back."

"We'll get it back," I said, not sounding overly confident. We *had* to get the microchip back. *What if it's right under our noses?* My eyes darted around the room. Would Mr. Phillips have hidden the microchip in his home?

"What are you looking for?"

My gaze returned to Emery. His eyes narrowed on me.

"So what now?" I deflected. "How do we find Moreau?"

"Riley is reaching out to her contacts. Hopefully they'll have information on his current whereabouts."

I gave him a moment to continue. When he didn't, I asked, "That's it? There are no other plans?"

"Other than you scouring the streets for Moreau, none at the moment. I've depleted every resource I have online. Even the FBI has little on him—"

I slapped a palm to my forehead. "*You* hacked into the FBI's database?"

"No need for alarm. They don't know. Riley's contacts may have more information. Would you mind switching the laundry?"

"What? Why? You're making my head spin."

"Well, I don't want to do *that*. If you could take care of the laundry?"

"Okay." Resigned, I slid off the stool. "Here I go to the washer and dryer, playing along."

"By the way, I was kidding about scouring the streets for Moreau," Emery said. "Looking for him would be futile."

"How can you be so sure?" I opened the dryer door to beige towels and slid a laundry basket underneath. "I know his scent." I reached deep into the dryer to scoop the towels out. "Besides, you don't have any better plans—" I stopped short as my mummy costume tumbled into the basket with the towels. "Emery," I gasped, glancing at the stairs. "Are you crazy? What if your dad had taken these out?"

"He wouldn't have. He told me to do it."

I twisted around to look at him scrolling through email, wearing a smug smile.

"What are you—a lazy, rebellious teenager?"

He shrugged. "I just don't like to fold."

"Well, who does?" I quickly piled towels over the costume. "You take too many chances. At some point someone is going to take *you* by surprise."

"I know a strong-willed redhead who does quite often."

"*I'm* strong-willed? That's the pot calling the kettle black. You want me to wear this again?"

"The costume? Eventually, after we've found Moreau. He and his men were terrified—"

"All of them?" Emery's dad hadn't looked very terrified to me.

"Granted, they're professionals. Soldiers of fortune would be my guess . . ."

Squirming, I snagged a towel from the basket to fold. I regretted asking the question. It could cause Emery to meditate on Moreau's men more than he already had.

Emery went on, watching me a little more carefully than he had been. "The way the gunmen handled weapons and maneuvered through the museum, they're obviously military trained. Soldiers are taught to hide fear, but that doesn't mean they don't feel it. Experienced or not, a frightened person is more liable to slip up."

"True." I dearly wanted to change the subject—although, frankly, I was shocked Emery couldn't see the obvious. The shooter was built like his military-trained father, who had come home three days before the robbery. If clues were snakes, they would have bitten him.

*But maybe Emery doesn't want to see the obvious.*

"The costume's thrashed," I pointed out.

"Do you think I would send you into the field with unsuitable gear?" Emery clucked his tongue. "Take a closer look."

Digging the costume free from the towels, I shook it out and examined the front. The rips had been meticulously repaired with tiny, even stitches of cream-colored thread. Without looking carefully, one wouldn't even notice the damage. "Serena is a great seamstress."

Emery huffed. "My mother? Please. I'm the seamstress in this family."

"Well, you've got some mad skills, Betsy Ross."

He gave me a sly smile. "I'm a man of many talents. You know, it would be a shame to waste the effort my mom is exerting to occupy my dad. Why not reward her with a vial of blood?"

~~~

After the blood draw, Emery said, "About those towels . . . why risk blowing your cover? You should fold them and put them away."

I was about to tell him where he could put the towels when a light bulb went off in my head. The linen closet was located on the second floor next to the master bedroom. Being alone on the second floor would provide a golden opportunity to have a look around. If Mr. Phillips had the microchip, he had to hide it somewhere, right? If anything, I might find a clue to where it was hidden, or to Moreau.

"Well, I don't want to blow my cover," I said, adding a nice bite of sarcasm to mask my excitement. "Or have you get off your backside."

"My thoughts exactly." Emery flipped open Serena's Mutant Girl journal, displaying no signs of suspicion.

"Glad we're of one mind."

"Well, then, commence folding." He waved a hand for me to begin.

While folding towels, I watched him transcribe his mom's notes on her laptop, a task he had been doing daily ever since Silver Tooth, i.e., Raul Diaz, created a bonfire out of Serena's file cabinet contents in her former laboratory. "Has your mom found anything new?"

"Nothing compelling. But I'm confident you'll be rid of us one day."

I stopped folding and stared at him, fear shooting through my heart. *Do they plan to leave when I'm cured?* The thought overwhelmed me.

"In that case," I said, finishing the last towel, "I hope she never succeeds."

I set the towel on the pile and swept up the laundry basket, glimpsing a satisfied expression on Emery's face as I turned to the stairs. I interpreted the look to mean he didn't want to leave me, either, which pleased me to no end.

"Make sure my dad sees you carry the towels upstairs," he called after me.

"I will, and I'll suggest he grounds you—or gives me your allowance."

"Allowance?" Emery laughed. "Good one, Cassidy."

I opened the basement door and stepped into the kitchen, pausing to take stock of what was happening in the living room. Serena giggled. It took a second to digest this. Serena wasn't exactly the giggling type.

Gripping the basket, I stomped loudly down the hall and cleared my throat for good measure.

"Busted," Mr. Phillips teased his wife in a muffled, husky whisper when he heard me clomping down the hall.

Serena giggled again.

I turned bright red. I had figured they were smooching.

As I entered the foyer, I saw Serena slide off her husband's lap and onto the sofa. *Couldn't she have done that, like, two seconds ago?*

"Ummm," I said, feeling awkward. As if I wasn't embarrassed enough, they sat a foot apart, grinning like a couple of teenagers who had been caught "necking," as my Grandma Jean would say. "I'm taking these upstairs."

"Thank you, Cassidy." Serena straightened her lab coat. "Would you mind taking the dirty laundry from our bathroom down to the lab, too?"

"I already have," her husband told her, poking her side.

With a coy smile, she slapped his hand away.

Sadness crept into the corners of my mind. This was no act. Gavin Phillips loved his wife, and she loved him. Looking at him just then, it was difficult to envision him as the killer who had emptied his gun into my stomach.

*Why would he risk losing everything? And for what? Money?*

"It's your move, dear." Mr. Phillips indicated the chessboard that sat on the coffee table.

Serena stifled a giggle.

I turned up the stairs, catching sight of Mr. Phillips wiggling his eyebrows devilishly at his wife, just as Emery did when he was teasing me. Downcast, I barely had the heart to enter their bedroom and snoop around.

When the nightstand, dresser drawers, and the closet produced nothing, I adjusted my vision and slowly scanned the room, to no avail. A microchip could be hidden anywhere, and it wasn't like I had the time to search properly. I couldn't very well turn their room upside down to do it.

*I've already taken too long putting towels away as it is*, I thought with frustration. *Besides, hiding the microchip right under Serena's nose would be super stupid—or very clever.*

Before leaving their room, I examined a few family photos on the dresser: the Phillipses' wedding picture, Emery as a baby, an awfully cute picture of him wearing a lab coat and big glasses at around age four, and a family photo when Emery looked to be about seven. After admiring the pictures, I slid the backs off each frame to make sure there wasn't a microchip behind them.

Then I hustled down the hallway and the stairs, slowing my pace to toss a tight smile to Mr. Phillips and Serena as they actually played chess.

"That took a long time," Emery remarked when I tromped down the basement steps.

"I was looking at pictures on your mom's dresser. You were a cute little guy. What happened?"

"I grew into these." He tapped the black frame of his glasses.

I dropped the laundry basket on the floor and began collecting dirty plates off the lab table.

"You don't need to do that." His eyes skimmed through the data he had typed into the computer.

"For appearance's sake, right?"

He grinned at the screen. "Whatever floats your boat, sugar," he said, quoting our deplorable neighbor, Jason

Crenshaw—or as I referred to him, the Henchman. Emery had hired Jason to drive us back and forth to Catamount Mountain when we were hunting a tiger and a metal man. Then Jason had blackmailed Emery.

"Thanks, *Slick*," I returned. Jason had given Emery the cool nickname Slick, while I got called every degrading pet name in the book. "I'll be back."

"And I'll be waiting with bells on."

I rolled my eyes. Emery could be such a dork.

While loading the dishwasher, I eavesdropped on the conversation in the living room, gleaning critical information. Mr. Phillips planned to grill steaks for dinner and made a bet with Serena that if he won their chess game she would watch a movie with him and Emery tonight, but if she won she would massage his feet. Obviously, he figured she would win. His bet and the dinner menu were irrelevant except for the fact that they revealed he had no plans to sneak off and sell biological weapons secrets that evening, at least not until after their movie was over. By then, it would be late enough for me to follow him.

*But what about during the day, when I'm at school?* I wondered while scrubbing encrusted chili from a bowl. Serena was a huge fan of canned chili.

*Cupcake, you do know one person who has all the time in the world and will do anything for a few bucks.*

"Well," I whispered to myself, sticking the bowl in the dishwasher, "looks like I'm hiring myself a henchman."

# Thirteen

# Henchman for Hire

A t 11:34 p.m., Emery texted me *good night* after he and his dad finished their movie. A few minutes later, I hid in the shadows of my fence line, waiting . . . and waiting . . . and waiting. Mr. Phillips never left his house.

At 2:00 a.m., jittery with energy and bored out of my mind, I concluded that Emery's dad was fast asleep and left my post to take care of the energy issue. If I didn't go for a run, I wouldn't get any sleep at all that night.

*Hopefully Mr. Phillips will make a move when Jason stakes him out during the day*, I thought, as if Jason had already accepted the job I planned to offer him in a few hours. I had no doubt he would, since I would be speaking his language: cold hard cash. Or at least the promise of cold hard cash, because I was broke.

~~~

"Darn!" I stopped dead in my tracks a couple blocks from school the next morning, slamming my palm into my forehead for effect. "I forgot my homework," I explained to Emery, Nate, and Miriam. And just so my scheme to talk to Jason alone wasn't totally deceitful, I actually *had* left my homework at home. "Gotta get it. See ya." With that, I turned on my heels, homeward.

"I'll go with you," Emery offered.

"Thanks, but no need." I waved him on. "We'll both be tardy then. I'll get my mom to drive me to school."

Emery didn't argue, though I could feel his suspicion hanging in the air between us.

*He won't follow me*, I thought, hoofing it. *He knows I'll smell him.* However, he would spy on me via GPS. I already had a plan for that.

At Miriam's house, I checked his location on GPS, or more accurately his phone's location. Emery could have left his cell at school and followed me from a safe-scent distance. GPS showed his phone at Queen Anne High. When deep, dragging breaths and a thorough visual scan from my front porch didn't reveal Emery to be lurking nearby, I placed my iPhone in the lavender plant next to the front door and walked over to the Crenshaws', smiling at my cleverness.

I rapped on the peach-painted door, which sported a *Welcome* wreath comprised of ornate flowers. The Crenshaws' wiry-haired mutt, Princess, answered with a howl and threw herself against the door. The dog was totally obnoxious. As I waited, I glanced around at the picture-perfect yard of the picture-perfect Victorian. Mrs. Crenshaw spent hours outside weeding, pruning and gossiping with Mrs. DeAngelo, who lived in the Dutch Colonial between our English Tudor and the Crenshaws' house.

"Princess, hush," scolded Mrs. Crenshaw from inside the house.

The dog kept barking.

The door cracked open, and Mrs. Crenshaw peeked out—pink bathrobe, hair in curlers, hazel eyes in a narrow face. I had forgotten how early in the morning it was.

"What's wrong, Cassidy?" She craned her long neck out the door to look in the direction of my house. Her foot held back the rabid mutt.

"Oh, sorry, Mrs. Crenshaw, everything is okay," I stammered, embarrassed. Of course she would assume something was wrong. It wasn't like I stopped by for a visit often—or ever. "Is, uh, Jason here?"

"Jason?" She blinked at me in confusion. Totally understandable. As far as she knew, Jason and I didn't know one another beyond sight. "Why do you want to talk to Jason?"

"Um, there's something I want to tell him. It's in regard to an employment opportunity." The words had sounded much more sophisticated in my head.

"An employment opportunity?" Mrs. Crenshaw's face lit up. "For Jason? Yes. Please, please come in." She opened the door, again telling Princess to hush.

The dog ignored her.

"Thank you." I entered the foyer, which was wallpapered in a pretty floral pattern. Princess backed away, snarling, with her balding tail tucked between her legs.

Mrs. Crenshaw shut the door and gestured to the living room, self-consciously touching the curlers on her head. "Please take a seat, and I'll get Jason for you," she said, and hooked her finger under Princess's collar.

While she dragged the growling dog away, I went into the living room, which was packed with ornate antiques, fancy bisque dolls, floral-print upholstery, and oil paintings featuring more flowers. Along with the flowers, lace dominated the room: lace curtains, lace fringe on pillows, dolls wearing lacy dresses, lace doilies gracing tabletops and the arms and headrests of the sofa and chairs. Unfortunately, the smell of stale cigarette smoke, which had absorbed into the surfaces of the room, stole from the ambiance, as did the yellow tinge on the lace curtains. It made me think of plaque on teeth.

Since dolls occupied the chairs, I sat on the sofa. Having trapped Princess in the dining room behind French doors, Mrs. Crenshaw smoothed out her robe, which had become disarranged in the struggle, and turned to me wearing a hospitable smile.

"Excuse me for a moment," she said. "I'll get Jason for you." She rushed up the stairs as if the opportunity of a lifetime was at stake. Maybe in her mind it was. Her twenty-five-year-old bum of a son finding gainful employment would be a dream come true.

I tracked her eager footsteps down the upstairs hall. They stopped, and a door opened.

"Jason," she whispered.

No answer.

"Jason," she said more sharply.

Jason groaned.

"Jason."

"What?" he snapped.

The door closed. Apparently Mrs. Crenshaw didn't want me overhearing them.

"You have company," she explained from inside his room. "Cassidy, Drake and Elizabeth's daughter."

"Who?"

I gritted my teeth. He knew exactly *who*—I think.

"Our neighbors, the Joneses." Mrs. Crenshaw sounded weary. "Cassidy wants to talk to you. Get *up*. It's impolite to keep her waiting."

"Tell her, *politely*, to take a hike." His words were muffled, as if he had buried his face in a pillow.

"You *will* talk to her," Mrs. Crenshaw insisted.

"Ma, knock it off!"

I pictured her pulling the covers off him. "If you weren't up playing that computer game all night . . ." Her voice was strained, suggesting that she and Jason were having a blanket tug-of-war. "She wants to tell you about a job."

"Yippee. Is Deluxe Burgers hiring?"

"Jerk," I muttered under my breath.

"Okay, I'm up!" he said. Footsteps stalked across the floor.

"Jason, put on a robe," Mrs. Crenshaw pleaded.

Jason blew her off.

A knot formed in my stomach as I listened to him come down the hall and stairs. I hated dealing with Jason.

He appeared a moment later wearing a holey T-shirt, pajama bottoms, and a sour expression. His sandy blond hair was in complete disarray, which would have been charming if it hadn't been on his head. "Long time no see. This better be good, Cupcake."

His mother came up behind him and gave me an apologetic look.

I cleared my throat and straightened my spine. "It's regarding a job opportunity." I tried to sound professional, aloof.

Jason mocked me with a look that announced I had failed.

"Is there some place we can talk privately?" I asked.

"As a matter of fact, there is." He dug sleep from his hazel eyes, just to be disgusting, I'm sure. "Get up, and you can proposition me there."

Mrs. Crenshaw gasped in horror. "Jason!"

I came to my feet, clenching my jaw and resisting the urge to march right out of that house. For the good of humanity, I would stomach Jason's rudeness.

"Relax, *Mother*." He flopped a hand in my direction. "She's, like, twelve. If she hits on me, I'll turn her over my knee and spank her."

"Apologize to Cassidy immediately!"

"For what? Warning her to keep her hands to herself?"

Mortified, Mrs. Crenshaw was speechless.

"I don't have all day," he said to me, and headed down the hall toward the back of the house.

"Excuse me, Mrs. Crenshaw." I felt sheepish, walking past her in pursuit of her deplorable son.

She nodded, wringing helpless hands. No wonder Jason got away with being such a loser. She let him walk all over her.

Jason collected the waist of his pajama bottoms, which had slid down on his narrow hips, and hiked them up. It was the only acknowledgement that he knew I was walking

136

behind him. I figured he also did this to make me uncomfortable.

Tall, broad back, cocky walk—he still resembled the high school football star he had once been, though I was sure if I poked a finger through one of the gaping holes in his T-shirt, it would sink into marshmallow flesh. In a few more years, his chosen career path, Professional Bum, would catch up with him. Spending long days lounging around, smoking and playing the online game *Gods and Kings* didn't do much for retaining muscle mass.

He flung the basement door open, releasing more cigarette stench.

*So this is where the magic happens*, I thought, crinkling my nose.

Jason flicked a light switch and started down the stairs while I trailed him. Fluorescent lights buzzed to life over an unfinished basement. Utilities lined the right wall, while shelves stacked with storage containers occupied the back wall. Jason's "command center" dominated the left side: two ratty recliners on a brown shag area rug, angled toward a wide-screen television with a loaded console underneath. The top of the console was coated in dust.

"So this is the man cave," I remarked.

Jason plopped into one of the recliners and swiped a cigarette pack from amongst open cans of soda, candy wrappers, and empty chip bags littering a side table. A bowl of fine china serving as an ashtray looked and smelled like it hadn't been emptied for weeks.

"Explain yourself." Jason tapped a cigarette from the pack.

"May I?" I asked, indicating the other recliner.

"You may."

I traversed the area rug, which literally crunched under my feet, and pinched a chip bag that had been deposited on the vacant chair. Pinky aloft, I transferred it to the side table with the other rubbish. "May I brush the crumbs off?"

Jason smirked around the cigarette he had just lit and waved for me to proceed.

I brushed the crumbs onto the carpet, which was filthy anyway, and sat gingerly on the edge of the chair while Jason watched, mildly amused.

"Now that you've made yourself comfortable," he said, exhaling smoke, "get on with it."

"Don't you know how bad those are for you?" I pointed at the cigarette.

"Yes, sweetheart. I saw the film about the black lung in fifth grade health, just like you."

"And that didn't deter you?"

"Apparently not. Note: *small talk* will be added to the tab."

"What makes you think I want to hire you for anything?" I waved his gray death away from my face.

"Ch-ching." Jason made a cash register hand motion, warning me to get down to business.

"I need you to follow someone for me while I'm at school."

"Who?"

"Mr. Phillips, Emery's dad."

"Interesting." He actually did look interested, which I found rather disturbing. He pushed back in the recliner and stared into the void, smoking and thinking.

*And plotting*, I added, regretting my decision to involve Jason. I had known hiring him presented a risk, but now, watching him churn information in his cunning mind, I realized I had underestimated the danger. This had been a mistake.

"Never mind," I said, standing up.

"Where do you think you're going?" His sly eyes slid to me, his mouth curling into a smirk. "You opened this can of worms, and there's only one way to close it." He rubbed his fingers together to indicate *money*.

138

I plunked back down, glaring. This had been a *huge* mistake.

"Now that we have an understanding, let's talk rates. Taking the threat level into consideration, twenty dollars an hour."

"Twenty dollars an hour?" I spluttered, though that was a third less than what he had charged Emery. "Five," I negotiated, since that was all I currently had to my name.

"Twenty. Take it or leave it, but I suggest taking it."

"Fine, but we're setting up a payment plan."

Jason barked a laugh. "Pumpkin, are you really this naïve? How much cash do you have available?"

"Five dollars—but I get paid twenty dollars a week. It's yours until you're . . ." I searched for an impressive word to prove I wasn't a complete idiot. "Compensated."

"Compensation will take a while. Interest rates compound."

I glowered. "*Interest rates?* In other words, you're blackmailing me?"

"Interest rates, blackmail. Tomato, tamahto."

"Whatever," I said, agreeing sourly to his shakedown. I should have expected Jason to bleed me dry. "And what do you mean by 'threat level'?"

"Please." Jason tapped ashes into his makeshift ashtray. "Do you take me for a fool? Mr. Phillips is not one you'd want to meet in a dark alley."

I couldn't argue that, and honestly was relieved that Jason knew the man was dangerous. As despicable as Jason was, I wouldn't let him go into this blindly. "Have you met Emery's dad?"

"I haven't had the pleasure." Jason yawned. "Shouldn't you be at school?"

"Meet me at four o'clock sharp at the halfway point in the woods," I instructed, ignoring his dismissal. I had to retain some semblance of control, or the *appearance* of control, at least.

Jason saluted me.

"Call me if he does anything suspicious. Do you have a paper and pencil so I can write down my cell number?"

"I believe I have it on speed dial."

I stared at him uneasily, and then remembered he had my phone number from when Emery had hired him. A smug grin appeared on his face when he saw that fact register on mine.

"Sorry, but you're not my type," he said.

I opened my mouth to retort, but held my tongue. I had to keep things professional. "I won't be using that phone."

"The plot thickens. Lay it on me, babe."

"Where's something to write on?"

He tapped his temple. "I'll put it in the locker for safekeeping."

At this point, I was too flustered to argue. I rattled off my phone number while he took a deep drag from his cigarette, appearing more focused on that than on anything I was saying.

"Four o'clock sharp," I reminded him.

Jason exhaled smoke. "You better run along. You can show yourself out."

"You're on the clock now, you know. Mr. Phillips could leave his house anytime—"

"I'm on it. Now scoot." Jason waved a hand for me to go.

Flaring my nostrils, I swung around and marched to the stairs, feeling like I had just sold my soul to the devil.

~~~

I walked into first period twenty minutes late. Emery looked at me questioningly. Smiling, I waved my sheet of homework at him and placed the tardy slip on Mr. Narin's desk.

Something passed over Emery's face that I couldn't quite identify before his standard calm expression slipped into

140

place and his gaze returned to Mr. Narin lecturing at the front of the room.

The rest of the day plugged along, while I sat on pins and needles waiting for my cell phone to ring. It never did. Otherwise, the day was run-of-the-mill, save for rumors about me stalking Chad. I laughed when my first friend reported the rumor, but by the fifth friend I wasn't laughing anymore. I told myself repeatedly that I didn't care what anyone thought, but who was I fooling? I cared, especially considering the disgusting nature of the gossip. I had a strong suspicion where it had originated: the supposed object of my obsession and his evil girlfriend, my self-proclaimed arch-nemesis, Robin Newton. Robin never could pass up an opportunity to talk trash about me. So when I saw the two of them walking toward me on the way to history class, I couldn't help but aim a pointed glare at Chad. I generally avoided looking at Robin.

His initial reaction was shock, which quickly turned to smug satisfaction. Inwardly I groaned, realizing the egomaniac had interpreted the dirty look as jealousy.

He came to a halt and swung Robin around to him. She staggered into him, opening her mouth to demand what he was doing, and at the same moment, Chad dove in for a kiss.

A couple of kids plowed into him from behind, causing Chad and Robin to stumble and foiling his kiss attempt. Robin lost her footing and slipped onto the floor between his legs. Somehow, Chad managed to keep hold of her and stay up on his feet, though the awkward way he lunged forward, with his legs spread wide and arms wrapped around her back, made it look like he had messed up a challenging dance move.

In other words, they looked delightfully ridiculous.

I escaped into the classroom, snickering quietly. Moments later, Chad stalked in, beet red, daggers shooting from his eyeballs, as if I had forced him to make a fool of himself. Whipping his nose in the air, he walked to his desk with as much swagger as he could muster.

*Fourteen*

# Busted

After school, I was extremely relieved to see Jason's and Serena's cars parked in front of their respective houses. I'd fretted all day that I would come home and find them both gone. I was dying to get Jason's report and happy to know where Emery's dad was, for the time being.

Nate, Emery, and I bid Miriam good-bye at her house and continued on to ours.

"Talk later," I said to Emery. Thankfully it wasn't a "housecleaning" day for Serena. She had gotten restocked with my blood the day before.

"See ya," Emery said, flashing his easy smile.

I looked at him carefully. I'd had a feeling something other than finding the microchip had been on his mind all day. Though outwardly he seemed fine, with Emery, outward appearance meant nothing.

He crossed the street, while Nate and I turned up our front walk. As Nate unlocked the front door, I peeked over my shoulder and watched Emery duck into his house and close the door. I entered our foyer and groaned.

"There's something I need to do real quick," I told Nate, without specifying.

He gave me a "so what" look.

"Tell Mom I'll be right back." I dropped my backpack on the floor and scuttled out the door, pulling it shut behind me.

Outside, I studied Emery's windows to make sure he wasn't spying. Not seeing anyone peering out, I jogged down the porch steps, picked up speed on the sidewalk, and didn't slow down until I was a hundred yards or so in the woods. I wanted to get to the meeting spot before Jason.

Then I stopped dead in my tracks. I had caught a whiff of Jared.

"You've gotta be kidding me!" I skidded to a stop on the gravel path. Judging by scent, he was very close. If I hadn't been running, I would have smelled him sooner. I had to have the worst luck in the world.

By the time I had collected my wits and come up with a plan—which was to hide—Jared strolled around the corner, carrying a guitar case.

He jumped when he saw me. I pretended to be taken by surprise, too.

"You startled me," he said, looking happy to see me nevertheless.

Normally, I would have been thrilled, especially since this crossing of paths was a total coincidence. It was as if fate—or some evil force—was at work.

"Yeah, what a shock." I put my hand over my heart, as if to calm it down. Yep, I had the worst luck *ever*.

"What are you doing here?" Jared stopped in front of me.

I shrugged. He gave me an odd look.

Groping for something to say, I nodded at the guitar case. "What's with the guitar?"

His mouth curved into a slow grin. My heart sped for *reals* this time.

"I play at Cherry Street on Tuesday and Thursday afternoons."

"You what?"

"I play guitar." He lifted the case. I must have looked like I needed a visual aid.

"At Cherry Street, the coffeehouse? You work there?"

"Yep, I work there. It's a good gig. I'm doing something that I love and getting paid for it."

"But you just started playing."

"A year ago."

144

"And you're that good? That people pay you?"

"Paul, Cherry Street's manager, seems to think so, but he isn't all that picky." Jared grinned again.

"Wow! That's incredible. You must be a fast learner," I said, attempting to mask my true feelings. I should have known Jared played guitar well enough to be hired. *I would have known if I hadn't been a total jerk last May and annihilated our friendship.* I shook my head to dislodge the condemning thought. I had to cut myself slack at some point.

"I'll have to come down and listen sometime—" I stopped, having smelled Jason's cigarette-laced scent. I could also smell Princess. "Well, you should get going," I urged Jared, giving him an overly bright smile. "You don't want to be late."

Jared studied me. "You've been acting strange all day. What's going on?"

"I have?" I thought I was a better actress than that.

"Be straight-up, Cassy," Jared advised. He was getting tired of my games.

So was I.

"Okay, I'll tell you. I got to thinking about what you said about Mr. Phillips, so I hired Jason Crenshaw to follow him. I'm meeting him here for a report."

A few silent moments passed while Jared stared at me.

"You're joking? Of course you're not joking. This is exactly something you'd cook up." He shook his head, amused.

I didn't quite know what to make of the remark, but the endearing way he had said it made getting riled up impossible.

"Jason Crenshaw's your neighbor, right?"

"Yeah. He's sort of like a private eye."

Jared stared at me for a beat, then peeled into laughter. I laughed, too. Jason didn't exactly scream *professionalism*.

"How do you come up with this stuff?" Jared asked between laughs, which stopped as his eyes fixed beyond me, narrowing.

I didn't need to turn around to know he was looking at Jason. I could smell him just fine and hear the gravel crunching under his leisurely footsteps.

"He's here," Jared whispered.

"You should go, then."

Jared frowned. "I think I'll stick around."

"No, no, you have to go." I gave him a little push.

Jared didn't budge.

Princess started barking as she noticed us, which made me wonder if there was something wrong with her sense of smell. She should have smelled us long ago.

"Jason is cool," I assured Jared. "We've worked together before."

Jared's gaze jumped from Jason to me. "You've *worked* together? What does that mean?"

"Nothing," I said, louder than I meant to. Princess's manic yapping had forced my voice to rise and put my nerves on edge. I could hardly hear my own thoughts, and Jason didn't even try to shush her.

"Well, fancy meeting you here," Jason spoke over his dog, sarcasm dripping from his voice. He was such a jerk.

"Hi," I said, swinging around. Princess strained at her leash, practically foaming at the mouth. "What a sweet dog." I blew the wretched mutt a kiss.

Princess went ballistic.

Jason gripped her leash with both hands and smirked, appreciating my smart mouth. "Appears she has taken to you." His mocking eyes moved to Jared. "If looks could kill," he remarked, his smirk widening.

I turned to Jared. Jason wasn't kidding.

"Really, it's cool," I assured Jared, lowering my voice. "Please go. I'm getting charged by the minute."

"That she is," Jason confirmed. "So take the hint, Sir Lancelot, and ride off into the sunset."

Jared's fists clenched.

I was stunned. Why would Jason provoke Jared? Any fool would know he could give Jason a run for his money, and Jason was no fool. So why wave a red cape at a young bull?

*Is Jason trying to pick a fight?* I prepared to catch Jared's fist if he took a swing at Jason. This was ridiculous, and exactly what I didn't need. As it was, I was ready to hike Princess like a football. She hadn't stopped barking once.

Jared's hands relaxed. "If you say it's cool, it's cool, Cass." His mouth turned up into a small smile as he stared Jason down.

Jason continued to egg him on with that smirk. I wanted to wallop him and tell him to make his dog shut up.

*What is it with these males?*

"I'll see you later, Cassy." Jared shouldered past Jason. The stupid dog ignored him and kept barking at me.

"You certainly get these young bucks in a tizzy," Jason remarked.

Something inside me snapped. My temper had risen to dangerous levels, but hadn't stirred the beast. It was just Cassidy who was furious.

Slowly, I lowered my chin and made eye contact with the dog. "Stop. Barking," I commanded, and she did, much to my surprise and Jason's.

Whimpering, Princess rolled on her back in submission to the more dominant female, her tail between her legs and pointing skyward in defeat.

"Wuss," Jason said, mocking his dog, but when he looked at me, the blasé had been replaced with uneasiness. His dog's reaction was odd, and though I didn't want to admit it, for a split second there was a connection between Princess and me, much like I'd had with Roga, the tiger who had been ready to feast on Mrs. Westing before I intervened.

"See, all your dog needs is a little discipline." I gave him a disarming smile, hoping it hid my own uneasiness. "Did Mr. Phillips leave the house today?"

Jason cast one last look at his cowering dog before meeting my gaze, his expression unusually serious. "Around eleven."

I wished I had just let that stupid dog bark.

Jason listed the places Mr. Phillips had stopped: Shell gas station, Ace Hardware, Peet's Coffee, and Trader Joe's. Then he fell silent. I turned my hand in circles for him to continue.

Jason's smirk returned. "Home," he said, back to his normal sardonic self.

"That's it?"

"What were you expecting him to do? Blow up Columbia Tower?" Jason delivered this in an offhanded way, but watched for my reaction. This was exhausting. I couldn't let my guard down for a second with him.

"Oh, yeah, that's *exactly* what I thought he'd do." I willed my face not to reveal that Mr. Phillips blowing up Columbia Tower was a completely feasible scenario. "How long did you follow him?"

"Sweetheart, if this is in regard to what you owe me, I was on the clock the moment you left my house this morning, remember?"

I began calculating. Jason saved me the effort.

"Eight hours, rounded down, out of the goodness of my heart: a hundred and sixty dollars."

"One sixty?" I sputtered. "For errands?"

"Disappointing, I know, but you're paying for a service. That's how it works in the big people world. Now, Cupcake, I'm getting a bad feeling that you're playing me. I strongly advise against reneging."

"I'm going to pay you. A deal's a—" I stopped, getting a whiff of Emery this time.

*No!* I shot my hand into my coat pocket. My fingertips jammed into my iPhone. Why hadn't I thought of powering down the phone? *Darn GPS.*

"You've got to go, *now*," I told Jason.

Alarmed, he jerked his head around to see who was sneaking up on him. The path was clear. Emery hadn't rounded the corner yet. Jason turned back around to me, irritated.

"No conning a con," he advised.

"I'm not conning you," I snapped. "And I *will* pay you. Just go!"

"I think not. Pay up now, and I'll be on my merry way."

"You know I don't have the cash right now," I hissed. Emery would be in earshot at any moment. "We agreed to a payment plan. But here's five dollars." I slapped the bill in his greedy mitt. "I'll get the rest to you when I have it. Just go, that way." I pointed in the opposite direction of Emery, but it was too late.

He came around the corner and was not the least bit surprised to see Jason.

"Now this is a fine kettle of fish," Jason said.

I felt my face turn a shade of green. I was going to be sick.

Emery briefly regarded the dog, still curled into a submissive ball on the gravel. Princess had been so quiet, I had forgotten she was there. His gaze moved to the five-dollar bill in Jason's hand.

"How much?" Emery asked Jason in a matter-of-fact way, as if he'd been the one who had hired him.

"A couple Bens should do," Jason replied, smug, as if Emery *had* hired him. It made me wonder what I'd missed.

I experienced a range of emotions as I watched Emery pluck out two hundred-dollar bills from his wallet. My stomach sank. He had come prepared. He knew I had hired Jason, but did he know what for? Rubbing my forehead with a shaky hand, I wondered if anyone else knew—such as Mr. Phillips.

Jason tucked the bills into his jeans pocket, then yanked the dog to her feet by the leash. Princess let out a yelp.

"Enjoy this fine afternoon, lovebirds." Jason winked at me. Good thing for him I was so devastated.

I watched him saunter away, dragging Princess behind him. She looked back at me, miserable. I knew how she felt.

"Would you mind explaining why you hired Jason to follow my dad?" Emery asked when Jason was out of earshot.

Unable to look at him, I lowered my face into my hands and cried. When tiny pools of hot tears had formed in my palms, Emery's patience expired.

"This isn't getting us anywhere." Irritation edged his voice. "Let's go to the park and sit until you can calm down."

I nodded and started walking, avoiding eye contact with him.

As we emerged from the woods, Emery broke the silence. "Let's go to the swing." He called it *the* swing, but I referred to it as *our* swing, since it was where I had taken him into my confidence about the changes I'd experienced after knocking over beakers of Formula 10X. *Our* swing was a totally appropriate place to spill my guts once again.

"Step into the confessional." Emery held the swing still for me, echoing my thoughts.

Stealing a glance at his stoic face, I stepped onto the slatted wood platform and collapsed onto a bench. Emery sat across from me on the other bench.

I wiped my eyes with my coat sleeve and allowed my gaze to crawl up to his face, which was calm. Why was he always so calm?

"I'm going to share what I've pieced together," he said. "Stop me if I have anything wrong."

Biting my lip, I jerked a nod.

"My dad was also in the tomb at the Denny."

I nodded, staring at his mouth.

"My dad shot you."

"He didn't shoot me. He shot a mummy," I corrected, only somewhat intelligently, since I had started crying again.

"Do you think he wouldn't have fired his weapon if he had known it was you?"

Unsure whether he was being rhetorical, I shrugged. Emery's dad was bad to the bone. I wouldn't put anything past him.

Emery placed his elbows on his knees and laced his fingers together thoughtfully, narrowing his eyes on the void before him. "An honest answer, not muddied by tiptoeing around my feelings," he observed. "Now we're getting somewhere. Tell me everything you've held back. Spare no detail."

I did as he asked with much difficulty. If it weren't for all the tears and apologies, I would have completed the account in half the time. Throughout it, Emery urged me on with nods and waved off apologies as if they were gnats.

At one point, he interrupted my agonized apology. "Stop apologizing, Cassidy. You were between a rock and a hard place. I understand that. In your position, I would have verified my suspicions before sharing them with you, too."

I couldn't handle his calmness anymore. "I don't understand how you can be so easygoing about this. You don't even look upset." I followed this with another horrified apology. Why couldn't I think before speaking?

Emery waited for me to fall quiet. Then he said, "I have a skill you don't—the ability to *compartmentalize*. Once we have the microchip, I'll sort through my feelings, but until then, I can't let emotion influence my decisions. Too much is at stake."

"But he's your dad."

"I know. To be frank, he and I are close, but at arm's length, if that makes sense. I'm allowed into one part of his life, but not another, which is fine, because the part I'm in is meaningful to him—"

Tears poured down my face. This was so heart-wrenching.

"I'm aware he has a dark side." Emery paused, and a gamut of emotions flitted across his face—worry, sadness, confusion, regret, anger. He cleared his throat and added, "But I always thought he was one of the good guys."

I couldn't take it anymore.

"Oh, Emery!" I grabbed his hands and bent over them, smothering them with weepy kisses. I tasted his skin and the salt of my tears. When I had sufficiently slobbered all over them, I peeked up at him through wet lashes.

His face was composed again, and his expression showed he was deep in thought. He also seemed unaware of me looking at him, as if a sobbing girl weren't kissing his hands and making a complete idiot of herself.

"However," he said as though continuing a sentence, "we can't forget that we only have a few data points to draw a conclusion from."

Releasing his hands, I straightened up. Apparently his moment of vulnerability had passed.

Now that he had his hands back, Emery relaxed into the bench. "Admittedly, the data points that we do have are damning. My dad *did* help plan a heist; he *did* break into the museum; and he *did* steal Queen Kiya's crown."

I considered sharing Mr. Phillips's joke about killing the security guard if he double-crossed Moreau, but dismissed it. Why rub salt in the wound? Emery had his dad's number now.

"So we will keep priorities straight and emotions at bay," he continued, "and take whatever measures are necessary to recover the microchip before damage can be done."

"Should we tell your mom about this?"

"Absolutely not. She is too emotionally driven and would be compelled to confront my dad."

I stared at him skeptically. *Serena driven by emotions?* I just didn't see it.

"Don't let her fool you," Emery said, answering my thoughts in his eerie way. "She isn't as rational as she puts on—like someone else I know." He grinned.

"You're *teasing* me?" I slapped his thigh, which made him grin more. "At a time like this? And when have I *ever* pretended to be rational?"

"I stand corrected. You have *never* pretended to be rational. What did Jason report?"

"Nothing. Your dad ran errands. That's it. By the way, how did you know I hired Jason?"

"My dad told me."

I just about had a heart attack. Judging by Emery's laughter, my expression was hysterical.

"Apparently some clarification is needed," Emery said between laughs.

I didn't hold this amusement against him. He probably needed it to cope.

"My dad casually mentioned when I came home that 'the blond kid from across the street' seemed to 'be about Seattle quite a bit today.'" He shook his head with a look of distaste. "Honestly, it was humiliating for him to think I was such an amateur that I'd hire Jason to follow him."

"I deserve that," I agreed, taking my lumps. "I am an amateur. What did you tell him?"

"Tell him? He made a general comment to which I cleverly replied, 'Huh.'"

"But obviously he knows Jason was following him. Doesn't he want to know why?"

"Of course he does, but he isn't going to ask me, since I'm a prime suspect."

"I'm going to be sick," I groaned, gripping my stomach. I had really made a mess of things. "How did he even see him? Jason's good at this stuff."

"My dad is better," Emery said. "We'll have to take extra precautions, since his suspicion is aroused."

"Are you okay with this?"

"I have no choice but to be okay. We should get back. We have to run surveillance on my dad."

"I'm so sorry."

"None of that," Emery reminded me. "The story isn't over yet. But we'll err on the side of caution and assume my dad belongs behind bars."

I started to say *sorry* again, but Emery covered my mouth.

"And *you* are never to keep me in the dark again. We're a team. We need to be straight with one another. Otherwise we're at a disadvantage."

"Sor—" I began to say into his hand.

He shook his head. "Nod yes."

I nodded.

"Glad we're in agreement." He released my mouth.

"So what do we do now?"

"I'll poke around my house for clues, probably to no avail. My dad won't leave any behind."

"You say that like you've looked before."

"I've looked for clues my entire life."

Hearing that Emery had been searching for the truth about his father had surprised me a little. He'd always acted indifferent about his dad's mysterious ways.

"I'm a known factor. You're not," he continued. "My dad won't anticipate what you're capable of. I'll run surveillance during the day, and you will at night. If we're lucky, he'll slip up, and we'll have the microchip well before Sunday."

Sadness filled me. Emery talking so impassively about his dad, as if we were discussing a complete stranger, bothered me. Could he really turn his feelings off like a faucet?

Instead of annoying him with another apology, I took his hand again. "Are we okay now?" I asked.

"We were always okay. Just be completely honest with me from here on out."

I nodded miserably, turning my face away so he wouldn't see that there were things I still hid, such as his dad being a paid killer, suspicions that he had something to do with Junior's prison break—and that he might be on the senior King's payroll.

*Fifteen*

## Chad the Cad

As Emery had predicted, he didn't turn up any evidence of his father's activities, business associates, or possible locations of the microchip. I didn't have any luck that evening, either. Mr. Phillips never left his house. Around 2:00 a.m., I once again gave up waiting for him to sneak out and got some exercise. Although I was dying to make sure that Joe was off the streets for the night, I decided to not venture farther than the woods, just in case Mr. Phillips pulled a fast one. From the woods, I could hear a car engine start on our street and catch up with him in under a minute.

I crawled into bed at quarter to three and woke up to my iPhone vibrating in my coat pocket at quarter past six.

Drowsy, I fished out the phone. The text was from Emery: *Doing a stakeout with Mickey today. Will text if we need you.*

I frowned. I didn't like Emery staking out his dad without me, but it was what we had agreed to. Mickey would look out for him.

I texted: *OK. Be careful.*

Immediately after sending the text, I regretted doing so. I shouldn't have told Emery to be careful of his own father, no matter how dangerous the man was.

~~~

My mind, for obvious reasons, was elsewhere all morning. I was on pins and needles, waiting for Emery to text and tell me he needed my help. Since I didn't want to be annoying, I resisted asking for an update, but did check

Emery's location often on GPS. They'd been stationed at a marina on Elliot Bay for most of the morning.

By lunchtime, my resolve not to pester Emery broke down. I had to find out what was going on.

I texted: *What's happening at the marina?*

Emery replied: *We don't know yet. Enjoy lunch.*

"Enjoy lunch," I muttered. How could I possibly enjoy anything today?

Walking to the cafeteria, I absently swung my lunch bag, pondering. How much had Emery told Mickey, and did Mickey believe him?

At the table my friends occupied, I stepped over the bench and sat down next to Bren. Lost in thought, I was vaguely aware of Miriam, Carli, and Natalie Fletcher sitting across from me.

"What are you thinking about, Cassidy?" Miriam sang. "Or more precisely, *who* are you thinking about?"

I glanced up. She gave me a mischievous wink. As far as Miriam was concerned, brainpower should be utilized only to fantasize about boys.

"Why do you always look like you're up to something?" I asked her.

"Because I am." Miriam grinned and sank her teeth into her sandwich.

"Stupid question."

Without warning, Chad squeezed in next me, sitting backward at the table with his hip pressed against mine. I recoiled and scooted closer to Bren.

With his back to my friends, he propped his elbows on the table, leaned back, and stretched his legs, gifting me a dimpled smile.

I tasted vomit in my mouth.

"Hey, Red Hot," he said, trying to sound seductive.

I cracked up, as did Bren.

The dimples faded.

"What?" he demanded and sat upright, looking annoyed and perplexed.

Was he really *that* dense?

Still laughing, I flipped my palms up to my friends and shrugged. Miriam wore a fiery grin, while Carli and Natalie appeared uncertain how to react. This was Chad Dunham, after all, one of the most popular boys in school. Snorting with laughter, Bren dropped her head to the table and drummed it with her fists. She didn't give a hoot about Chad Dunham or his popularity status, and wanted him to know it.

"What's so funny?" he asked me, scowling.

"I'll tell you," Bren offered between laughs.

His haughty eyes didn't waver from my face. It was as if Bren hadn't spoken to him. Now I was getting angry. Who did he think he was, blowing Bren off like that and keeping his back to my friends?

"What do you want?" I snapped.

His dimples deepened into a cheesy smile. Clearly he lacked talent for interpreting tone and body language. If I moved any closer to Bren, I would be sitting on her.

"Have lunch with me, over there." He gestured to the left with his chin. My gaze moved in the direction he indicated, to a group of kids I would rather swallow nails than eat with. Robin sat among them. Momentarily meeting my gaze, she gave me a death glare. I could hardly blame her. This was just plain cruel of Chad—but then again, remora Jessica Blanchet sat next to Robin. Chad had dumped Jessica for Robin.

Before I could tell Chad to "just shoot me instead," Miriam took matters into her own hands.

"Cassidy eat with you? But, Chad, that would make me so *sad*," she mocked in a cherubic voice.

Chad's spine stiffened.

"I mean, I know you're totally *rad*, but—"

"Miriam!" Carli cut her off. "Don't be rude, or Chad might tell his *dad*."

158

I sputtered into laughter, spraying spittle everywhere.

"Yuck," Bren choked out in laughter, pretending to wipe my spit off her face. "Maybe you *should* eat with the *cad*."

Chad got to his feet.

As he strutted away, Miriam called after him, as if devastated: "Chad, *please, please, please* don't be *mad*! I know I'm *bad*, and not just a *tad*. But *bam*, you look hot in those skinny jeans, even though they're no longer the *fad*."

Chad flipped her the finger over his shoulder.

Giggling, Natalie shouted, "That's not nice, *lad*. Say hi to *Brad*."

We looked at her questioningly.

"Who the heck is Brad?" Bren barely got out.

Natalie shrugged. "I dunno."

We laughed harder, if that were possible.

~~~

Because I was watching the little red dot indicating Emery in Mickey's jeep as it drove east on Elliot Drive along the water, I didn't see the door to the girls' locker room swing toward me.

*Bam!* The door smacked me, sending blood gushing from my nose. Robin stood in the doorway, hatred gleaming in her flat blue eyes and a challenging smile curving her lips. It caused her nose, which I had busted, to bend slightly to the left.

"Are we even now?" I cupped my nose to catch the blood.

"It's an improvement." Robin smirked and shouldered past me into the gym, a couple of remoras fluttering after her. They threw me disdainful looks, too, being the good little minions that they were.

In the locker room, concerned girls instantly came to my aid. Waving off their offers of help, I thanked them and said I was fine as I made my way to the restroom. I slipped my phone into my hoodie pocket, pulled open the door with my clean hand, and stepped inside. My vision adjusted instantly to the dark. I locked the door and walked to the sink, where I dumped out the blood cupped in my hand. There wasn't much. Whatever damage Robin had done had healed soon after the door hit me.

"Hope you got it out of your system, Robin," I muttered, cleaning my face. "Otherwise, we're going to have an interesting time in P.E."

Utilizing the mirror, I wiped the last of the blood from my face and frowned at the red spatters on my hoodie. *Now that just looks gross.* I shrugged out of the hoodie and used a clean portion to pat my face dry. Then I wandered back into the locker room and got dressed.

Robin didn't even look in my direction when I straggled into the gym. I'd been sure she would greet me with a gloating smile. Even someone totally predictable can be unpredictable at times.

"Are you all right, Cassidy?" Mr. Saunders asked, obviously privy to my *accident.*

"Yes, thank you." I stood next to my friend Josie.

"You can't even tell it was bleeding," she whispered as Mr. Saunders announced, "We're running track today."

Groans.

"But it's cold," whined remora Melissa Whipple.

"Well, it won't be cold when you get your blood movin'," Mr. Saunders replied. "You have thirty seconds to grab a sweatshirt from the locker room. Move!"

About three-quarters of the class scrambled for the locker rooms. I stayed put. I didn't want to wear my hoodie.

A couple minutes later, we were on the track.

"Guys, I'm running ahead," I told my friends, who shuffled their feet along the dirt, doing what I used to call "running," too. None of us girls were athletes like Jared, Emery, and Robin—or more accurately, my friends *thought* we all weren't athletes.

160

*I could give a racehorse a run for its money around this track.* I took off at a moderate speed, promising my legs a real workout later that night.

Jared, Bobby, and their friends led the way, as they always did. I noticed with each extension of my legs, however, that Jared's seemed to shorten. *Maybe he's slowing down so I can catch up*, I humored myself, and was genuinely shocked to discover that that was exactly what he was doing. I caught up to him within seconds.

"Hey, Cass," he greeted me.

"Hey." I glanced at him quickly and then ahead again. Shyness, that strange creature I sometimes battle, descended upon me.

Jogging side by side, we fell into an awkward silence. I sensed Jared wanted me to say something. What, I wasn't sure.

He chuckled.

I glanced at him, befuddled. What had I done to make him laugh?

"You're going to make me drag it out of you, aren't you?" he said, slightly out of breath.

"Drag what out of me?" I seriously had no clue.

He popped my upper arm with his fist, just like I had seen him do a hundred times with his buddies. "What did Jason say?"

"Oh, that." *Duh.* Of course he was curious to hear Jason's report. I could be so dense at times. But in all fairness, a lot had happened since we had crossed paths in the woods. "Emery's dad ran errands. That's it."

"Hmm." He shrugged and changed the topic. "I saw you with Dunham at lunch. Is he giving you a bad time?"

Now it was my turn to laugh. "If you call being extremely annoyed a bad time—then, yeah, he's giving me a bad time."

"Did you tell him to lay off?"

"Sure, but nothing penetrates his enormous ego."

161

With a frown, Jared ruminated. I was about to tell him not to worry about Chad when he suddenly smiled. "Pick up the pace. It's killing me," he said, and sped away.

Grinning like a goofball, I took off after him.

~~~

Leaving the school that afternoon, I spied Emery slouched against the light post, backpack slung on his shoulder. I waved. He smiled in return.

"I wasn't expecting you to be here," I said, thrilled that he was. School days dragged without him.

"You weren't tracking me on GPS? Haven't I taught you anything?"

I hugged him. He hugged me back.

"I hate it when you're not at school." I gave him an extra squeeze. "Why are you here, anyway?"

"To walk you home, of course." He grinned and jerked his head homeward. "Let's go before someone sees us."

On cue, Miriam bobbed up to his side.

"How's it goin', *ditcher*?" she said and hugged him, too.

Emery stiffened. His arms stayed at his side.

Miriam released him, looking none too comfortable herself. I felt uncomfortable for them both.

Collecting herself, she bestowed upon him a dazzling smile. "Next time, we're playing hooky together," Miriam announced. Despite her brazen demeanor, I could tell Emery's uneasiness bothered her.

He grimaced in response.

Miriam began laughing. I figured this was her attempt to chase away the tension. What she did next eliminated that theory.

She gave Emery's face a playful slap, taking him aback as much as it did me. His standard calm mask slipped into place, hiding whatever he was feeling.

162

"Dude," Trevor Young said, coming up and giving Emery a high five. It provided Emery the perfect opportunity to extract himself from one of the most awkward scenes I had ever witnessed. He turned away from us to talk to Trevor.

Miriam looked brokenhearted, which broke my heart, too. I knew how unrequited love felt.

"Let him make the first move," I advised her in a whisper.

Her face reddened. "*That* will never happen."

"Why would you think that?" I challenged gently.

"I don't know." Miriam's pretty blue gaze wandered. Her face suddenly erupted into a smile. "There's Nate. Now we can go." She flagged my brother down, shouting, "Nate, get your butt over here!"

"Yeah, like that'll get him to do what you want," I teased, and then had an epiphany. Beautiful, bold Miriam knew less about the opposite sex than I did.

*I have to help her,* I thought. *I have to help her win Emery over.*

## Sixteen

# Cat and Mouse

After leaving Miriam at her white picket fence, Emery, Nate, and I continued to our homes.

"Here." I shoved my backpack at my brother. "Take this in. I have to talk to Emery real quick." I was dying to hear what he had to report.

When Nate shut our front door behind him, I asked Emery, "Well? What happened at that marina?"

"My dad boarded a yacht named—" Emery's front door opened before he could say the name of the boat, and our heads snapped to his house. His father stood in the doorway, smiling, with a small duffle bag over his shoulder. He waved. My stomach twisted, and I felt fear freeze on my face. Emery saw it, too.

"Hi, Dad," he called, and then advised me through a smile, "You'd better stay here. You won't be able to act naturally around him."

"And you will?"

"Yes," he answered, his face relaxed.

"Ready to practice?" his dad asked, coming down their front walk. The casual smile lingered on his face, but he watched us like a hawk. My stomach dropped another inch. His suspicion had most definitely been roused.

"Be right there," Emery called back.

"Where are you going?" I asked in a low voice.

"To the shooting range, not that he needs practice."

"Do you think he knows you were following him?"

"It's possible," Emery replied, unconcerned.

"This is like a cat and mouse game. Oh my gosh, I think I'm going to be sick."

"Everything is under control." Emery displayed not a shred of doubt. "This would be a good opportunity for you to see my mom. She can draw your blood today."

"I can't do it," I said, unable to tear my eyes from Mr. Phillips as he loaded the guns into the trunk of their car. "And not because your mom's blood-drawing is just shy of torture. You're right. I won't be able to pull off acting natural, not even with her."

"I understand. We'll talk later, and don't worry about me. I'll be fine."

He took off to join his dad. Mr. Phillips waved good-bye to me, and I gave a quick wave back, forcing a smile. Strangely, as I watched them drive away, panic didn't grip me—just sadness. Emery had to be dying inside.

~~~

Emery and his dad didn't come home until eight o'clock that evening. I considered asking my parents if I could go over to his house, but thought better of it. What was I going to do, ask Emery to go down to the basement where we could talk about his father? Mr. Phillips's suspicion was already stirred. Why rouse it even more by showing up on their doorstep unannounced and for no good reason?

Around nine, I texted Emery: *Did you have fun?*

I figured the less said the better, in case his dad was nearby. His reply confirmed this had been a wise decision.

*Yes, but still have homework. Will be up late.*

I gnawed my lip, contemplating his obvious code, and concluded that he was telling me to come over at midnight. But what about his dad? If Mr. Phillips left the house before Emery and I had a chance to talk, was I to follow him anyway?

Racking my brain for a cryptic way of asking this question, I came up with this: *Me, too. Watching this old spy movie, Eagle Eye. Seen it?*

*Yes*, Emery replied.

I took this to mean that he wanted me to follow his dad if he left the house, rather than meet Emery for an update.

~~~

At midnight, I landed on the grass in my side yard, crouching as I whipped my head to Emery's house.

To my dismay, light from the television flickered between the gaps in the living room curtains. I'd been a nervous wreck for the last three hours, anxious to learn what had transpired during the ominous father-son outing. Had Emery gathered any information about Moreau? The yacht? The whereabouts of the microchip?

Was his dad even more suspicious?

I contemplated Emery's bedroom window and decided he would have turned off his light if it wasn't safe to come over.

*Bright side: his dad is home*, I thought, darting across the street. I knew Serena wouldn't be watching television. I ducked behind the Phillipses' car and studied the gap between the curtains. No one peeked from them. No shadows indicated movement inside.

I ran forward and leapt to the awning outside Emery's window, landing with a light thud. I froze and listened, but only picked up noise from the television. Emery's lamp turned off, and his footsteps moved quietly to the window. The curtains pulled apart, and he opened the window.

"That was stressful," I whispered, scrambling into his room.

"My dad fell asleep in front of the television," he whispered back. "I checked on him about ten minutes ago."

"How do you know he's really asleep?"

"Good point," Emery granted, gesturing to his bed. "Have a seat."

"Are you okay?" It was a lame question. Of course he wasn't okay.

"Yes," he said, which made me feel lousy for asking.

We sat down, and I removed my ski mask. Emery leaned in to my ear.

"The yacht was rented by a Hector Duvall—i.e., Julian Moreau, or so I'm presuming." His breath smelled of peppermint toothpaste. "I ran the credit card number used to rent the yacht. I won't go into why, but the number is fishy."

"You mean it's fake?"

"Yes. Moreau was on the yacht, along with three other men. Their builds were similar to the men who broke into the museum. I'm assuming they're the same men—"

"But it doesn't matter," I interrupted in an excited whisper.

It was too loud for Emery's liking. He brought his index finger to his lips. "My ear," he murmured.

I leaned forward and went on. "We know where the microchip is now: on the yacht. I'll tear it apart until I find it."

Emery shook his head. "The microchip isn't on the yacht. Moreau isn't a rookie. He wouldn't keep a key component in developing a biological weapon close to him. Being apprehended by the authorities is the least of his worries."

I nodded, understanding what Emery was driving at. Moreau had to be dealing with some scary folks, perhaps even Arthur King. "So what happened on the yacht?"

"Two men stood guard while Moreau, my dad, and the third man went below deck, I'm assuming for a meeting. A couple hours later, they emerged. What I would have given to be a fly on the wall."

"What's stopping you now? We can plant a bug."

"Armed guards," he reminded me.

"What about your dad, then? Plant a bug on him."

"Good idea with any other person. My dad would sniff out a bug like a bloodhound. That's what makes keeping tabs on him difficult. I can't risk using any electronics, even on the car. As it was, Mickey and I had to abort soon after my dad left the marina. It was obvious he suspected he was being followed."

"How do you know? Did he know it was you?" I asked in one breath.

Emery cautioned me to keep my voice down again. "He made it seem as if he was unaware of being followed, in answer to your first question. When he turned down an alley, we kept driving. If we'd followed, he would have slammed on the brakes and pulled a firearm. In answer to your second question, I don't know."

That wasn't reassuring in the least—on either account. "Did he hint around that he knew you were following him at the shooting range?"

"No, but he wouldn't. He would wait for me to slip up."

"And he thinks Jason was a slip-up?" I asked, furious with myself. I was about to proclaim myself the stupidest person on the planet for hiring that slacker when I heard a step creak on the staircase.

"He's coming," I whispered in a panic.

"Under my bed."

I slid under the bed, while Emery, moving lightly on his feet, unlocked his bedroom door. He had just made it back and under his covers when the door cracked open.

Bright light from the hallway spilled under the bed, illuminating the left side of my face. I held my breath and prayed.

"Emery," his dad said quietly.

"I'm awake," Emery replied, to my surprise. Why hadn't he faked sleep?

*Because he's curious about what his dad has to say,* I surmised. I pressed my hands over my pounding heart in a desperate attempt to insulate the sound. Thank heavens I was the only one in the room with enhanced hearing.

"Mind if I come in?"

"Of course not."

Bedsprings protested under Mr. Phillips's weight as he sat on the edge of the bed. I hadn't taken a breath and had no intention of doing so until he was gone.

"I had a great time today."

"Me, too, Dad."

"There was something I meant to discuss with you."

"What's that?"

"Cassidy."

*Cassidy? What about me?*

"Go on."

"You spend a lot of time together."

*Not even*, I inwardly groaned at what appeared to be the introduction to a birds-and-the-bees discussion. My mom had started her conversation about Emery spending so much time with me in the exact same way. Of course, he wasn't in the room at the time. This would be torture.

"We do," Emery agreed, his tone wary. He was probably squirming inside as much as I was. "We're friends."

"But you'd like to be more than friends?"

Emery paused. "Yes."

My eyes widened, but then I remembered our charade. *Emery is in love with me. Duh.*

"She likes someone else," Emery added when his dad didn't respond.

"I've noticed," Mr. Phillips said, unsettling me. Mr. Phillips had only seen me with two other possible candidates: Jared and Bobby. Somehow I doubted anyone would mistake me for being smitten with Bobby. "Have you told her how you feel?"

*Why do I have to be trapped under this bed, at this very moment?*

"No, and I don't plan to until I see a sign that the feeling is mutual."

"It is. Cassidy just doesn't know it yet."

There was a gentle patting sound, and I pictured Mr. Phillips giving Emery's shoulder an encouraging pat. This made me sad beyond words. How could he be so corrupt and heartless on one hand, and then so loving on the other? And how could Emery handle this?

"You're much better off than I was at this stage of the game," his dad continued. "Your mother couldn't stand the sight of me."

"You were cramping her style," Emery said, a smile in his voice.

"Only your mother would think a *dashing* young Navy SEAL assigned to protect her would cramp her style." Mr. Phillips chuckled. Curiosity momentarily overruled despair. I made a mental note to wheedle this story out of Emery one day.

*What's there to romanticize, anyway?* I thought, bitter and sad again. *The dashing young Navy SEAL became a mercenary. The end.*

"I think your humbleness won her over," Emery teased.

"Just as yours will win Cassidy's heart. Lucky you, inheriting your old man's charm." Mr. Phillips remained silent for a moment before adding, "Good night, son. I love you."

"Love you, too, Dad."

Tears flooded my eyes.

After Mr. Phillips left the room, the breath rushed out of me. I remained still and quiet, listening to him lumber to his room. My heart felt like it had been ripped out.

"Did you hear him go into his room?" Emery whispered tonelessly.

"Yes," I choked out.

"Come out then."

I slid from under the bed and stood up, wiping tears off my face. Back against his headboard, Emery stared at the tan comforter that covered his legs, thinking. Like his voice, his face revealed no emotion.

170

"I'm sorry," I said, pushing it past the constriction in my throat.

"It is what it is. We can't lose sight of the mission, or we won't succeed. Please lock the door."

After doing so, I returned to his bedside. He remained deep in thought and hadn't changed position.

"When you leave here, work off your energy but stay close by. I'll keep an ear out for my dad. If he leaves, I'll text you."

A sudden weariness overcame me, and I dropped down on the edge of his bed. The exhaustion was purely emotional, because the rest of me was ready to spring out the window and run like a crazed werewolf chasing down its prey.

"I'm sorry this sucks so bad," I said for the zillionth time. I closed my eyes and massaged my forehead. "I wish I could make it go away."

"Me, too," Emery said. "Not to belabor the point, but push down your emotions and focus on the task at hand. If you and I allow feelings to get in the way, we'll fail. Here—" He pulled my ski mask from under his covers. I had forgotten that I'd left it on his bed.

"Sorry," I apologized again, taking the mask. *Sorry* was even annoying to my ears now. "I'm glad you remembered this."

Emery shrugged. "Me, too. His suspicion is elevated enough."

"He doesn't seem suspicious." I rewound their conversation in my head.

"Oh, he is."

Something occurred to me. "What if he's bugged your room?" I mouthed, glancing around with alarm.

"He isn't the only one who's suspicious. I swept the room for bugs earlier. You should go for your run."

"No running tonight. I'll stick to the woods."

"Sounds like a plan. I'll talk to you tomorrow."

171

Immediately, he lost himself in his private thoughts.

I left, realizing as I ran down the steps to the park that this had been the first time Emery hadn't escorted me to his window.

# Seventeen

# Champions and Cowards

M r. Phillips did not leave his house during the night, which frustrated Emery, whereas my feelings were mixed. On one hand, I'd hoped Mr. Phillips would lead us to the microchip before the exchange so we would avoid the unpleasantness that was sure to ensue around midnight Saturday or early Sunday morning. All parties would be on high alert, armed and ready for trouble. That would make taking them by surprise difficult and more dangerous.

That said, I also wasn't opposed to delaying the inevitable, which would surely involve turning guilty parties over to the authorities after we recovered the microchip. What wasn't certain was how gaining possession of the microchip would play out, especially since I was the only one who was bulletproof.

"Emery probably won't make it easy for me to keep him alive," I mumbled to myself while pulling on sweats for Fight Club.

I had wanted to opt out this morning and hang at Emery's house. That way we could keep an eye on his dad. But Emery had vetoed that idea, pointing out that his dad would be watching for anything out of the ordinary. Emery and I ditching Fight Club to watch television would definitely be out of the ordinary.

"Emery shouldn't even be involved in recovering the microchip," I continued as I yanked on a T-shirt. "It isn't like he's indestructible. He is *so* stubborn."

The doorbell rang.

I snatched up a brush and hurried out of my room to answer the door, assuming Emery had come over early to give an update. Last he texted, his dad had just woken up and was making coffee, as if today were like any other day.

"Got it," I called to my dad, who was headed to the front door from the kitchen. Turning bolts and unhooking the chain, I opened the door to Miriam.

"Mornin'," she greeted me, wearing her most fetching grin. "I'm here for Fight Club." She said this as if I had invited her.

"Cool." I cruised my memory banks, coming up with nada. I couldn't even recall ever having talked about Fight Club with her. "Come on in."

As we went upstairs to my room, I felt an overwhelming need to apologize. "I would've invited you before, if I'd known you were interested."

"Oh, I'm *interested*," she hinted.

I laughed, understanding where her interest lay.

Miriam banged on Nate's door. "Room service."

Nate groaned. "We don't want any." He sounded groggy and irritated.

"Liar," Miriam declared with a smile. "Get your butt out of bed! It's almost time for Fight Club."

"Not even," Nate groaned again. "Go home."

"You are *so* rude." Miriam laughed and grabbed the doorknob. But before she could open his door, I yanked her into my room.

She stumbled in, yelling, "Nate, I am so kicking your—" Catching herself, she swung wide eyes at me.

*Your mom and dad?* she mouthed, as it occurred to her they could be upstairs sleeping.

"In the kitchen," I answered, shutting my door.

"*Shwooooo!*" Miriam giggled. "Thought they were still in bed for a sec. Nate cracks me up. He is *soooooo* adorable. I think I'm in love with him. Does Emery wear a shirt?"

"In Fight Club?" I asked, trying to keep up with her train of thought, which was similar to one of those bouncy balls from a gumball machine. "Yes, he does. Sorry."

Normally, I wouldn't deny her the opportunity to be with Emery, especially since I believed the interest was mutual. Emery insisted he didn't like Miriam, but I knew better. However, I didn't think he would be in the mood for her antics today. Frankly, I wasn't either.

"Miriam, these guys are serious about this stuff."

"Are you suggesting I'm *not*?" She feigned offense. "I totally know karate. Want me to prove it? I'll flip you."

Miriam seized my arm and tried her best to flip me. Eventually, we both ended up piled on the floor, laughing hysterically.

"You'd better put your hair in a ponytail, or things could get ugly," I advised, eyeing the tumble of dark, silky ringlets spilling over the taupe carpet. Miriam had the most beautiful hair.

"Oh, I hope so. Can I borrow a scrunchie?"

"Top drawer on my nightstand," I said as I stood up. "I haven't eaten yet. Want a protein bar?"

"Yeah, thanks."

I went down to the kitchen where my parents were reading the newspaper and Chazz was silencing Rice Krispies in a bowl of milk, submerging the puffed rice with a spoon until it no longer *snapped*, *crackled*, or *popped*. I grabbed two protein bars and bottled waters from the fridge.

Moments later, I returned to an unusual sight in my room. Miriam sat cross-legged on my bed, frowning and playing absently with my rainbow scrunchie. She was so immersed in thought that she hadn't noticed me come into the room.

"What's wrong?"

Miriam jumped and looked up at me. "Nothing." She shrugged. "I'm not in the mood for this anymore. I think I'll go home."

"What? Why?"

175

"I don't know." She shrugged again, avoiding eye contact.

My mind raced. *What happened in the last two minutes?*

"Stay!" I urged, feeling inexplicably panicked. "This is fun." I had never seen Miriam sad before and couldn't shake the feeling that I had caused it. "You'll have a good time. Think about it. Sparring with Emery."

"I don't care." She flopped her hand dismissively, looking away. "I'm over him."

"Since when?"

"Since—now!" She shot the scrunchie at me. It missed, of course. Miriam had horrible aim. "Don't think this doesn't mean I can't do one of those karate kicks," she said, laughing.

I laughed, too, relieved that she had decided to stay.

"Tell me . . ." Miriam put her hand out for a protein bar. "Is Aiden Pruett in Fight Club?"

"Yes. Why don't you like Emery anymore?"

"Because I am *over* him," she repeated, seeming more interested in the wrapper of the protein bar than the current subject. I recognized evasion when I saw it.

"Fine, you're over him," I relented. "So let's talk about Aiden. Oh, and by the way, he wears a shirt, too."

~~~

Kicked back on my bed, Miriam and I shot the breeze while ten or so boys made their way to the attic at intervals. By unspoken unanimous decision, we had elected to arrive fashionably late, which I didn't mind at all. I was having a blast. Miriam and I hadn't talked, gossiped, and laughed like this since premutation.

"Shall we?" I asked, once the noise overhead suggested the boys had started warm-ups.

"In a few." Miriam twisted her ponytail of ringlets around one finger while she stared up at my ceiling. "Do *any* of them take off their shirts?"

"No, *but* there's always a first time." With that, I flung myself off the bed, threw open the door, and dashed for the attic at a speed Miriam could keep up with.

"Oh, no you don't!" she shouted.

At the foot of the attic stairs, she shoved me out of the way. We laughed and pushed, forcing our way in front of each other for the entire ascent. At the top, we lost our collective balance and fell face down on the Berber carpet, making an entrance that would have embarrassed me if Miriam hadn't gotten me all wound up.

"Hi, guys." She giggled, pushing escaped ringlets from her face. Propped up on her elbows, blue eyes sparkling, midriff exposed where her hot-pink tank top had ridden up during our struggle—Miriam made a stunning mess.

"Don't mind us," I said and scrambled to my feet, assisting Miriam to hers.

Surprisingly, she didn't resist my effort. This was the sort of opportunity she would normally seize in order to create a scene.

"I know. Way to make an entrance," I added.

Noting that the room had fallen oddly silent, I glanced around at the boys. Tension was thick in the air. Their sliding glances to one another proved I wasn't the only person who felt it.

"Join in," Emery said to us, his expression inscrutable.

I lifted my eyebrows.

He gave me a half-smile and looked away. "Switch legs," he instructed the boys, who were stretching.

My questioning eyes cut to Nate. He shrugged, but looked none too pleased about what he obviously sensed, too. My gaze then swung behind me to Jared, who smiled, exuding the same sort of alert energy that I had prior to a confrontation.

From the corner of my eye, I could see Chad watching me. I pretended not to notice.

*What the heck is going on?* I wondered, shifting my eyes forward. I caught a glimpse of Miriam blatantly scoping out the boys who were doing warm-ups, oblivious to the tension in the room.

"On the floor," Emery instructed.

*Who cares what's going on with these boys? I've got enough to worry about.* I followed Emery's instructions and redirected my concern to him. As he led us through floor exercises, I marveled at how calm he appeared. *He has to be freaking out. I know I am.* I grabbed my right foot and stretched forward over my leg. *Everything comes crashing down tonight. What are we even doing here?* I switched legs.

By the time we finished floor warm-ups, the bad vibe hadn't diminished.

"We're going to do a conditioning drill that I did when I was a kid," Emery announced, clapping his hands as if that would break up the tension collecting in the air. "Holding one leg up"—he grabbed his knee, balancing on one foot to demonstrate—"you'll try to knock your partner off balance."

There were grunts of approval.

"I claim Nate!" Miriam shouted, running over to him and clutching his arm. He was shocked. We both were.

*Nate?* I thought, dumbfounded. *Why not Emery?*

"No—*I* claim Nate!" Bobby bellowed over the snickers and harassing comments from the boys and grabbed my twin's other arm. A tug of war for Nate ensued.

I laughed with the boys, but still sensed an undercurrent. I looked at Emery to get his take. He was grinning and appeared not to have a care in the world.

"Dudes, enough!" Nate broke loose from Bobby and Miriam. "There is plenty of me to go around. Bobby, you can have me after Miriam."

"Sicko!" Bobby shouted and shoved Nate.

Clasping Nate's hand, Miriam hooted and swung their arms in the air like they had just won an Olympic gold medal. "Emery," she said, pointing at me, "you and Cass be partners."

My brain hurt. *What is going on today?*

She dragged Nate off. The other boys started pairing up.

"Why are we even here?" I muttered to Emery under my breath. His cell phone vibrated in the pocket of his sweatpants. Collecting it, he looked at the screen.

"Who is it?"

"Riley." He answered the phone. "Hi, Riley. Hang on a moment." He asked me, "Mind if I take this in your room?"

"Not at all. Do you want me to come?"

His gaze swept over the boys. "No," he said, looking back at me. "Stay here. I'll be right back."

Emery walked in long strides to the stairs, bringing the phone to his ear. As I watched him go, Chad's smell invaded my space. He tapped my shoulder.

I turned around to him. He smiled.

"I need a partner," he said, dimples deepening. A quick survey of the room revealed that he most certainly did. All the other boys had partners.

"I guess I do, too," I admitted, feeling charitable. What was I going to do, make him stand there until Emery came back? "Lead the way."

Following Chad to an empty spot in the upper corner of the mat, I ran through reasons why Riley could have called. She had a lead on Moreau? She had learned what was going down tonight? She'd found out Emery's dad was involved?

*Why are we even here?* I asked myself again, pulling my leg up.

Chad tucked his left knee in his forearm, and we began circling one another, bouncing on one foot. While he looked for an opening to knock me over, I reminded myself to pay attention, make this look challenging, and not accidentally hurt him.

179

*I should have gone with Emery*, I thought, absently evading Chad's shoulder. I looked longingly at the stairs.

Chad's forearm grazed my chest.

"Hey!" I dropped my leg and jerked around.

Chad threw his hands up in surrender. "I'm sorry, it was an accident," he claimed, appearing embarrassed. A few boys watched us, including Jared. This embarrassed me.

"Well, watch it," I muttered, blushing, and we continued the drill.

With each passing second, I became more distressed about Emery as my body naturally and automatically eluded Chad, though he did get in one good body slam when I glanced at the stairs. I didn't even teeter.

"You're like running into a brick wall," he complained.

*Try it when my skin is hard*, I grumbled in my head.

The attic door opened then, and I whipped around to face the stairs. Chad took the opportunity to throw his full body weight at me. Our feet got tangled, and we fell.

*Umph!* My back slammed into the mat, and Chad landed on top of me. We stared at one another in shock, as sweat dripped from Chad's face and splashed on my cheeks.

The next thing I knew, his warm, sweaty mouth covered mine—and the next thing *he* knew, he was face down on the mat with his right arm craned straight up and my bare foot digging between his shoulder blades.

"Criminy!" Ahmid shouted.

Instantly, boys flocked around us, staring in stunned silence.

Heaving furious breaths, I glared daggers at the back of Chad's head, wanting to spit out the taste of him. He turned his head to the side and cussed up a storm.

"If you pull his arm to the left, you'll dislocate his shoulder," Emery advised, appearing at my side.

Chad told him where to go, and then pleaded with me, "I'm sorry. I misread you. I thought you wanted me to kiss you."

"You kissed her?" Nate shouted, furious.

"I'll say you misread me, *jerk!*" I hissed, cranking his arm a little higher.

Nate charged forward. Emery grabbed his arm.

"I'm killing you, Chad," Nate said through his teeth. He looked like a deranged madman.

Despite my disgust, I busted up, accidentally putting more pressure on Chad's arm.

"Please!" he wailed in pain.

"That's all I was waiting for." I snickered. "Nate, don't go loco on him when I let him up."

Eyes blazing, Nate didn't reply.

I took the chance that my twin would behave himself and let Chad go. If Nate punched him, then so be it. It wasn't like Chad didn't deserve it.

With surprising dignity, Chad climbed to his feet.

"Did I hurt you?" I asked, just to embarrass him.

Glowering, he called me a rude name and stormed off.

"Not cool, dude," Zach called after him. The other boys voiced their agreement.

Miriam hissed, "He's a pig."

I wiped my contaminated mouth and said to her, "Please tell me that doesn't count as a first kiss."

Jared's head snapped around, and his angry eyes held mine. My heart galloped in alarm. Resolute, he turned away and walked to the stairs in measured steps.

"Dude," Tyler called, scampering after Jared. "He ain't worth it."

The other boys followed. Miriam and I took a step forward, but Emery stopped us. "Stay here," he commanded, looking at me. "I'll take care of this."

I nodded, understanding his concern. There was no way I would let Chad hurt a hair on Jared's precious head.

"Don't let anything happen," I called after Emery, worried out of my mind.

The door closed behind him, and Miriam and I didn't move an inch for about ten seconds.

"Forget this," she said, and we ran for the stairs.

~~~

We threw ourselves onto the porch as the mob of boys rushed down the walk toward Chad and Jared.

"Chad," Jared said, his voice razor sharp.

On the sidewalk, Chad puffed out his chest and turned to glare at him.

Jared stopped in front of him. "I told you not to pull your crap with her!"

"You don't tell me what to do. Besides, she wanted it."

"I can't hear. Let's go down," Miriam urged.

"No, stay here," I said, horrified.

Something inside warned me that if I left the porch, I would do more harm than good—most likely to Chad's face. If reason hadn't told me this, the stern look Emery threw me over his shoulder would have.

"Stay away from her." Jared delivered each word like the strike of a cobra.

Emery broke through the crowd of boys and stood next to Jared, preparing to intervene.

"Sure. Later." Chad stepped away, giving the impression that he was leaving, and then swung his arm around.

My mind slowed his fist, and my mouth formed into a scream as I took in everything during that millisecond: Chad's fist, Emery not making a move to block the blow he saw coming, and Jared seeing the sucker punch too late.

In my mind's eyes, the beast lurched from the recesses, howling like a savage and straining at the chain gripped in my hand. I felt the fury in every fiber of my being, and heard the cry of animal instinct to feed the violence.

Chad's fist connected with Jared's jaw, thrusting his head to the side.

I stumbled backward, fighting an internal battle—one I would win.

*No,* I commanded, exerting every scrap of willpower I possessed to resist the powerful impulse to tear off the porch and attack Chad. The shadowy embodiment of my feral nature dissolved into blackness. *Victory,* I thought, as my scream synchronized with Miriam's.

Jared took the blow and turned his head back to Chad slowly. He smirked. Chad kept his fists up, ready to fight.

"That's your free one," Jared said.

Arms at his side, he stepped forward so he and Chad were chest-to-chest, nose-to-nose. Displaying no fear, Jared stuck his chin out ever so slightly, inviting Chad to throw a punch.

Unflinching, they stared one another down. The swift intake of breath from the other boys, Miriam's alarmed squeaks, and random urban background chatter were the only sounds that joined the wild pounding of my heart.

Chad's eyes dropped. "Some other time. I'm outnumbered," he explained, as if he could fool us. He avoided eye contact with the other boys as he turned away and strutted off in the opposite direction of his house.

The boy was scared spitless.

When he'd put enough distance between himself and the other boys, Chad pivoted around. Smugness, anger, and embarrassment mingled on his face. "Phillips," he shouted, walking backward, "she's all yours."

He said this as if he had gotten the last word.

Before Emery or Jared could retaliate, Chad swung around and continued his cowardly retreat, throwing his shoulders back in empty bravado.

I wondered about the point of that, especially because I belonged to *no one*.

Zach was watching Chad with obvious disgust. "Jared, why didn't you kick the crap out of him?"

Jared shrugged and glanced at me. Heat flooded my cheeks, and I quickly looked down.

Nate clasped Jared's shoulder, regarding him with admiration. "Thanks, dude. Now, I say, *let's fight*."

The boys whooped and made their way back up the walk, joking, pushing, and harassing one another. The confrontation and Jared's valor had obviously triggered some testosterone. I was furious at my cheeks for burning crimson as the boys filed past Miriam and me into the house, and at my body for the trembling, the rush of adrenaline, and the subtle, shameful disappointment I always felt when tempering the beast. A sliver of me still howled for blood and longed for the freedom I knew I would feel if I were to give in completely to the savage inside.

*Something I will never, ever do . . .*

Jared reached me. I peeked up at him and smiled shyly.

His lips curled at the corners. The left side of his jaw where Chad had sucker-punched him pulsed red and already showed signs of swelling.

My smile flipped. "Your jaw! Do you want ice?"

"Thanks, Cassy, but no worries." He ducked into the house.

"Nate!" I shouted. "Get Jared some ice."

Emery chuckled. I swiveled my head to him and glared. "You said you were going to take care of things," I accused, bringing my hands to my hips. They were trembling from the spiked adrenaline, so I quickly moved them behind my back.

Emery had the gall to grin. "What makes you think I didn't?" he replied and stepped through the doorway, leaving me to ponder.

"What is that supposed to mean?"

He smiled and closed the door.

"Get Jared an ice pack," I bellowed at the door, baffled. The boy was a riddle.

"Look at me," Miriam said. "I'm shaking like a leaf—"

My hands flopped against my back like beached fish.

"I need to sit." Miriam plopped down on the top step.

I sat next to her, numb and dazed. The last five minutes had been surreal. I drew in a deep breath and asked on the exhale, "Did all of that just happen?"

"You mean, you sucking face with Chad Dunham? Uh-huh."

I pinched her.

She laughed, then grew serious. "Are you sad it wasn't Emery?"

I looked at her. "What do you mean?"

"You know—are you sad it was Jared who defended your honor, and not Emery?"

"Oh, my gosh! Don't make me laugh. Defending my *honor*?" I chuckled, thoroughly confused. "Why would I be sad?"

"Because, you know," Miriam said, sheepish.

"No. What?"

"Oh, you're going to make me confess I'm a slimeball, aren't you?" She drummed my upper arm with her fists. "I know how you *really* feel about Emery. I read your poem about him in your nightstand."

"My poem?" I recalled my sad attempt at a poem and burst into laughter. "Oh my gosh. I'm so embarrassed. That's why you suddenly lost interest in Emery? You thought *his* eyes were like *pools of chocolate*?" My laughter abruptly ceased as Miriam's sacrifice dawned on me. "I love you, Miriam." I threw my arms around her. "You gave up Emery for me."

"Well, yeah." She yanked my hair. "I'm not letting some boy come between me and my best friend, no matter how hot he is."

I pulled back to look at her, touched beyond what words could express. Emery wasn't just *some boy* to her. Yet she was willing to give him up for me.

"You're making me cry," I told her, and I wasn't kidding.

Miriam's eyes misted, too. "Stop!" she wailed, shaking her fists in protest. "Now you're making *me* cry."

"But I'm also about to make you very, very happy. Those *eyes like chocolate pools*—" I paused to snicker.

"Tell me!" Miriam punched my arm.

"They're not Emery's eyes." I lowered my voice just in case. "They're Jared's."

"What? Jared *Wells*?"

"Shhhhhh," I cautioned her, bringing a finger to my smiling lips. "Yes, Jared Wells. I've liked him forever."

She stared at me, absorbing the information. A dazzling smile broke out over her face. "Yes! Emery is mine—mine, mine, mine," Miriam sang, moving her upper body to the rhythm of her snapping fingers.

I laughed so hard that I almost fell off the step.

"Mine, mine, mine, mine. All mine. Mwa-ha-ha-ha-ha-ha—" A cross look followed her maniacal laugh. "Hey! Why didn't you tell me you liked Jared?" she demanded. "Not cool. Not cool at all. But. Oh. My. *Gosh*!" Miriam shook me. "How perfect is this? The boy you're in love with took a punch for you!"

"Shhhhhhh," was all I could get out, too giddy to even speak. It was true. Jared had taken a punch for me while defending my honor.

"Okay," Miriam whispered, already conspiring. "Fess up about Jared. Tell me *every* gory detail."

And I did.

*Eighteen*

# Dire Miscalculation

Saturday afternoon evolved into one of the strangest I'd ever had, which is saying a lot, considering that I'd fought a tiger and a supervillainess in an afternoon.

After Fight Club, Emery and I went over to his house to make lunch. Then, on a whim, we decided to have a *Doctor Who* marathon. Much to my surprise—but not Emery's—Mr. Phillips was also a *Doctor Who* fan and joined us.

I couldn't have told you what happened in any of the six episodes we watched, I was so rattled by the man relaxing in the recliner, munching on popcorn, like he had nothing better to do than watch television all day. Every so often, Emery would jam his elbow into my ribs, subtly signaling me to watch Matt Smith and not his father.

Around six thirty, Mr. Phillips announced he was hungry and was going to order Chinese food, and invited me to stay for dinner. I accepted, blushing and getting tongue-tied in the process, which didn't come across as suspicious at all. I was pretty sure Mr. Phillips thought me an odd duck, so making a fool of myself would come across as totally normal.

Mr. Phillips and Emery discussed *Doctor Who*, while Serena and I slurped down chow mein. Her thoughts were elsewhere, probably mulling over the microbes that had invaded my body, whereas I concentrated on reminding myself to chew and swallow. Getting food past the nervous lump in my throat was no easy task.

Mr. Phillips was reaching for another eggroll when he snapped his fingers like he had just remembered something.

"Serena, I forgot to tell you—" He paused, waiting for her to look up at him so he knew she was listening.

My gaze riveted on him, I chewed faster. Emery kicked me under the table.

"Serena, dear," Mr. Phillips tried again.

Serena looked up. "Did you say something, Gavin?"

Mr. Phillips winked at Emery. "I forgot to tell you, I'm meeting a former client for drinks at eleven thirty."

My spine stiffened, and I willed my expression to appear natural.

"Would you like to join us?" he finished.

I could have answered for Serena. She responded the way we all knew she would.

"You want me to join you and this former client for drinks?" she repeated, as though needing confirmation that she had heard the ridiculous invitation correctly.

"I know it's a little late. He's meeting me after another meeting."

"You want *me* to join you and this former client for drinks at eleven thirty this evening?" she said again.

Despite the situation, a smile tugged at my mouth.

"If you'd like," Mr. Phillips said.

"I have nothing in common with this person," Serena protested as if she knew who this person was. Which she didn't, of course—since he didn't exist.

*You boldfaced liar.* I captured a rice noodle between chopsticks and shoved it in my mouth. *Clever.*

"Why would I want to go?"

"Don't get your knickers in a twist, love. I was only asking," Mr. Phillips teased in a perfect English accent.

I was stunned to hear this accent coming from his mouth. The fact that it sounded so authentic was unnerving. If I'd heard his voice over the phone, there was no way I would have recognized him.

Serena frowned at her husband. "You know I disapprove of idioms."

Emery and I lost it. How could we not?

Ignoring our laughter, Serena said to her amused husband, "I'll have to decline, but you enjoy yourself."

"I'll try, dear," Mr. Phillips replied, pleased as punch.

*And don't wait up,* I silently added for him, jamming another noodle in my mouth.

Emery kicked me under the table—again.

~~~

I couldn't sit still. I had gone upstairs, presumably to bed, at nine thirty, and immediately clipped on my phone earpiece and dressed in the mummy costume, pulling it on over a tank top, workout shorts, and thermal underwear. I was preparing to apply face paint when I realized it was too early to costume up. What if my mom came in to check on me, as she was still compelled to do from time to time? Sleeping in thermal underwear would be reasonable, but wearing face paint and a mummy costume? Reluctantly, I took the costume off.

After fifteen minutes of pacing the floor and strategizing a solution for every scenario I could foresee cropping up in the next several hours, I decided to throw caution to the wind and put the costume and face paint on. I would much rather have my mom catch me dressed as a mummy than not be ready if Mr. Phillips left early to meet his "former client."

Over the costume I donned loose black sweatpants and a black windbreaker, pulling the hood over my mummified head. After tugging on my Nikes, I busied myself with creating a decoy under my covers, spending more time than ever forming pillows into my body shape.

I got tired of fussing with my decoy around ten. Instead, I snapped up *The Tennant Of Wildfell Hall* from my nightstand and kicked back on my bed with my head on my decoy's stomach, turning page after page that might as well have been printed with invisible ink. When I'd had enough of reading, I took to staring at my phone, waiting for Emery's text.

When Emery had walked me home after dinner, he'd decided to take a chance and plant a tracking device on his parents' car. That way, when Mr. Phillips left the house, I could follow him, while Emery tracked his movements on GPS in case I lost him or he drove down a main thoroughfare or something. If I were to lose him, Emery would guide me to his dad's destination.

We didn't have a plan beyond that, other than a mummy taking the baddies by surprise if need be, which is why I wore the costume under my clothes. Once Mr. Phillips led us to the microchip, we would improvise, or, as Emery was fond of saying, we would cross that bridge when we came to it.

At 10:55 p.m., the anticipated text came: *My dad is heading out. Jump.*

I breathed a prayer and did just that, landing as Mr. Phillips walked out his front door. He looked like he had stepped out of *GQ* magazine, duded up in a leather jacket over a knit shirt, slacks, and dress shoes—all black, of course. Black shades were the only thing missing from the ensemble. I wondered how many weapons were tucked away under his slick outfit.

I crept along my shadowy fence line, watching him circle around to the front of his car, his eyes never resting as they scanned the nearby vicinity. He directed the remote on his keychain at the driver's side door, then lowered his hand again, as if thinking. Suddenly, he dropped into a squat and reached under the car, feeling around.

I held my breath.

He extracted his arm from under the car empty-handed and stood. Shaking his head at his suspicion, he opened the door. My breath came out in a relieved *whoosh*. Emery had obviously hidden the tracking device well.

When he closed the car door, the phone vibrated in my hand.

I answered it. "Hi, Emery."

"Put the phone away," he said, his voice coming through the earpiece. "I'll tell you his movements. Don't speak unless necessary."

The car started, and Mr. Phillips pulled from the curb and made a U-turn. I zipped the phone into my windbreaker pocket and watched him drive in the direction I had hoped he wouldn't: Queen Anne Avenue, a main thoroughfare.

"Cut through the park," Emery instructed, his voice edged with frustration.

"Copy that." Was it the route Mr. Phillips had taken that caused Emery's frustration, or did it cover other emotions? No matter how well he could compartmentalize, this *had* to be getting to him. If all went according to our plan, his father would be arrested within hours.

*But what choice do we have?*

My feet flew across the dark expanse of grass in the park. There was no choice. Mr. Phillips had set the wheels in motion. Emery and I were just along for the ride.

~~~

Mr. Phillips returned to the same marina that Emery had previously followed him to. I showed up five minutes later.

"I'm at your car," I whispered to Emery as I crouched behind it. I surveyed the deserted parking lot. Thumping music from a nearby dance club penetrated the air, its deep bass throbbing against my eardrums. "I don't see your dad."

"Can you hear him?"

I cocked my head and concentrated. The music and other sounds that came with late-night city life receded. I picked up a murmur of voices and turned up the mental dial. Mr. Phillips's voice struck my inner ear.

191

"Moreau, Sanchez, after you." The soles of shoes scraped wood against a background of lapping water.

"They're on the docks," I whispered to Emery. "Getting on a boat, I think, probably the yacht. I'm going down."

Slinking low, I scuttled across the parking lot to the chain-link security gate that gave entrance to docks lined with moored boats. There wasn't a soul in sight.

An engine powered up. The high frequency sounded like a speedboat.

I hurriedly climbed the chain link, jumped from the top, and landed on the asphalt in a run. A speedboat appeared on the other side of a moored yacht's stern. Mr. Phillips, Moreau, and another goon, Sanchez, were in it.

*No, no, no, no, no*, I thought, sprinting onto the dock too late.

The villains' boat backed out of the marina and zoomed into the dark waters of Elliot Bay.

Despairing, I stopped at the end of the dock and watched the thieves race away, presumably with the microchip. Why couldn't I have gotten there two minutes earlier?

While I updated Emery on the situation, the boat sped toward a ship floating about a mile offshore. I squinted to pull the boat into my enhanced vision. It was a huge fishing trawler with *Enchantress* plastered across her stern.

"I'll swim after them," I told Emery.

"Bad idea. That water is forty degrees. Find another way to pursue them."

"Done," I said, spying a rowboat tied to a floating dock. Seven sea lions slumbered next to it.

I shot toward the dock, leapt over the steps, and landed on the metal structure, causing it to rattle violently and bounce on the water. The sea lions lifted their heads in my direction and barked their irritation.

"Hush," I barked back, and looked around to make sure they hadn't woken anyone sleeping on a nearby boat. No lights switched on, and no heads popped out of portholes to investigate.

"Sea lions?" Emery asked.

"Loud sea lions," I confirmed as I weaved my way around their yapping, blubbery bodies toward the rowboat. One sea lion tried to drag his body after me along the dock. His friends followed suit.

"Weird. They're following me," I said as I stepped into the rowboat. The crazy sea lions lined the edge of the dock, barking.

"They actually harmonize." Emery's voice echoed my own irritation. Clearly he hadn't worked a sea lion encounter into the evening's equation.

"Will you hush," I hissed at them and went to work untying the rowboat.

One lurched forward and caught hold of my windbreaker between its teeth.

I yelped in surprise. "He bit me!"

"Cassidy, keep it down."

"I can't get him off." I shook my arm. The sea lion clenched the fabric like a rabid badger. His buddies cheered him on.

"Fine," I growled. I unzipped the windbreaker and wiggled my arms out of the sleeves. "Take it!" I went back to work on the knot.

The choir of sea lions grew louder, celebrating their buddy's victory.

"Psychos," I muttered. "I had to give him my jacket," I told Emery.

The sea lion slid into the water, clenching the prize between his teeth.

Emery said, "Your phone—"

The earpiece went dead.

"—is in your pocket," I finished for Emery through my teeth, "which is now submerged in forty-degree water. Sorry, Emery, and forget this."

Abandoning the knot, I ripped the hook clean off the dock with the rope still laced through it and tossed it over my shoulder and into the boat.

The other sea lions slid into the water as I took up the oars.

"What is wrong with you demented beasts?" I complained at the half dozen heads bobbing up around me. The thief wasn't among them.

I dipped the oars into the water and pulled back, expecting the rowboat to shoot in a straight line like in the movies, but this wasn't the movies. The rowboat veered left, ramming into the boat moored next to it, the *Annah Lee*.

My progress out of the marina was slow and frustrating. I turned in circles, knocking into boats, while a parade of sea lions mocked me. It would have been hysterically funny—if I hadn't had to catch up with a speedboat that was in the process of being lifted onto the *Enchantress* by a crane. And there I was, still in the marina, spinning a rowboat in useless circles. Just when I thought things couldn't get worse, a shout rose from the direction of the music.

"Whoa, what the—?"

I jerked my head around to the nightclub at the edge of the marina and saw a man with a wild mop of hair standing on the patio that hung over the water, staring at me. Mouth ajar and wobbly on his feet, Mop Head rubbed his eyes and looked at me again. Another man joined him.

"Dude, do you see what I see?" slurred Mop Head as the rowboat clipped another boat.

I caught a glimpse of my arm. The white costume seemed to glow in the harbor lights. I knew what was coming next.

"You see a mummy in a rowboat?" the second man said, leaning so far over the rail I thought he might fall in.

Mop Head unsteadily made his way to the patio's door.

The sea lions swam around the rowboat, mocking me with their barks.

"Hey, everyone, there's a mummy!" Mop Head bellowed into the nightclub. "It's rowing a boat."

Five club goers stumbled onto the patio.

"If I don't get this right now, at this very moment, I'm going in with you and swimming to the *Enchantress*," I told the sea lions. As if some magical pixie dust had been sprinkled over me, I pulled back on the oars, and the rowboat shot forward in a straight line. The next stroke was even better. Six perfect strokes later, I cleared the docks and entered Elliot Bay. Then I threw some real power into it, leaving behind the cheering club goers and sea lions alike. The rowboat sliced through the water in time with the oars' rhythm, the cold wind licking my costume and biting through the layers of fabric like icy needles. The temperature had dropped significantly.

Within minutes I was approaching *Enchantress*, which was much larger than it had appeared at a distance. Around three hundred feet long, the deck loomed at least twenty-five feet above me at its midsection and forty feet in the bow. The three-story cabin and bridge, lined with a row of windows, doubled the height. Through the window, I saw a couple of men sitting at a control panel.

I slowed my paddling and surfed the airwaves, picking up a conversation between two males from somewhere on the deck. Moreau was one of them. The other man had a Dutch accent.

*Now to be the element of surprise*. I evaluated the exterior of the vessel. An anchor chain had been lowered into the bay off the bow. It appeared to be my best way on board.

I paddled to the bow and contemplated the chain. I considered tying the rowboat to it, but promptly dismissed the idea. If the anchor were drawn, the rowboat would come up with it, clattering against the trawler and revealing that an intruder had snuck aboard.

*It isn't like I can't swim,* I thought, untying my shoes. If I was going to do this, I was doing it right. What mummy would wear black sweats and Nikes?

After removing shoes and sweatpants, I grabbed hold of the thick, corroded anchor chain and climbed. Stopping about six feet below the guardrail, I listened to the conversation being carried on by the two men exchanging pleasantries. *Some lighthearted conversation before buying top-secret biological weapons*, I thought, trying to gauge where the men might be on deck. It proved to be a nearly impossible task, since I didn't know how the deck was laid out. Two sets of footsteps strolled past at a pace that suggested they belonged to men patrolling the deck. Fortunately, neither sounded as if they were directly overhead—for now.

*Please don't let anyone see me*, I prayed, swinging my legs back and forth like a pendulum. When my momentum had increased so that my body swayed horizontally in the upswing, I released the chain and soared over the guardrail feet first. Landing on the deck, I pivoted around, preparing to come face-to-face with crew members. There was no one on the bow, and the conversation between the men flowed without interruption. I had boarded undetected.

I ducked behind the anchor winch and peeked down at the lower deck where the criminals had congregated. Moreau wore a navy peacoat and cap, getting into the seafaring theme. The robust man he talked to looked equally harmless, bundled in a mud-colored down jacket and a striped knit hat that rested above bushy gray eyebrows on his weathered face. The five men surrounding them looked anything but harmless: powerfully built, watchful, silent, and poised to pull out concealed weapons. Stony-faced Mr. Phillips was the most intimidating of all.

Scattered around the deck were objects I expected to see on a fishing trawler: nets, big spools wound with chains, gaffing poles, a hoist to lift nets from the sea, and barrels—

lots of barrels. What they were for and what was in them, I hadn't a clue.

The smell was what I expected, too: fish, salt, and diesel. Apparently, the trawler was used as it should be—to catch fish—and as it shouldn't be—to sell out humankind.

Something clanged against the metal stairs leading to the bow. I scrunched down lower, assuming one of the guards was coming up.

A rumble shook the lower deck, and the footsteps on the stairs paused. Mr. Phillips and Sanchez had their weapons out in a flash, sharp eyes darting around. The other men drew their weapons in turn, training them on Mr. Phillips and Sanchez.

"Visser, what was that?" Moreau demanded of the man he had been talking to.

"*De Duivel*," the man on the stairs whispered to himself in Dutch. The words sounded like "the devil."

Visser put his hands in the air. "Gentlemen," he said with a disarming smile. "There is no need for concern. We are working on our engines. Please—lower your weapons."

Moreau looked skeptical. Mr. Phillips displayed no emotion whatsoever and kept his eyes and weapon on Visser's men.

"Lower your weapons," Visser ordered his men, to show good faith. They obeyed.

Sanchez looked to Mr. Phillips for direction. Mr. Phillips nodded, and they both lowered their weapons, too.

"You had better not be up to anything, Visser," Moreau warned.

Visser smiled. "I wouldn't think of it, my friend. We've conducted business in the past. You know I am an honest man." Both men laughed at this. I gathered it was a joke.

Feet clanged up the steps. I ducked lower.

"Honesty is relative." Moreau jovially slapped Visser's shoulder. "And overrated. Why don't I show you what you came all this way for?"

A rough-looking face appeared at the stairs. I curled into a ball and mentally cursed the sea lion for taking my windbreaker. If it hadn't, I wouldn't have gone for dramatics and taken off my sweatpants. And I wouldn't have resembled an enormous snowball.

"Spectacular," Visser said. I assumed he was looking at the crown.

The man's unhurried footsteps moved toward me. He hadn't seen me yet.

"Yes, it is," agreed Moreau.

The man's foot came down next to me. I sprung up like a jack-in-the-box and clamped his mouth and the back of his head between my hands, I brought my knee into his groin and he doubled over, screaming into my hand.

"Priceless, as is what is behind the amber," Moreau said. "Take a closer look."

I slammed the man's head into the anchor winch, hard enough to knock him out. He went limp. I lowered him to the deck, grabbed his collar, and dragged him to a round hatch door several feet away.

"Observe that the stone hasn't been tampered with, as requested by your employer," Moreau said to Visser as I lowered the unconscious man through the hatch. When my arms wouldn't stretch anymore, I released his collar. He dropped with a thud, sprawled in the narrow corridor like a discarded rag doll. Cringing at the sight, I closed the hatch door and crept forward on my belly to get a better look at the deck.

Visser examined Queen Kiya's crown, specifically the amber stone behind which the microchip was hidden. The other man who patrolled the deck sauntered down the right breezeway toward the stern.

Eyeing the crown, I contemplated what to do. I could grab it and go overboard before anyone realized what had happened.

"Yes, I can see that," Visser answered Moreau as I pulled up into a crouch. I mentally prepared myself to launch onto the deck. "The boss will be very pleased. He's due anytime."

The surprise crossing Moreau's face gave me pause. I glanced at Mr. Phillips and caught surprise on his face, too, but his expression immediately went blank. I lowered myself to my stomach again. Clearly, Visser's boss making a personal appearance had not been on the agenda.

*But he won't be here anytime soon*, I thought, not hearing a single boat motor in Elliot Bay, nor in the Puget Sound, for that matter.

No sooner had I thought this than my ears picked up a disturbance in the water to the left of the trawler. I pulled myself to where I could see the waters swirling into a whirlpool fifteen feet from the deck. Moreau ran to the side of the ship to see what was happening as a black submarine broke through the surface of the water.

Visser's men drew their weapons, aiming them at Emery's dad and Sanchez, who had drawn their weapons, too.

"He has arrived," Visser announced smugly. "Gentlemen, I suggest we don't greet him with firearms. Lower your weapons."

Eyes narrowed on Visser, Mr. Phillips gave him an amicable smile. "Your men first."

Sighing, Visser motioned for his men to comply.

When all barrels were pointed downward, Mr. Phillips kept his cold gaze on Visser and said to Sanchez, "Stand down."

Sanchez lowered his gun, as did Mr. Phillips.

At this point, the submarine had fully surfaced and the trawler's spotlight had been directed on it. A hatch door opened on top of the submarine, and a brawny man in a black leather trench coat emerged, armed with an Uzi. Dread slithered through my stomach when I observed the empty expression on his face. I had seen this show before.

As anticipated, the henchman sidestepped to the right, and an almost identical henchman followed him out of the submarine: Uzi, black leather trench coat, slicked-back hair, a face familiar with brutality.

The next henchman did take me aback, however. For whatever reason, we had not been informed that there had been two prison breaks.

Sultrily, Selma Heart appeared from the hatch, wearing that mocking smile I remembered so well on her full, blood-red lips. Raven hair slicked back and tucked behind her ears, round blue eyes, fair complexion, a button nose . . . She had the face of an angel and a heart as black as tar.

Hips swaying, she moved into position, her Uzi swinging casually at her side. Her smile never let up as she snapped the weapon to her eye and put Emery's dad in the crosshairs. The other two henchmen on the submarine and Visser's men followed her cue. Moreau and Sanchez looked from gun to gun. Unruffled, Mr. Phillips stared at Selma. Her smile expanded behind the Uzi.

"Your firearm, Mr. Meyer," Visser said, as if trying to stay patient with a spoiled child.

With a grin at Selma, Mr. Phillips gripped the gun by the handle and held it out to Visser.

"Nice try, handsome," she called, holding her gun steady on him. "*Mr. Meyer,* put the gun down ever so slowly, and keep those gorgeous eyes on me."

"You're scaring the children," Mr. Phillips quipped, referring to Moreau and Sanchez, who looked baffled. He followed her orders.

Selma laughed. "My favorite pastime. Watch him carefully over there. Don't fall for that charming smile. He'll fill you up with bullets, if given the chance."

"I see my reputation precedes me." Mr. Phillips gradually straightened up, hands in the air, weapon at his feet, his eyes and smile never leaving Selma.

Moreau found his voice. "What is going on here, Meyer?"

"A dire miscalculation on my part," Mr. Phillips replied, loud enough for Selma to hear.

"None of us are perfect," she called back, smiling. "Slowly put your hands behind your head and take four big steps back from the gun. Boys, give him plenty of room."

While Mr. Phillips did as he was told, I tried to digest the scene taking place before me. It felt a lot like watching a movie. Of course, all that would change if bullets started flying, and if they did, some were sure to hit their intended target: Emery's father.

*I can't intervene yet*, I concluded, *or Mr. Phillips's blood will be on my hands.*

As to why those guns were trained on him, I could draw no conclusions, other than Emery's dad wasn't as bad as I had assumed. Or was he even worse? Selma certainly wasn't taking any chances with him.

Once Mr. Phillips's gun had been cautiously secured by one of Visser's men, Selma pumped her fist in the air, striking a rock star diva pose. "Let's get this party started!"

As if that was his signal to enter, Arthur King Jr. popped out of the hatch, flipping his palms up to present himself. He wore a rainbow vest and bow tie under a red cloak, blue knickers, white knee-high socks, pointy black shoes with big gold buckles, and a top hat. He looked like a clown attending an opera. His four-foot-ten frame and weasel-like face added to the disturbing and ridiculous display.

"Did someone call my name?" He grinned, revealing the sharp, pointy teeth he had sunk into my arm on the roof of King Pharmaceutical. Removing the hat, he took an elaborate bow.

Behind him, a figure in a black cloak rose from the submarine like smoke. His scent triggered the same reaction in me that it had in the museum: aggression.

My muscles tensed. I resisted the instinct to pull up into a defensive stance, but couldn't stop the growl that rumbled deep in my throat. My gaze locked on the cloaked man as he glided into place behind Selma and Junior.

I had to force my eyes from him to the next person exiting the submarine, a dignified older gentlemen wearing a full-length gray fur coat. He had a thin face, high cheekbones, wavy gray hair neatly combed to the side, and an aristocratic air. Without question, the newest addition to the bizarre cast of characters was no other than the infamous Arthur King Sr.

"It's him," Moreau breathed.

"We are privileged," agreed Visser.

"Gavin," King greeted, his voice as refined as his appearance. His steely, calculating gray eyes regarded Mr. Phillips with the sort of excitement one might regard a winning jackpot on a slot machine. "What a pleasant surprise."

"Gavin?" Moreau repeated, dumbfounded, eyeing Mr. Phillips.

"The surprise is all mine, Arthur," Mr. Phillips called back, grinning.

King laughed. "Indeed, my old friend. Permission to board, Mr. Visser?"

*Nineteen*

# Wrath

---

Amid my primal reaction to the hooded man's scent, a very human emotion rose to the surface: fear.

I chewed my lip as I watched the Kings and their henchmen climb the stairs that Visser's men had lowered to the submarine. The hooded man boarded first, gliding like a phantom. The other men were visibly shaken when he appeared among them, standing before Mr. Phillips, who calmly sized him up. Selma boarded next, never allowing Emery's father to stray from her gun's crosshairs. Last came the Kings, strolling between the robotic henchman, who acted as armed bookends.

"Mr. Visser." King shook his hand. "I assume my cargo is receiving your utmost attention."

"Of course, Mr. King. Rest assured."

*Cargo? What cargo?* I could see on Mr. Phillips's face that he was asking himself the same question.

King released Visser's hand and offered it to a bewildered Moreau, who grabbed it eagerly. He held the crown in his other hand.

"Julian Moreau," said King. "How nice to meet a man with your reputed skills. May I?" He flipped his hand out for the crown.

"By all means, Mr. King." Moreau stumbled over his words. "It would be my pleasure." He gave King the crown.

"Unequalled," King remarked as he examined the crown. He frowned at the amber stone that hid the microchip, and nodded to his son. "Mr. Moreau, my son, Arthur."

Mr. Phillips's mouth curved into a small, satisfied smile.

Moreau offered his hand to Junior.

Junior produced a cigar from inside his colorful vest. He bit off the end and spat it out on the deck, then snapped his fingers at one of his henchmen, who took a lighter from his trench coat pocket and held the flame to the cigar.

Moreau kept his hand extended during this process, all the while looking extremely uncomfortable.

Finally, puffing out smoke, Junior extracted the cigar from his mouth and looked at Moreau.

"How are ya, chief?" He ignored Moreau's hand. "Let's have a look-see, Pops." He wiggled his stubby fingers at his father in a *gimme* gesture.

"The craftsmanship is as exquisite as we had anticipated," his father remarked as he handed the crown over. I detected a hint of sarcasm in his voice, along with underlying anger.

With the cigar trapped between his small, pointy teeth, Junior admired the crown. "Yep, nifty," he said around the cigar. With that, he flung the crown into the bay.

Moreau gasped. "Are you mad?" he exclaimed and ran to the rail.

Junior doubled over in laughter and slapped his knee. "You're a card, Phillips," he said between hoots, waving his cigar at Emery's dad. "A *real* card."

Mr. Phillips smirked, although behind his eyes, I knew the gears were spinning. My heart twisted. This very same expression appeared on Emery's face when he was plotting an escape.

*I'll get you out of this*, I sent to him. *For Emery's sake.*

"Mr. Moreau, the crown is a fake," King said with disgust when Moreau appeared ready to dive in after the artifact. He redirected his gaze to Mr. Phillips. "Isn't that right, Gavin?"

Moreau whipped around from the rail. "It most certainly is not!" His pinched expression suggested he regretted the harsh tone. He had forgotten that he was speaking to a powerful man with significant clout in the underworld. "The crown has been in my possession since I acquired it," he explained.

"You're rather slow on the uptake, Mr. Moreau," King chastised.

Junior snickered around the cigar. Moreau's jaw tightened, but he kept silent.

"Allow me to clear the mud from your eyes," King continued. "The crown you stole was a plant. The real crown and microchip are safe and sound with the United States government—*for now*. Correct me if I'm wrong, Gavin."

"Will do." Mr. Phillips smiled.

King smiled, too, a slithering, venomous smile. "I hope you understand that I had to follow through with this charade on the off chance you would make a mistake—"

"And that was your entire motivation," said Mr. Phillips, his expression indicating that King was full of it.

Hatred burned deep in King's eyes, but he kept his composure. "I learned long ago not to presume anything."

"We all have." Contempt flashed in Mr. Phillips's eyes, too.

I surmised that they were making a reference to something from the past, and that Junior was savvy to their history, given the smug, careless way he blew smoke rings into the cold night air.

Moreau glared at Mr. Phillips and demanded, "Who are you, *Gavin*?"

"The very best the CIA has to offer," King explained for him. "Put in simple terms, Gavin Phillips is a spy, an extremely skilled and dangerous operative, as I am sure you have witnessed on several occasions. He takes his assignments very seriously and is thorough when he infiltrates an organization. I believe the term used to describe his brand of expertise is 'hard man.' The end justifies the means, the end of this particular assignment being the apprehension of a criminal topping the world's Ten Most

Wanted list: myself. By the way, that is *top secret*. I am dead, after all."

Junior burst into a fit of giggles.

Mr. Phillips sighed. "You're itching to tell me, Arthur. So get on with it. Brag away. When did I tip my hand?"

"WHEN HAVE YOU *NOT* TIPPED YOUR HAND?" King raged.

My breath caught at his unbridled fury, and for a split second he looked every bit as insane as his son, who also had a tendency to explode in anger.

Summoning every ounce of control, King exhaled a slow breath that ended in a smile. "We have an interesting history, you and I. Your commanding officers' assigning *you* to root me out was a stroke of brilliance on their part. Hatred fuels you. Look at what you have sacrificed in order to bring me to justice. Precious time that could have been spent with Serena and Em—"

"Careful," Mr. Phillips interjected, his tone cold and lethal. The murderous look on his face caused my mouth to go dry. Without a doubt, if there hadn't been six gun barrels pointed at him, Emery's dad would have grabbed King by the throat and snapped his neck.

King seemed to realize this, too, and the knowledge that he had elicited this degree of malice from Emery's father pleased him immensely. "But I digress. You asked when I became aware of your cover, Frank Meyer. Approximately one year ago. It has been truly fascinating watching you work—an education, really. Incidentally, I have helped you along the way, most recently by sending my pet to intercede with any obstacles that would have prevented you from acquiring the crown—pardon me, I mean the *plant*. And an obstacle did arise, quite literally. A mummy, of all things. A curious and unforeseeable event indeed, yet one that did not throw fate off course. For here we are, face-to-face, exactly what you have been striving for all of these years. Yes, I

206

know, it isn't quite what you envisioned, but alas, what is? Any other questions, my old friend?"

"Yeah." Mr. Phillips jabbed his thumb toward the submarine, paying no mind to the gun slides pulling back in response to the abrupt movement. "When did you get the new ride? And how did you get past our radar?"

King narrowed his eyes on Mr. Phillips. Without answering, he said to his henchmen, "We've given him too much time to plan an escape. Gavin is very resourceful. The only thing holding him back is uncertainty about my pet." King motioned to the cloaked man. A thin yellow tongue flickered from the hood. "Visser, lower the net."

Visser walked over to an operating panel and pushed a button. A small motor powered up. The deck rumbled again, and an unearthly howl rose from within the ship's belly.

The strange cry caused the hair on the back of my neck to stand up. I shifted to my knees, readying myself for anything.

Moreau and Sanchez looked around in terror, while King's crew and Visser's men didn't react. They knew the source of the scream.

"It awakes." King's face glowed with the excitement of a child about to rip open a Christmas present.

A large fishing net dangling from a pulley was lowered to the deck.

"Your carriage awaits," King said to Mr. Phillips, sweeping his arm toward the net. He ordered his henchmen, "Escort Special Agent Phillips—*cautiously*."

A knot formed in my stomach as I watched Mr. Phillips ushered into the net at gunpoint with his hands on the back of his head. *King is going to drown him*, I realized. When the net was lowered into the water, the henchmen would lower their guns. That was when I'd go in after Mr. Phillips, free him from the net, and swim him to shore.

Turning my head to Bainbridge Island, the nearest shore, I estimated it to be less than a mile away. *If I swim fast enough, he might not get hypothermia.* That would be the best-case scenario. Worst case: Mr. Phillips would be dead before he hit the water.

*But King wants Mr. Phillips to suffer. Shooting him would put him out of his misery too soon,* I consoled myself as Emery's father was hauled into the air.

At the control panel, Visser stopped the net halfway to the rail, causing Mr. Phillips to sway back and forth over the deck.

"Gavin, you have been a most worthy adversary," King solemnly said, placing a hand over his heart to honor the man that he was about to murder. "My greatest desire has always been to better the human condition through science, to overcome the frailty that plagues our race, thus enabling every man, woman, and child to live to their full poten—"

Mr. Phillips cut him off. "Save it. I'm well aware of how you like to play God."

King crossed his arms and shook his head, as if disappointed. "You're a small-minded man, Gavin. What Serena saw in you mystifies me to this day. If she had been more selective and thought more like a geneticist than a love-struck teenager, there may not have been a need to experiment."

Mr. Phillips's face darkened with rage.

"Frankly, I have never understood your objection to the results. Granted, the means of attaining success weren't ideal, but you cannot deny—"

Mr. Phillips launched himself forward violently, stunning King into silence. The net swung at the henchman closest to Mr. Phillips, who was paying more attention to King's blathering than the CIA operative he had his gun on. Mr. Phillips saw an opportunity and took it. Getting hold of the Uzi through the net, he brought an angry fist full-force down on the man's skull. The henchman crumbled to the ground, and Mr. Phillips swung back in the net, whipping the gun around at King.

He shoved his fingers through the fiber weaves and clamped onto the slide, just as Selma rammed the butt of her gun into his forehead. The blow snapped his head back, causing him to lose hold of the weapon and his opportunity to make Swiss cheese of the man he hated so vehemently.

"I warned you to watch him," King reprimanded his henchmen. He frowned at Emery's dad, who was pulling himself up by the net, blood dripping from the gash Selma's gun had made. The men exchanged malevolent stares.

I shuddered, wondering what had generated this much hatred between them. It was then that I noticed I had jumped to my feet. Quickly dropping down, I willed Visser to lower Mr. Phillips into the bay so I could rescue him. The longer Emery's dad and King talked, the more likely he wouldn't be lowered into the water alive.

As if we were in cahoots—a horrifying thought—Junior released a puff of smoke and said, "Pops, let's get on with the swan song already. I don't want to waste another Cuban on this joker." He pouted at what was left of his cigar.

"As you wish." King nodded at Visser.

Visser flicked a switch on the control panel, and the large steel door to the cargo hold began to slide open underneath Mr. Phillips, releasing a scent that set every nerve in my body humming. I had never smelled anything like it. Equal proportions of predatory aggression and excitement seized my mind, and my body drew into a deep crouch. I instinctively prepared to defend myself.

Another ominous howl rose from the cargo hold. Terrified, Moreau and Sanchez backed up.

Mr. Phillips squinted into the dark opening beneath him, trying to make out what fate awaited him. Judging by the foul odor, it wasn't anything good.

"Have no doubt, I will look after Serena and Emery," King said, as if this was a comforting thought. "Emery is quite an accomplished young man. You must be very proud of him. I'm sure I will find much use for him in the near future."

Mr. Phillips shot him a furious look, and my hands clenched into fists. If either of the Kings came anywhere near Emery, I would make them live to regret it.

"Perhaps Serena will see things in a new light without your influence. I have never forgiven you for poisoning her mind against me and destroying what she and I had worked so hard to create. Assassin was more than a weapon. It was the key to a new existence. The organisms we were harnessing held secrets, secrets that could advance our race faster than centuries of evolution. I have not given up on them, and I know Serena hasn't, either. I'm speaking of her Formula 10X, which brings me to the blood sample we found in her laboratory."

My racing heart skipped a beat. *The towel soaked with my blood. King has had it all along.*

"We haven't had success identifying the particular properties of the sample. This will be another mystery that Serena will have to explain. Perhaps she'll be willing to collaborate. I've made great advancements on my own. Exhibit A." King motioned to the hooded man who had stood curiously still, even when Mr. Phillips attacked the henchman.

"I have had failures, as well." His eyes dropped to the cargo hold. His *failure* let out another blood-curdling howl. "But failure is to be anticipated. I look forward to Serena's assessment of our test subjects. She has always had a remarkable ability to—"

Mr. Phillips barked a mocking laugh. King's gaze jumped to him.

"Dream on," Mr. Phillips said, antagonizing King with a grin. "This story doesn't end with you winning the girl and living happily ever after."

"You'll never know how it ends," King returned coldly. "But you can spend the last few agonizing moments of your life speculating. Good-bye, Gavin." King's arm rose in the air, signaling Visser to lower the net and feed Mr. Phillips to whatever lurked in the cargo hold.

I sprung from my crouch. The tips of my toes had just left the ground when something caught my ankle, and I felt a stabbing pain in my left calf. I whipped around and saw long, clawed, scaly fingers clutching my ankle. A hooded head was pressed against my burning calf.

*It's biting me*, I realized in the same split second that I was hurled violently downward. My skin reacted, hardening, but the searing pain underneath didn't decrease, as pain normally did when my armor came up. The sensation rippled through my calf muscle like a wave of hot lava.

*Venom. It injected venom into me.*

My back slammed into the deck, and the hooded creature leapt on top of me, grasping my neck with its claws. My hands dove into the hood and got a handful of tough, scaly skin.

The creature hissed rancid breath. Blood-tinged saliva dripped from the hood, followed by a stream of venom that barely missed my eyes, instead saturating the gauze underneath them. The claws dug deeper into my throat, and the dull pressure turned acute—excruciating—as if razors were slicing my skin.

*My armor is down,* I realized in a panic, feeling my skin vacillate from hard to soft. Searing pain shot up my leg in the moments when my skin returned to a normal state. *I'm poisoned, and my body isn't fighting it.*

Gasping for air, I forced my fingers deeper into the creature's thick, leathery throat. It let out a strangled hiss and flew backward, landing in a crouch.

I pressed my palms against the deck and began to rise, closing my eyes and shaking my head to clear the haze. A heavy net fell over me and knocked me on my back again.

Woozy with pain, I strained my blurred vision until I could make out the shadowy, hissing figure through the ropes of the net. As it loomed over me, its thin, spidery fingers hooked the hood and eased it back to reveal a grotesque, inhuman face.

A scream stuck in my throat. Crimson reptilian eyes with slit pupils regarded me on either side of a whiskered snout. Tufts of hair grew between patches of scaly bronze skin. My eyes rose to the thick black hair atop its head, streaked with white like a lightning bolt, and then down to the holes where ears should have been. The snout lifted in a ghastly smile, revealing sharp teeth and fangs. Light shimmered off a metallic canine tooth.

*Silver Tooth*, I realized, horrified beyond comprehension. This monster before me—King's *pet*, his experiment—was Raul Diaz, the thug who had kidnapped Serena and my dad for Junior and set fire to the data for Formula 10X. *This is the price he paid for betrayal. He became King's test subject.* I felt more strength drain from me.

Silver Tooth pounced. All I saw was a streak of black and then his face inches away. His serpentine eyes bore into mine, and his claws dug into my throat.

*He's killing me,* I thought, frozen with terror, unable to breathe. The claws cut deeper into my skin each time my armor faltered. *He'll rip my throat out if I don't stop him.*

Summoning strength, I flattened my palms against his chest and pushed. The force would have sent the human Diaz flying off me, but now it moved him mere inches. Straddling me, he snapped his teeth and slashed at me with his claws. I blocked his attacks from under the net as best I could, but he was too fast and too strong. My body sustained numerous cuts and bites, and with each bite, more venom entered my bloodstream, weakening me further.

I was dying—truly dying.

The attack seemed to go on for hours, but the distant sound of a chain releasing and cheers suggested only seconds had passed.

Then Mr. Phillips screamed.

*NO!*

My eyes closed to the flash of teeth and claws, and all noise muted into nothingness. Against my eyelids, I saw the formless beast within me snarling, straining for freedom. My thoughts turned to the fingers I always kept firmly wrapped around the chain. My fingers, my hand. *What if I let go and never come back?*

Then so be it.

I relinquished control.

# Twenty

# Release the Beast

In my mind's eye, I saw my fingers unfurling as I gave in to the beast, watched the thick chain slide over my palm and away . . .

I opened my eyes to see Silver Tooth's jaws coming down on me. My fist plowed into them.

The impact sent him flying backward and skidding across the deck on his backside. He slid up into a defensive crouch, fear registering on his hideous face.

"*Los muertos vivientes*," he hissed, his thin tongue flickering between bloodstained fangs in the space where teeth had been moments before. The right front tooth dangled from the root. He spit out blood and teeth and lifted his snout to spray venom. Shaken nerves disrupted his aim, and venom splattered on the deck.

I gripped the netting and pulled savagely, gritting my teeth with rage. *Pop! Pop!* The tightly woven fibers broke, and I burst free, springing to my feet.

"The undead," hissed Silver Tooth, taking a step back.

Chest heaving, I bolted forward, ready to shred him to pieces like I had the net. I caught hold of his black hair and flipped him, slamming his back into the anchor winch. Bones crunched as his spine collapsed grotesquely around the winch, as if he were made of rubber.

No mercy, no regret over what I had done, I kept my hold on that handful of hair and flung the crumpled body at the guardrail.

Silver Tooth's raccoon-like hand hooked the top rail as he went over, causing his body to snap back like a stretched bungee cord. He hit the hull of the trawler like a hammer striking a gong.

Unable to see him on the other side of the guardrail, I expected the spider fingers to slide off the bar as gravity pulled his broken body into the bay, but the fingers gripped tighter, and then the other hand was slapped down next to it.

A hiss came from the other side of the rail as if the wind was whispering a prayer. "Heal me," it said. "Heal me."

I willed my own body to heal as my eager eyes clung to those hands. I breathed heavily with anticipation, and my fingers twitched at my sides, ready to continue the fight.

"Yesssss . . ." Silver Tooth's face appeared over the top of the rail, wearing a wolfish grin. The missing teeth had grown back.

I felt a sick smile twist my face, and my muscles tensed with excitement. He pulled himself up, locked his elbows, and swung the lower part of his body over the bar, legs together like a gymnast on a pommel horse. He landed gracefully on his feet and snapped the cape back over his shoulders, exposing black pants and the white ruffled shirt one would expect to see on Zorro. His eyes seemed to burn a brighter red.

*He wants my blood*, I thought, thrilled—because I wanted his, too.

"*Venga a morir*," he hissed, gesturing for me to come to him with his long, scaly fingers.

We ran for one another.

The next several seconds were a flurry of fists, feet, and teeth. We fought hard and fast, so fast the naked eye wouldn't have been able to track us. I sensed Silver Tooth's determination beginning to wane, his desire to kill me surrendering to fear. His blows became desperate, his snake eyes widening and losing their fury. He eluded a bone-breaking kick aimed at his chest and shot past me. I swung around to see him crouched on the rail overlooking the lower deck.

215

"You are cursed," he hissed, fingers poised to defend himself.

Beyond his cape flapping in the wind, I glimpsed the Kings and their henchmen, looking down into the cargo hold. Junior smiled around a fat cigar, and it all came rushing back, why I was there and what I had to do without further delay.

I redirected my gaze to Silver Tooth and flew at him, catching his throat with an outstretched hand. We tumbled over the rail and plummeted end over end toward the lower deck, Silver Tooth's cape thrashing around us. I glared into his bulging eyes and squeezed his throat in my death grip, while my other fist pummeled his snout. Poisonous saliva and blood spewed from it like water from a burst pipe.

Startled eyes turned upward from the lower deck. Junior's mouth slackened, and his cigar fell from it and into the cargo hold, spinning wildly as it descended. Before anyone could move or draw weapons, Silver Tooth and I were upon them, knocking three henchmen into the opening of the hold with us. As we went down, I never lost hold of Silver Tooth's throat.

We hit the floor and tumbled upright. Silver Tooth's bloodied and crushed snout reformed as if by magic and curled into a snarl.

"Do not shoot." King's command rang through the cargo hold as I yanked my head around to the monster looming over Emery's father, who was now a bloodied heap on the floor.

Fifteen feet tall, with a slug-like body, tusks, hoofed legs, and a golden mane running down a bulbous back—it was as if all creatures, great and small, had been thrown into a blender. This atrocity against nature was about to make a meal of Mr. Phillips.

Beady, milky eyes peered down at me between flaps of warty skin.

"Atrocity," I growled at the slithering monster. "Why don't you two have some fun?" Taunting it with a smile, I bid, "Enjoy," and threw Silver Tooth at it.

Silver Tooth smacked into the creature's round, warty gut. Atrocity whinnied and bit at him, trapping the cape between big, square teeth, and then vigorously whipped Silver Tooth back and forth like a dog playing with a toy— only Atrocity wasn't playing.

I gripped Mr. Phillips's collar and ran full speed up Atrocity's back. I leapt for the deck and landed on the edge as a bullet grazed my shoulder. Mr. Phillips banged hard against the opening to the hold. Tossing him to the deck, I backhanded the shooter, Selma Heart, and sent her flying, while simultaneously planting my foot into a henchman's stomach with a sharp kick. Selma's gun clattered across the deck as she tumbled, taking out Sanchez and another henchman and landing smack-dab on top of Junior. He lay sprawled underneath her like flattened road kill, with his arms and legs sticking out.

I darted back to Mr. Phillips, grabbed his collar again, and flung him into the bay, then leapt up onto the rail to go in after him. Before doing so, I took one last look at King.

The crime lord ignored the chaos around him as he observed me, rubbing his chin the way my dad sometimes did when intrigued. This infuriated me, as did his cavalier attitude. Did he think he was safe—too good, too rich, too powerful to be harmed? The beast wanted to see him cowering, crying, and begging for mercy. Luckily, there was still enough of Cassidy left in charge to keep my priorities straight.

Turning my back to him, I dove into the bay.

*Twenty-One*

# Rescue

I swam about a hundred yards from the *Enchantress*, towing Mr. Phillips behind me, when it became apparent that my body had not overcome the venom. Adrenaline and rage must have temporarily covered the symptoms.

My head dipped under the rippling icy saltwater as I kicked my legs with all my remaining might. Once again, I broke through the surface. I repositioned Mr. Phillips's head on my shoulder and anxiously assessed him.

He looked like death itself, with an oozing head gash, bruises forming against his pallid skin, and his head lolling unconsciously against my shoulder. If it hadn't been for his shallow breaths and his chest expanding against my arm, I would have thought he had already entered Davy Jones's locker.

*Maybe I'll get there first*, I thought, feeling the weakness in my muscles. They contracted and felt like pitiful worms squirming under my skin. Nausea gripped my stomach, and my heart raced at a pace that couldn't be good, even for a mutant.

"Looks like it takes a mutant to kill a mutant," I said, and got a mouthful of saltwater. As I choked it up, my attention turned to the rapid pop of automatic weapons behind us. None of the gunfire appeared to be directed at us.

Images of bloodshed flashed through my mind. It sounded like a war.

I shook my head to dislodge the gruesome thoughts and encouraged Mr. Phillips, in case he could hear me: "We're almost there. Hang on." I coughed out saltwater. "You won't be another notch in King's belt."

Instantly regretting this last part, I glanced at Mr. Phillips's bloodless face and knew that if I didn't get him out of this freezing water soon, the next time Emery saw him would be at the morgue.

My legs moved like pistons. A minute later, I dragged him onto the beach of an extravagant waterfront home. I lifted him into my arms—not an easy thing to do, considering his size and the venom working its lethal magic in my body. Behind us, the distant gunfire had ceased. I didn't even want to think about what that could mean.

My arms shook as I carried Mr. Phillips to the back patio of the mansion ten yards from the water. A security light switched on, spotlighting us as if we were on a stage, and a Doberman Pinscher barked furiously from behind French doors. A man in flannel pajamas appeared next to the dog. Eyes wide, he watched me gently place Mr. Phillips on the flagstone.

I stared into the man's stunned face and brought my palms together in a pleading gesture, then made a phone gesture. His eyebrows knitted in confusion. I could almost read his thoughts. *What would a mummy know about telephones?*

Not wanting to delay medical care a moment longer, I swung around and jetted for the water, stumbling a few times. At the water's edge, I doubled over and heaved. I hadn't been physically ill since my mutation.

*I'm not sick*, I reminded myself, wiping my mouth. *I'm poisoned, and I need help, too.* I took a deep breath and dove into the freezing water toward the *Enchantress*. I knew it was a bad idea, but it was my quickest way to help. Emery would wait for me at the last place he had known me to be: the dock at the marina, three miles across Elliot Bay.

*I can do this.* I rallied, fighting against the current, the cold, sickness, pain, and increasing disorientation. I swam underwater and forced my throbbing legs to kick while weird, semi-lucid visualizations of mutant microbes battling it out with toxic invaders went tripping through my head. Never before had I rooted for my virus to prevail.

When my lungs began to burn, I came up for air, hoping the oxygen would clear my head. I could hardly think straight. Gulping in a deep breath, I glanced at the *Enchantress*, which floated an eighth of a mile or so away. I listened for voices and heard none.

*Who cares what happened to them?* I thought, and truly didn't care at the moment. My mind was singularly focused on one objective: Survival.

With my teeth clenched in pain, I dipped underwater and swam a couple yards until I heard an engine rumble to life. It filled the water with an eerie noise that sounded like an alien communiqué. Cocking my head left, I saw King's submarine cutting through the water at me, its nose angled downward. I swam in place, confused about what to do. King was escaping. I had to stop him.

*How? Grab onto the submarine, get pulled into the depths of the sea, and drown?* I reasoned, ending the ridiculous deliberation. Even if I were healthy, I doubted I could stop a submarine. *And you're not healthy*, I reminded myself as the submarine dove beneath me. *Keep going before you do drown*. On the tail end of this thought, I was caught in the submarine's wake and turned round and round as if I were in the drum of a washing machine. My head and stomach felt like they were in the spin cycle. Then an explosion thundered, sending a shockwave through the water. My eardrums nearly burst.

In excruciating pain, I clamped my hands to my ears. The water illuminated, as if a light switch had been turned on, and I caught a glimpse of the source of the light above me, burning like the sun. Releasing my ringing ears, I forced my way out of the turbulence and swam toward the ball of light, bursting through the surface to find the fiery remains of the *Enchantress*. A lone tusk floated amongst the debris.

A siren wailed from the shore, and I began to swim aimlessly, having no idea where I was going, other than *away*.

*King blew up the Enchantress!* My jumbled thoughts mixed with hot, salty tears and the cold salt water that slapped my face. My arms stroked, and my legs kicked for dear life. *He was getting rid of the evidence. They were probably all dead before he even lit the fuse.* All at once, the last of my energy reserves drained from me. I sank under the surface, unable to fight the current, the cold, the pain, the despair. I was tired of fighting, and I was just tired . . .

Everything went black.

My eyes fluttered open to murky water and a stream of air bubbles buffeting my face, colliding with my eyelashes. Muted sounds of engines and sirens raged above me. I realized with confusion that I was sinking. Clamping my lips to trap my remaining oxygen supply, I dimly remembered where I was and what had happened. I felt the evidence all over my body. Every part of me ached and trembled, and I was so very, very cold.

Above me, I watched the shadowy bottoms of boats glide over the surface. Slowly, I crawled up, feeling as if in a dream world, and broke through. Reality overloaded my senses. Sirens, motors, voices on loudspeakers, boats, smoke, waves, engine exhaust—it was all too much.

I took a haggard breath of air and sank back under the water, where it was quiet, and swam without direction. As far as I knew, I was headed out to sea, but in my current state of mind I didn't give a rip. My will to live was rapidly dissolving.

*I hurt.* My eyes closed. My feet and arms moved sluggishly. *Body, mind, and soul—all hurt.* I wanted my old life back.

*So let go,* a voice—my voice—urged. *Stop swimming, stop fighting. Let the venom do its job. No more lies, no more fear, no more anything.*

*This is the venom and cold talking,* a more reasonable thought retorted. *Remember the movie in fourth grade? The one where the man with hypothermia gave up, lay down in the snow, shut his eyes, and died? Open your eyes!*

*Can't,* I whimpered. *I'm sick of swimming, of thinking. Can't think anymore. I'm lost. I need help.*

*Cassidy, where are you?* I heard Emery whisper.

My eyes sprung open, expecting to see him, but there was only water. Miles and miles of water.

*Cassidy . . .*

I spun around toward the voice. Still, only water.

*Where are you?*

*You're in my head, Emery,* I thought. *No, you're not in my head. It's only my imagination, but don't worry. I'm coming back.*

Forcing my arms and legs to move, I swam toward Emery's voice.

*Come on, Cassidy . . .*

His voice felt closer. I fought harder.

*It's been hours . . .*

Piers and the outline of land appeared dimly ahead. I kicked and stroked with everything left in me.

*Where are you?*

Cold air struck my face as I wrestled my way up.

"Here," I gasped, arms flailing. "I'm here."

A slap of water knocked me back under, and I took a fateful breath, filling my lungs with surf. I couldn't get my arms to move, and panicked as the surface moved farther away. Arms slipped around my waist, and I felt myself being tugged upward.

My face reunited with air, but I couldn't take a breath. I choked out seawater and thrashed in desperation for oxygen.

"Easy, or we'll both drown," Emery commanded, his hot breath against my ear, arms tightening around me.

Willing my limbs to still, I sank into his chest.

"You're safe, Cassidy," were the last words I heard before passing out.

~~~

"Cassidy, I need you to help me."

Emery's voice brought me back to consciousness. I rolled my head to the side and pried my eyes open to see his face, pale as a sheet and strained with exhaustion. His hand clung to the rung of a ladder.

"Emery, you need to get out of the water," I said, pushing the words out through a throat that felt shriveled.

"Can you climb the ladder?" he asked.

I bobbed my head, grabbed a rung, and climbed slowly with Emery's help. At the top, I crawled onto the dock and curled into a ball. I closed my eyes for what felt like a split second. When I opened them, Emery was carrying me.

"Your dad's safe," I breathed, shivering against him. "I saved him. He's a good guy."

Emery nodded. His teeth chattered. The world went dark again.

~~~

"Cassidy." There was an incessant patting against my cheek. "Cassidy."

My eyelids pulled apart to find a concerned face hovering over mine. Dim light created a stark contrast of milky skin, black hair with water dripping from the ends, and dark eyebrows slanted over piercing black eyes, which brimmed with worry. Emery's lips were tinged purple, as if he had been out in the cold.

"You're so handsome," I mumbled groggily, "and wet." I brought my hand to his hair in confusion, then let it flop to his knit shirt. "But your clothes are dry."

"Cassidy, what happened to your leg?"

"My leg?" I pulled my head up, and my gaze traveled down to a hoodie I recognized as Emery's. Underneath, the damp clothes clung to my skin. The shorts were cut off at the upper thigh, exposing my bare legs. My left leg was black and blue, swollen to twice its normal size, and the muscles contracted like . . . *worms squirming under my skin.*

Then it all came rushing back.

I looked around and took in the unfamiliar bedroom. The movement made me dizzy. My head dropped to the pillow like a bowling ball. "Whose bed is this?" The room spun. "Where are we?"

"In a yacht. I let us in," Emery said, meaning he had picked the lock. "There are two puncture wounds on your left calf. Did something bite you?"

"Silver Tooth. I mean . . . Raul Diaz, but he isn't human anymore. He has fangs."

Emery searched my eyes, trying to determine if I was delirious.

"King is making mutants," I pressed on, trying to order the thoughts that eluded me like greased pigs. "He tried to feed your dad to Atrocity, but I saved him. Not Atrocity, your dad. He's one of the good guys. King blew Atrocity up." When he didn't respond, I asked, "Are you happy?"

"Far from it." Emery frowned, and I wondered if I had only imagined that I'd said his dad was one of the *good guys.* "I'm sorry," he apologized, which confused me even more. "Your leg threw me. I wasn't expecting that. Are you in pain?"

I thought about it, and shook my head. The pain was gone. "Is that bad? That my leg looks like this and doesn't hurt? And why are the muscles moving around like that?"

"You'll be fine," Emery said by way of an answer. He attempted a reassuring smile, but gave up quickly. "You're shivering," he pointed out, and sure enough I was. I hadn't even noticed until he'd mentioned it. "We have to raise your core temperature. The comforter you're lying on is wet. I'm going to find another blanket."

He stood up and stepped away. His movement gave me vertigo. I closed my eyes to calm the spinning sensation and managed to capture a thought from the whirlwind in my mind. "Where's my costume?"

"On the floor, along with your second layer of clothing." A door squealed on hinges.

"Did you take them off me?" Another door opened.

"Yes, but I was a perfect gentlemen."

There was something I wanted to say to that, but I couldn't think of what it was.

"Eureka."

I cracked an eye open. Emery had emancipated a wool blanket from a cabinet. Returning to the bed, he helped me to my feet. The room spun. I pressed my face to his shoulder, clinging to his neck as if he were a life preserver, and closed my eyes, but the sensation didn't subside.

"I'm going to be sick," I groaned.

"Hang on, almost there . . . I'm going to lower you to the bed." Gingerly, he guided me down to the mattress, which didn't help the spinning sensation.

"Is that better?" he asked, arranging a blanket over me.

"I'm cold." My insides felt frozen through and through.

"Me, too. This will help." He climbed under the blanket with me and pulled me to his chest.

I sighed, snuggling my cheek over his heart. "You're like a heating pad."

"You'll feel better soon," he assured me. But I detected something in his voice, something I hadn't heard before: doubt.

225

He wrapped my wet hair around his hand, squeezing some excess moisture from my locks. "I should have towel-dried your hair," he scolded himself.

I wanted to tell him to give himself a break—to thank him for rescuing me—but his warmth, comforting smell, and heartbeat were lulling me to sleep.

"You're not shivering anymore."

"Your dad is safe," I murmured, drifting. "He's a secret agent."

"I suspected as much." Emery's tone was thoughtful. "That's why I never nosed around his business, and why his involvement with King was a shock. I'll be frank. It put me in a tailspin. If it hadn't, I would have pieced together that he had infiltrated Moreau's gang to locate King. It's so obvious now . . . Cassidy?"

"Mmmmm . . ."

"Thank you."

I traveled from that place between sleep and wake, feeling warm lips press gently to my forehead.

~~~

"Mom, she slipped into a coma." Emery's voice echoed in the silence. I had never heard so much angst or fear in his voice. "No, stay there. I'm fine. As you said, there isn't anything we can do. She'll have to fight the side effects of the venom. Now that she isn't suffering from hypothermia, her chances are better."

*Emery is talking about me. I need to tell him I'm okay.* But I couldn't do that. I couldn't speak, open my eyes, or move. My control over my body had been severed. I could only listen.

"Yes, I'm positive that's what she said: 'King is making mutants.' Granted, she was delirious, but considering her current state, she obviously had that fact straight. The venom was most likely produced in a species that shares a similar genetic makeup—I say species because I have no other way to classify what Cassidy encountered . . . Yes, of course, I know what this means. Your former employer has never given up the dream, either." He paused. "Mom, I'm sorry. Forgive me for lumping you in with that psychopath. I know your intentions were for the greater good. I'm just worried about Cassidy and Dad. I *hate* feeling helpless."

There was a *bang*. The wall vibrated behind me. *Emery hit the wall*, I realized, and tried to tell him again not to worry.

"Have you had any luck with the hospitals? . . . No, focus on Bainbridge. The ship was anchored only a mile offshore, according to the news. That's where Cassidy would have taken Dad. I wish I had my laptop. Are you listening to the police scanner? . . . Nothing? . . . Mom, he's fine. Cassidy would have made sure of that . . . No. As we agreed, when you find out what hospital he's at, get his status, and if his condition is stable, wait for the hospital to contact you. If Dad knows you had prior knowledge, he'll also know *the mummy* told you . . . Yes, I know we can't let that happen. Dad will be obligated to file a report, and Cassidy will become government property."

There was pressure on my forehead.

"She's still clammy, feverish."

Footsteps moved away. The blanket lifted off my left leg.

Emery let out a breath that hissed through his teeth. "Her leg is unchanged. No signs of gangrene, thank God. Raul Diaz's saliva must be a bacterial cocktail. Correction: must have *been* a bacterial cocktail. No one could have survived that explosion. The only bright side is King's sinister ambitions came to an end tonight. He's likely scattered all over Elliot Bay."

*He escaped in a submarine*, I tried to say. Then silence fell.

~~~

"Cassidy . . . Cassidy."

A hand gently jostled me.

"Cassidy, wake up."

"Mmmmmm." My eyelids fluttered open.

Emery gave me a smile as warm as the sun, despite the dark circles under his eyes. "How do you feel?"

"Fine," I answered, unsure why he was in my bedroom. Then I remembered. I wasn't in my bedroom. I sat up and looked around. "It wasn't a dream?" I asked.

"I'm afraid not." Exhaustion and relief showed plain on his face. He brushed back some hair that had fallen over my eyes. "But you're fine now."

I flipped the blanket off my legs. The left leg looked like the right—normal, healthy, and flawless, with chipped lavender nail polish on all five toenails.

"Your immune system got the upper hand about an hour ago." Emery yawned. "Your leg healed within the last thirty minutes, but I wanted you to sleep. You needed it, and still do. You'll be able to rest more at home. It's a quarter to five. My mom should be pulling up in the parking lot any minute."

"Where's your dad?"

"Virginia Mason. He's registered under the name Seth Harrison. He was brought in by ambulance at one twenty a.m. and is in stable condition, thanks to you."

"How do you know it's your dad?"

"Seth Harrison suffered hypothermia and matched my dad's description. Plus, there's an interview on the front page of today's *Seattle Times* with the man who called the ambulance. He claims a mummy carried Harrison to his back patio and then returned to the depths of the bay." Emery grinned; his coal-black eyes twinkled. "I bet you'll be trending again by midmorning."

"But this isn't good. Your dad is a secret agent. He can't have his picture all over the place."

228

"He won't. The CIA will move him from Virginia Mason soon, if they haven't already. Let the government worry about government business, and we'll worry about ours." He mussed my hair and stood up. "Time to go home."

"Wait! Will you show me your tattoo?" Suddenly this became very important to me.

Without hesitation, Emery slid his right arm out of his shirt and angled the back of his shoulder to me. Sure enough, he had the same knotwork tattoo as Mickey's.

"Thank you." I smiled. "I love you, Emery."

He smiled back. "I love you, too."

## Twenty-Two

# Exposed

"You had quite a night, my dear," Serena remarked once Emery had pulled their car out of the marina's parking lot. We had been silent up until then, shell-shocked from the wild events of the night.

Serena turned in the passenger seat to scrutinize me as I nervously twined the fleece of Emery's sweatpants that billowed around my legs. Her face showed signs of worry and lack of sleep, but her eyes were sharp and focused, as if she didn't want to miss a thing. Her husband had almost died at the hands of the same madman who had been using her Assassin research to create monsters. Her world had been rocked to the core.

"I'm just glad Mr. Phillips is okay," I said, and looked down at the fleece I'd wound tightly around my finger.

When neither Serena nor Emery responded, I said to fill the silence, "It's a good thing you brought extra clothes, Emery. I guess you thought water plus my luck would call for dry clothes, huh? How I didn't capsize that rowboat, I don't know. I forgot to tell you about that, and it's probably all over the news by now. A bunch of club goers saw me—the mummy—*trying* to row. They cheered me on, and then there were those sea lions."

Laughing, I glanced up and met Emery's gaze in the rearview mirror. He was frowning.

"It's crazy seeing you drive," I rambled on. "I need to get my driver's permit, too. I don't know why I haven't yet." Finally I ran out of things to say.

"My dear." Serena stretched her hand out to me. I took it. "I understand you've been through a traumatic experience, but it's time Emery and I understand precisely what happened. As difficult as this may be for you, please collect your thoughts and tell us everything."

Nodding, I obliged. Words spilled from my mouth, so quickly that I could hardly catch my breath between them. Concerned that I wasn't making sense, I looked to Serena periodically for reassurance, and she urged me to continue, letting me know that she and Emery were keeping up, soaking in the information.

The only part I left out was the conversation between Mr. Phillips and King. Their exchange was cloudy. I couldn't remember everything that had been said, but a gut feeling told me not to disclose anything until I'd had time to process what I'd heard.

However, I did impart that King had referred to Silver Tooth as his "pet" and that Diaz and Atrocity were test subjects for experiments, based on Assassin research. At this, Serena clamped her lips together. She'd had less of a reaction when I described the monster that had been killing her husband before I interceded. Although, when I explained where I'd left Mr. Phillips, tears pooled in her bloodshot eyes.

"Thank you, Cassidy," she choked out, squeezing my hand. "You're a good girl."

Tears sprang into my eyes, too. I nodded, afraid I would start bawling uncontrollably if I opened my mouth.

"King escaped in the submarine," Emery concluded, before I had a chance to share that part.

"Yes," I confirmed, wiping my eyes.

Emotions warred on Serena's face: anger, fear, regret, and shockingly—relief.

*Is it possible that she's relieved King survived?* I wondered, flabbergasted at the thought. *So he can experiment on people and make them into monsters? Why wouldn't she want him gone for good?*

The questions firing through my head must have been evident on my face, judging by the sheepish expression that appeared on Serena's. Releasing my hand, she turned around and left me to draw my own conclusions.

~~~

Emery pulled up to the curb in front of his house. An unexplainable sadness fell over me as I stared at the dark windows of our English Tudor, where my family slept peacefully, unaware that I'd ever been gone.

*It's the secrets*, I thought, brushing away sudden tears. *I'm tired of the secrets.*

Emery cut the engine and turned around to study me. "Ready?" he asked, exhaustion written all over his face. It had been a long night, perhaps the longest either of us had ever had.

"Very," I said, more sharply than I had intended. I wasn't even sure what prompted my cutting tone.

*Living a double life*, I thought. *It's taking a toll.*

"The street is clear," Emery observed, forgiving my rudeness. "Let's go."

We got out of the car. I closed my door, careful not to make noise, and turned to say good-bye to Serena. Before I could do so, she caught my face in her hands and placed a sweet, motherly kiss on my cheek.

"Sleep well, my dear." Her doe eyes brimmed with affection. "We'll sort this out later."

"How? Snap our fingers and *voila*, King is in handcuffs?" I retorted. I instantly regretted it. "I'm sorry. I'm just tired. I hope the hospital calls you soon."

"Gavin is fine," she replied, not looking so sure. Her obvious concern made me feel even more like a jerk.

"I know he is," I agreed. "I'll come right over after I wake up."

"I'll walk you home," Emery offered.

I nodded, and we crossed the street silently. I kept my eyes glued to the ground.

Under my window, I started to whisper good-bye, but Emery seized my arm and spun me around to him. He took my face into his hands, as his mother had, and brought his face close to mine, staring deep into my eyes beneath the flickering light of the streetlamps. The intensity in his gaze caused my heart to thump like a rabbit.

"We'll sort this out later," he whispered his mother's words. The promise affected me very differently this time. I believed it.

"It'll be okay," I whispered in agreement.

He smiled. "I wouldn't let it be any other way. But we should stop tempting fate. Your dad could wake up early and open the family room blinds—"

Before he could finish, I squirmed out of his grasp and bent my knees, prepared to spring to my window.

"Get rest, Cassidy," I heard him whisper as I dove into my room.

Catching the carpet, I flipped up onto my feet, whipped around, and ran back to the window. I leaned out to smile down at my friend and waved. Emery waved back, then turned to leave.

A voice came from behind me. "Are you waving at Emery?"

I almost fell out of the window.

The blood drained from my face as I straightened up and shut the window. Slowly, I turned around to face my little brother.

Chazz sat up in my bed, sporting Spiderman pajamas and staring at me. He scratched his head on the right side where his red hair was flattened from sleeping.

My mind raced a million miles a minute for an excuse. How much had he seen?

His next remark answered that question. "You can jump real high."

I groped for words.

"I like how you do flips," he went on, and added while yawning, "How many people did you save in the night?"

I fell to my knees. *He knows. I am in so much trouble.*

Chazz's eyes widened. "What's wrong?" he asked loudly.

Alarm knocked me to my senses. "Shh," I cautioned, putting a finger to my lips. "You'll wake Mom and Dad. That's the last thing I need right now."

His cheeks reddened with embarrassment, filling me with regret. There was no reason to speak harshly to him.

"No worries, buddy." I got up and went to the bed. "Brrrrr, it's freezing in here. You should have shut the window."

"But then you couldn't get back in," he pointed out in a very soft whisper. Clearly he didn't want to make any more mistakes.

I sat on the bed and pulled off Emery's socks, which were disgusting from the damp grass in our side yard.

Chazz continued talking in that breathy voice: "I always leave the window open for you. No matter how cold it is."

"You can talk a little louder," I whispered, climbing under the covers and scooting down so we were eye to eye. "How much do you know?"

He beamed. "I know you're a superhero."

"When did you figure it out?" I asked, deciding not to dispute the *superhero* label.

He gave me a patient look, as if I were thick as a brick. "You wore Nate's ninja costume when you saved Daddy, and you used my purple face paint—but that's okay. I don't like that color."

I wondered how he knew I had used his face paints. The kid was more observant than I had given him credit for.

"You'd make a good detective," I told him.

He nodded in agreement.

"What else have you deduced?"

"Huh?"

"Figured out."

"That you dressed like a Sasquatch and saved that old lady from being eaten by Roga. You're real fast, and strong, and a really good fighter, and you protect people in the middle of the night from bad guys with your superhero friends."

"Superhero friends?"

"Yeah, those other guys."

I thought for a moment and realized he was referring to the Rain City Superheroes, a group of Seattle residents who wear superhero costumes and patrol the streets at night.

"You're right about everything, except me teaming up with other superheroes. I work alone."

"No, you don't," he countered. "Emery is your sidekick."

Burying my face in the pillow to smother laughter, I imagined Emery and me running around in Batman and Robin costumes, which probably wasn't far from what Chazz envisioned. When I was done laughing, I pulled my face off the pillow and looked at Chazz. Lips puckered, he appeared perturbed.

"I'm sorry," I said, grinning. "I wasn't laughing at you. I just pictured Emery and me in Batman and Robin costumes."

He didn't see the humor in this.

"Now I'm going to be really serious, because this is a serious matter." I dropped the grin and became all business. "Who have you told?"

He gave me a stunned look. "Nobody."

"Not even Mom?"

"*Nobody*," he asserted, like I was slow on the uptake.

"Wow. I'm impressed." I truly was. What six-year-old could keep a secret this big, even from his mom? "Why haven't you told anyone?"

He rolled his eyes. I seemed to have worn his patience thin. "Because superheroes need secret identities so the bad guys can't find them and hurt their family."

I stared at him, feeling like I had been kicked in the gut. *How long has he lived with this fear? Four months?* It had never occurred to me that if Chazz suspected my secret, he would also be scared for our family's safety.

"Oh, Chazzy." I hugged him, heartsick. "Our family is safe."

Even as I said this, I knew it was a lie. Chazz was right. If my "condition" became known, we were all at risk. *And King has the towel soaked with my blood, my DNA. He's probably using it to make mutants.*

Pulling back, I looked into my brother's trusting eyes. I had to be straight with him, to a degree. Leading him to believe there was no danger could have devastating consequences.

"You're very, very smart and wise. There are evil people who can't find out about me, so keeping my secret is *very* important. You, Emery, Mrs. Phillips, and me are the only people in the whole wide world who know it"—*for now*—"and we have to keep it that way."

He nodded, eyes wide. "I will. Cross my heart, hope to die."

I winced. I hated that phrase.

"Thank you." I considered asking him not to draw pictures of me in superhero costumes anymore, but decided against it. The request would embarrass him, and who would take his drawings seriously anyway? "This is important, too. Act like you don't know a thing around Emery and me. We don't want anyone to get suspicious. But if you need to talk about it, let me know. How about we come up with a secret signal?"

"Like this?" He held up his index and middle finger to form a V.

"Peace?"

"No," he said, giving me the eye roll again. "V for Victory, 'cause we're going to have victory over the supervillains."

"I like that."

"Thanks." He laid a wet kiss on my cheek. "You taste like popcorn," he remarked.

"Kind of salty?" I assumed he'd tasted saltwater.

"Yeah. You should take a bath."

"I will after I sleep. Cuddle with me?"

Chazz scooted closer and nestled his head on my shoulder. "Cassidy? Oh, wait." He held up his fingers in a V, as if raising his hand in class to speak.

I giggled. "Yes, Chazz?"

"How many people did you save in the night?"

"One. Just one."

~~~

I woke to loud banging on my bedroom door.

"Breakfast!" Nate yelled. "Get your lazy butt out of bed."

I jolted upright, sending Chazz tumbling to the floor. "Nate, you jerk! You made me knock Chazz on the floor," I yelled back, feeling cantankerous. I'm not what you would call a morning person.

Chazz stood up, rubbing his head. "I'm okay. My head's tough." He knocked it with his fist in case there was any doubt.

I cracked a smile. "So I see. Tell Mom and Dad I'll be down after I shower. Chazz—" I gave him our secret signal.

He made a V in return and ran out of the room.

My smile lingered as I listened to him trot down the stairs. For some reason, having my little brother privy to my secret comforted me, maybe because it was nice having one member of my family that I no longer had to deceive.

"Better call Emery," I said to myself.

The smile pulled down into a frown as I momentarily grieved the loss of my iPhone, which could have been halfway to Alaska for all I knew. Sitting up, I swiped my other cell phone off the nightstand and poised my finger to dial. My eyes slid to the alarm clock: 8:00 a.m. Emery could still be sleeping. It had been a long, exhausting night for him, after all.

*I'll just go over after breakfast*, I decided, gathering clean clothes.

After a heavenly shower, I joined my family for eggs and bacon. When Nate and I finished doing the dishes, I headed to Emery's house. I rapped softly on the door and gathered my coat collar around my neck to ward off the cold, glancing up and down the street. The door began to open. I turned and almost jumped out of my skin. Mr. Phillips stared at me with annoyance, his head bandaged and his face purple with bruises.

"Well . . ." I smiled and resisted the urge to rub my eyes, in case he was a mirage. *How can this be possible? He was at death's door only seven hours ago.* "Well . . ." I said again, scrambling for something to add. "Ummmm . . ."

Mr. Phillips winced, as if my voice caused him pain.

In a stroke of genius, I flipped my palms up and commented with forced cheer, "It feels like snow in the air, doesn't it?"

He stared at me like I had a screw loose. "Are you here to do work for Serena?" He winced again, as if his own voice hurt his ears, too.

"Yep, yep." I snapped my fingers. "That's why I'm here."

He shook his head and looked like he immediately regretted doing so. Atrocity had gone to town on him. "Serena and Emery are still asleep, strangely." He paused, as if considering just how strange this occurrence was. "But you're welcome to come in."

He stepped aside for me with some difficulty, flinching as he turned his torso, which suggested broken ribs. I could commiserate. It also occurred to me that I might be responsible for some of the damage. I hadn't exactly rescued him gently.

"After you." Mr. Phillips gestured toward the kitchen. Apparently, the kitchen was where he thought I planned to start working. It was as good a place as any.

"Thanks," I said with an abundance of brightness. Brightness requires loudness. I couldn't believe Serena and Emery were sleeping through this.

The trek down the hall was uncomfortable with Mr. Phillips behind me. We walked in silence, aside from an occasional grunt of pain here and there.

In the kitchen, I made a beeline for the sink, grateful to see dirty dishes, but bummed that Emery's dad had followed me in. As if I couldn't wait to get the dishes in the dishwasher, I flipped on the water with vigor and went to work.

From the corner of my eye, I watched Mr. Phillips turn on the coffeemaker, then lumber to the table. Chair legs scraped across the floor. I cringed, feeling his pain when I heard him fall heavily into the chair.

"Cassidy," he said seconds later, as I rinsed and stacked dishes like there was no tomorrow.

"Yes, Mr. Phillips?" My voiced pitched. I gave myself a mental kick in the rear and continued to work.

"My appearance has obviously made you uncomfortable," he surmised, partially correctly.

His physical appearance hadn't thrown me; his being there did. I had thought that I would have more time to prepare before seeing him again, and I certainly hadn't anticipated that I would be alone when I did.

"A little," I admitted. Being truthful was probably wise. Who wouldn't be uneasy about someone being so beat up? Forcing myself to turn around, I teased, "Bar fight?"

This was a joke he'd used to explain why he looked like he'd been on the losing end of a fight when I first met him—right before he'd fed me some line about falling down airplane stairs.

Mr. Phillips barked a laugh, which turned into a coughing fit. He went rigid, and his face turned pale as he struggled to catch his breath.

"Do you need help?" I rushed over and sat beside him, placing a hand on his arm. "Do you want me to get Serena?"

Coughing and doubled over in pain, he waved me off.

"But your ribs are broken," I persisted, panicked that a rib may have pierced his lung. "Oh, why didn't you just stay in the hospital?"

His head jerked up, and his eyes met mine. I froze.

As he got the coughing fit under control, he stared into my eyes like a mouse mesmerized by a cobra. Neither of us blinked. Unable to look away, I watched the pupils in those black orbs expand with understanding and could almost see the equations running through his head, adding up everything that had occurred over the last four months:

$$2x(52y+19z) + 32(30 +15x) + 9x(22x+10) = C+A+S+S+I+D+Y$$

"Y-you?" he stammered with shock on his face. "How?"

"Gotta go." I jumped to my feet and hightailed it to the front door.

"Cassidy!" Mr. Phillips called from the kitchen.

I grabbed the front doorknob with trembling hands.

"Cassidy!" he called again, struggling to the hallway.

Emery came running down the stairs.

I bolted out the front door and slammed it as Mr. Phillips bellowed, "Serena! What did you do to that child?"

# Twenty-Three

# What Fate Awaits

I flung myself into our foyer and slammed the door, flattening my back against it. My heart hammered behind my ribs so hard that I thought it might crack a few of mine, too.

*Keep it together, Cassidy. Keep it together.* I spun around and set the locks on the door, as if they would keep out whatever might be coming our way.

*He knows. Mr. Phillips knows.*

"Cass, are you back?" Mom called from the kitchen, where she was probably scrubbing grout with a toothbrush.

"Yes," I squeaked and pounded my palm into my forehead. I had to calm down. *Keep it together. Keep it together.*

"That didn't take you long." Mom poked her head out of the kitchen, while drying her hands on a dishcloth.

I gave her a wide grin that made my cheeks feel ready to shatter.

She looked at me oddly. "Are you all right?"

I cleared my throat and nodded, slumping against the door in an attempt to look casual. Her expression told me that I hadn't succeeded.

She sighed, as if giving up on trying to figure out her peculiar daughter. "Your brothers are stripping the sheets off their beds. Why don't you do the same? I wrote out a chores list. It's on the kitchen counter."

"Okeydokey," I lamely responded, and jetted up the stairs.

I had my bed stripped in seconds flat, dropped the sheets off in the laundry room, and then got right on the chores list, engaging in them with enthusiasm, all in an attempt to ward off worry and paralyzing fear.

*Mr. Phillips knows. He knows!*

When I couldn't numb my mind any longer, I turned on the stereo and sang along to whatever song blasted through the speakers—rock, pop, hip-hop, jazz, country, polka—it didn't matter. Anything to keep my mind off what was going on across the street.

*Mr. Phillips might be dialing the Pentagon right now. Oh, why didn't I blink? If I would have blinked, he might not have figured out that I'm a freak.* "OOOOOOH, BABY, BABY—"

"My ears are *bleeding*!" Nate shouted over the vacuum.

I sang louder.

After finishing my chores and the ones my brothers hadn't gotten to yet, out of desperation I assigned myself to reorganizing the pantry. Shutting the accordion door to the pantry closet, I pulled neatly stacked cans off the shelves and decided to order them by expiration date. Amidst this brainless task, I allowed my mind to reflect and plot. Just when I had concluded that fleeing to South America to live in the jungle was probably the best solution, Nate opened the pantry door.

He looked at me sitting in the dark amongst the cans and rolled his eyes. Then he held the phone handset out to me.

"Phone, psycho," he said with his usual tact.

*Who is it?* I mouthed.

*Emery, duh,* he mouthed back.

*What does he want?*

Nate grinned impishly. "She wants to know what you want," he told Emery.

I *so* wanted to chuck a can at his head.

"He wants to *talk*," Nate reported, satisfied with himself. "So get off your butt and go."

I did, pegging Nate in the arm on my way. *Jerk.*

I marched out of the house mad as a hornet, planning to give the Phillipses a piece of my mind.

"Who do they think they are?" I muttered between my teeth as I stomped across the street. "They *ruined* my life!"

My boiling-hot temper had simmered down to stewing dread by the time I reluctantly climbed their front steps. I took two deep, shuddering breaths before knocking. Emery opened the door, his expression inscrutable. I began to pivot on my heels. No way was I doing this.

"If you run, I'll hunt you down," he said, securing my wrist. "The worst is over, trust me."

Emery pulled me into the house. I stumbled over the threshold and turned to the living room, where I smelled Mr. Phillips and Serena. She sat on the sofa, staring down at her hands. Mr. Phillips relaxed in the recliner, as if he had just finished a big meal.

"Cassidy," he greeted me as Emery locked the door.

I lifted my chin defiantly, pushing back the hair that had fallen over my face when Emery had yanked me inside.

A grin tugged at Mr. Phillips's mouth, as if insolence amused him. "Please take a seat." He motioned to the sofa.

To show that I wasn't afraid of him or whatever he planned to do to me, I marched to the sofa, plunked down next to Serena—who still hadn't looked up—and crossed my arms, glaring at him boldly. Emery sat next to me. The three of us lined up on the sofa made me think of elementary school kids who had been naughty, sitting in front of the big, bad principal's desk.

*I won't let him cow me. I won't!*

"Serena and Emery have apprised me of the situation," Mr. Phillips said, looking me in the eye. "First, I want to assure you that you and your family are safe."

His words extinguished the fire in my belly. That wasn't what I had expected him to say—at all.

"And I will do everything in my power to protect you and your secret—"

"You're not going to report me?" I choked out.

Serena gave my knee a reassuring pat.

"You don't appear to be a national threat," Mr. Phillips replied with a slight smile, "so I don't see how you are any of the United States government's concern. I'm still upholding my oath to protect the Constitution against all *enemies* foreign and domestic."

"I can vouch for her." Emery made the Boy Scouts' hand gesture.

Serena clucked her tongue with disapproval.

Mr. Phillips grinned at his son. "Smart aleck."

Normally, I would have punched Emery's arm for joking about a serious situation such as this. But I was too overcome with relief to do much more than blubber at that particular moment.

"It's all right, dear," Serena cooed as she gave Emery a significant look. "Well, don't just sit there. Get her a tissue. You should have anticipated this."

"My bad," Emery agreed, getting up.

*He's in rare form*, I thought as Emery fetched a box of Kleenex. But I understood why. His dad was safe and the man Emery had always believed him to be.

"He's just happy," I said, using my coat sleeve to mop up some tears.

Serena patted my knee again. "We know, dear."

Mr. Phillips looked on silently. His expression revealed nothing, though his thoughts were probably along these lines: *Is this really the fearsome mummy that pulled me out of the cargo hold and tossed me into the bay? Or does my doctor have me on some mighty strong painkillers, and I'm dreaming this?*

"I'm glad you're okay, Mr. Phillips," I snuffled.

Emery handed me the box of tissues and took his seat again.

244

I grabbed a handful and blew my nose in as ladylike a way as possible. "I was super worried about you," I added to Mr. Phillips. "I'm sorry I just left you at that house like that, but I'm sure you understand—"

A look crossed his face, as if he hadn't completely believed everything Serena and Emery had shared until that very second. He raked his hand through his hair as I continued my apology.

"And I'm sorry for any injury I might have caused when getting you off the ship. I get a little crazy when I'm like that, and I'm sorry for chucking you into the water—"

Mr. Phillips raised a hand for me to stop talking. "You have nothing to apologize for. You saved my life. Thank you." He looked as if he couldn't believe what he was saying. I think it was more likely he couldn't believe the situation, and I couldn't blame him.

"No problem." I blew my nose again. "I'm sorry I couldn't get to you sooner, but I had trouble of my own." I looked at Emery. "Did you tell him about Silver Tooth?"

"Raul Diaz," Emery explained to his dad, which answered my question.

"I call him Silver Tooth because I didn't know his name when he tried to murder Ben, so I named him after his capped tooth," I explained. "Did you tell him about that, too?" I asked Emery.

Emery appeared on the verge of laughter.

"Not yet," his dad answered for him. Mr. Phillips's expression had become calm and friendly again. I noted it was similar to the expression that Emery wore when concealing what he really felt. "I look forward to hearing more."

"I look forward to telling you. Anyway, like I was saying—" I paused, losing my train of thought. What had I been saying?

"As I told you, Gavin," Serena said, taking over for me in her clinical tone, "Cassidy is extraordinary. Her abilities are unprecedented—"

"Until now," I pointed out, thinking of something halfway intelligent to contribute. "King is making mutants. Oh, I forgot to tell you in the car—he has the towel with my blood. But he says his scientists, or whoever, haven't figured out the *properties* of the blood, or something like that. What exactly did he say, Mr. Phillips?" I looked at him, catching alarm on his face.

Diligently, he composed his expression and became calm and friendly once again. "That's what I remember as well," he confirmed. "Serena and Emery, would you mind letting Cassidy and I have a few moments alone?"

The two regarded him with suspicion, but obliged, rising to their feet. My heart galloped as they left me. I felt exposed, as if I had suddenly lost an article of warm clothing.

"Cassidy, may I sit?" Mr. Phillips asked, gesturing to the sofa.

I nodded, heat pouring into my cheeks. The blush had crawled down my neck by the time he carefully lowered his achy body onto the sofa next to me.

"Ow." He gently rubbed his side. "I've had my share of broken ribs, but I don't remember them being quite so uncomfortable. I must be getting old."

"No, it just hurts. I've had broken ribs, too—well, for about thirty seconds, when I jumped off a car and hit a tree. Only thirty seconds, you know, because of the healing thing. Did they tell you about that?"

"Yes, they did." He regarded me thoughtfully. "Do you know where they are right now?"

"In the lab," I said, and then amended, "Wait! I listened to them go down the hall, but I should double-check." Mr. Phillips didn't breathe as I concentrated, listening. "Yes, they're in the lab," I confirmed.

"How do you know?"

"I can hear them talking."

Mr. Phillips didn't try to conceal his astonishment.

"But," I whispered, "Emery could've bugged the room."

"That's my department," he replied with a grin. "The house is clean. Emery and I make our daily secret bug sweeps." He winked at me, and I cracked a smile.

*What a strange family this is.*

His expression sobered. "I hadn't realized you'd overheard Arthur King. Ridiculous on my part, considering your hearing."

"Yes, I heard everything," I confirmed, blushing again. I knew what he was getting at. Now that I'd had time to digest everything that King and Mr. Phillips had said, it was evident that there had been a love triangle many years ago. That was the reason for Serena's emotional conflict about King surviving the explosion. There was a time when she'd loved him.

"So I see." He smiled thinly, gesturing to my pink cheeks. "I know I don't have the right to ask this, but please don't share what you've overheard with Emery—"

"Because King did something to him." This was also a conclusion I had come to. King had experimented on Emery when he was young. "What did he do to Emery? And why?"

Mr. Phillips's face darkened. "Has Emery said anything to you?" he asked, watching me carefully.

"No. Does he know King tampered with him?"

Mr. Phillips winced at the word *tampered* and looked as if he regretted broaching the subject.

When he didn't respond, I rushed on, surmising, "You don't know if he knows, and how could you? Emery isn't exactly an open book. But nothing gets past him, believe me. Why did King experiment on him?"

"You know Emery well, or as well as anyone can know him."

His voice still sounded deceptively calm, belying the glint of rage I could see burning in his eyes. I knew I was treading on forbidden ground, but I wanted the truth. I nodded, encouraging him to continue.

"True, Emery is a need-to-know-basis kind of guy. That's in the blood. And you're right—he doesn't miss a thing, unless that thing involves him. Emery's intelligence is beyond what I can comprehend, but he has proven, time and time again, that he shares a common human weakness—the inability to see oneself with clarity."

I didn't agree with Mr. Phillips, but held my tongue. "Doesn't Emery have a right to know?"

"In due time, when I feel he can handle it."

"Handle what?"

His eyes bored into mine. "If you care about Emery as deeply as I believe you do, you will trust me and not repeat what you overheard."

"You want me to lie to him?"

"I want you to withhold information until I feel he is ready to hear it."

Foreboding crept through me like a thief in the night—a perfect metaphor, since I was essentially in the dark. Nevertheless, I relented.

"Okay, I won't say anything. What's another secret, anyway?"

Mr. Phillips studied me for a long moment. *Determining my sincerity*, I assumed.

"Thank you, Cassidy," he said when the analysis concluded. "Would you mind calling Serena and Emery up?"

"Sure, Mr. Phillips." I started to stand.

He touched my forearm. "Gavin. Please call me Gavin."

I nodded, but didn't test it out. I wasn't comfortable calling him by his first name just yet.

Emotions slammed through me as I walked down the hallway and into the kitchen. Swinging the basement door open, I called, "Mr. Phillips wants you." To my irritation, my voice cracked.

As Serena and Emery came up the stairs, I turned the doorknob back and forth, willing the emotional storm raging within me not to show. I didn't want to keep a secret from Emery that involved him. Why had I promised not to say anything?

"I understand how you feel, dear," Serena commiserated. Squaring her slight shoulders, she headed for the living room. Apparently my poker face was a failure.

Emery appeared behind her, scrutinizing me. "Are you all right?"

"Yes," I lied. *But what's new?*

"I'm sorry, Cassidy," Emery said, though I wasn't sure what for. "Let's get in there before World War III breaks out."

In the living room, Serena sat in the chair Mr. Phillips had vacated, her arms and legs crossed, her foot flicking with irritation. They stared one another down, each trying to bend the other to their will.

*Serena doesn't like whatever she thinks he's about to say*, I deduced, lingering in the doorway. I glanced sidelong at Emery. He appeared to know what was about to transpire.

"Well!" Mr. Phillips clapped his hands. "Obviously we're all in agreement. Cassidy's family will be told the truth immediately."

And World War III broke out.

*Twenty-Four*

# Eyes Wide Open

"Do you realize the risk of what you're proposing, Gavin? We must contain the situation."

"Serena, get your head out of the laboratory and think like a mother. Cassidy's family has a right to know."

And so Gavin and Serena fired back and forth, nose-to-nose, fiercely arguing their points of view regarding my fate.

Emery and I observed from the sofa, our eyes shifting between them as if watching a tennis match. I found myself conflicted. Both of their arguments were valid. My heart leaned toward Gavin's standpoint, of course, but my mind stood by Serena. The more people who knew a secret, the more likely it would be revealed. Things slip out in conversation, intentionally and unintentionally. I trusted my family, but they were human and subject to making mistakes, like anyone.

"'If you would keep your secret from an enemy, tell it not to a friend,'" Serena quoted.

"So we're reduced to famous quotes? Benjamin Franklin, I'd wager, since he's your favorite strategy in trying to win an argument. Two can play at this game. 'A secret at home is like a rock under tide.'"

"Ha! How ironic of you! 'Loose lips sink ships.'"

"'No one keeps a secret so well as a child.'"

"That is true," I chimed in, lifting my index finger.

Gavin's and Serena's heads snapped to me, almost as if they had forgotten that Emery and I were in the room.

"I haven't had a chance to tell you," I continued. "Chazz has known about me since King Pharmaceutical."

"Oh, dear." Serena dropped into the recliner.

"We're *presuming* he knows," Emery said, correcting me.

"Nope." I explained what had happened when I came home that morning.

"I'm astonished," Serena said, looking every bit of it. "I cannot believe he hasn't said a word to anyone."

"'No one keeps a secret so well as a child,'" Emery repeated, and something in the way he delivered the quote made me think he intended a double meaning. "In light of this new development, I see we have only one option—it's time to enlighten Cassidy's family."

"And we'll make it very clear to them that it's *her* head on the chopping block if tongues wag," Gavin added.

My hands automatically went to my throat. "They won't say anything," I assured him, thrilled and terrified at the same time. My parents would be livid about the lies, after they finished freaking out.

I recalled the last time my mom had freaked out—when she'd found out about the prison break. This naturally led to Lily White.

"Emery, did you tell your dad about Lily?" I asked.

"I didn't get that far in our earlier conversation. But we should now. I'm sure the FBI will appreciate a heads up, in case Detective Cruz didn't give my anonymous warning credence." He paused and said to his dad, "We'll start in 1938 when the Roman god of fire and metalwork, Vulcan, came to German scientist Dr. Josef Richter in a dream—"

Gavin's mouth dropped open.

*Oh, Emery is going to love this*, I thought, making myself comfortable on the sofa for the tale that ended with me being responsible for the creation of a supervillainess.

~~~

It was eventually decided that Gavin and Serena would break the news to my parents while Emery and I talked to

Nate and Chazz, which was fine by me. I didn't want to be anywhere near my parents when they were *enlightened* about my condition, exploits, and deception.

The four of us sat at the kitchen table as Emery broke the news. Nate burst into a fit of laughter, laughing so hard that he fell from his chair.

"Cassidy." Emery motioned to my twin rolling on the floor, holding his gut and laughing his head off.

I got up from the table, bent over, and gathered Nate in my arms.

"Whoa, whoa, whoa," he said in disbelief as I easily picked him up.

Enjoying his shock, I tossed him high in the air.

"Holy—!" he screamed on the way down, arms and legs flailing about. I caught him, and he stared at me, gaping.

"Yay!" Chazz cheered, clapping.

Emery grinned and leaned back in his chair. "Showoff."

"More, more, more," Chazz chanted.

I set Nate on his feet and leapt onto the island, which earned a gasp from Nate. "How 'bout this, Chazzy?" I said, and did a back flip, landing on my feet. "Ta-da!" I threw my arms back like an Olympic gymnast.

"Wahoooo!" Chazz applauded, giving me a standing ovation.

Nate finally found his tongue. "I always knew you were a freak of nature," he quipped.

"Now that Cassidy has given you proof, we need to lay down the ground rules," Emery said, all business again.

Ten minutes later, after Emery was satisfied that my brothers understood how imperative secrecy was, I did more tricks for them.

At one point, as I wowed them with my prowess in the living room, contorting my body like Gumby, Nate joked, "It's like having our own circus monkey. Does she fetch, too?"

I swung my leg high like I was going to kick his head. Nate dropped to his belly. We all exploded in laughter.

I heard the front door shut and turned my head to the foyer, smiling. Four somber faces observed us, as if they hadn't heard the sound of laughter before. My mom's eyes were red and puffy from crying, and my dad's face looked a decade older. My heart sank. By their appearance, you'd think there had been a death in the family.

"Sweetheart," Mom choked out, forcing a sad smile.

She made a beeline to me, as if I was the only person in the room, and my melancholy father followed her. She fiercely pulled me into her arms and pressed her cheek to my head, stroking my hair like she had done to console me after a nightmare when I was a little kid.

"It's okay, Mom," I reassured her, taken aback. I had expected anger, not grief.

Dad grabbed my face. His eyes were so haunted. "I almost shot you," he whispered with shame, as if confessing a terrible, dark secret.

An image flashed through my mind—of his crystal blue eyes narrowed lethally behind a gun barrel.

"You didn't know it was me," I protested. "You were protecting everyone." I smiled, believing my next words would comfort him. "Besides, even if you had shot and killed me, I would have come back to life."

A stricken look materialized on his face, as if my words were a blow between the eyes—eyes that were completely open now, and seeing the rough road ahead. He might have seen it more clearly than even I could.

With tears brimming, he enveloped Mom and me in his arms and wept.

*Twenty-Five*

# Magical

I woke up Monday morning with a smile on my face. I sprung out of bed, stretched, and did a couple back flips to the window, my smile expanding as I caught upside-down glimpses of my bedroom door, which was wide open. It didn't matter anymore.

"No more secrets," I cheered, landing before the window. I flung the curtains apart and welcomed the day with glee. The sky was still dark, the weather cold and gloomy, but I felt as if the sun blazed.

Much had been settled yesterday. After my parents had pulled themselves together, we'd gotten down to business. Assembled around the dining room table, our two families had orchestrated a collective plan.

My mom had suggested we disappear and create new identities so the likes of Arthur King Sr. would never find us.

To this, Gavin had replied, "Don't let the movies fool you, Elizabeth. If King, or the government, wants to find you, they eventually will. A life of running and looking over your shoulder is no life at all, and once you leave this house, you'll have tipped King off. At this point, you're only the nice family that lives across the street from us."

He assured us that King was watching and always had been. But we weren't to live in fear. Instead, we would fortify our walls—literally. Gavin would take over the security for the operation, and as soon as he could persuade the owner of their rental house to sell— which we had no doubt he could accomplish— the remodeling of both our houses would begin. Nate had looked excited at this, probably picturing something along the lines of the Batcave.

Now, feeling light as air, I moved through the school day with a smile on my lips, earning many comments and raised eyebrows.

"What are *you* smiling about?"

"Who put that smile on your face?"

"What are you up to?"

"Come on, fess up. What are you hiding?"

In my head, I replied to each question: *Wouldn't you like to know?*

My cheer even caught Chad's attention. With his arm slung over Robin's shoulder, he gave me the stink eye and the finger, assuming that I was taking pleasure in his humiliation. It was an unsurprising assumption on his part, since the world *did* revolve around him, after all. Robin smirked, her nose angling left.

Smiling back, I mentally sent my best wishes to the dastardly duo as they undertook another round of "ChaBin." I gave it two weeks, tops.

~~~

After school, while walking home with Emery, Nate, Miriam, Jared, Bobby, and Zach, I tuned out their chitchat to reflect on my *team*—which was what we were now, the Phillipses and us. I dashed away all of my fears about the future one by one as they encroached on my good mood. Instead, I made a conscious decision to enjoy the calm—while it lasted.

*I couldn't be happier than I am at this very second*, I told myself as Emery, Miriam, Nate, and I turned down our street and the other boys continued down the hill, or so I thought.

Jared's voice pulled me out of my head. "Cassy."

I stopped and turned around. Everyone else stopped, too. I'd been wandering several paces ahead of them, unaware of doing so, and had no idea why Jared had come down our street. This wasn't his usual route home.

"Can we talk, down at the park?" He gestured to the stone steps with his head.

I caught a look on Emery's face that instantly melded into his standard easygoing expression. If I wasn't mistaken, the look had been dread.

"S-sure," I said, moving my gaze from Emery to Jared reluctantly. *What does Emery know that I don't? Is Jared mad at me?*

"Give me your backpack," Miriam demanded, and practically ripped it off my back. She shoved the backpack at Nate and pushed me toward Jared. "Talk!" She waved at me to go.

"All right," I shot back, distressed. Why did it feel like I was the only one who was clueless? I looked at Emery, hoping my self-consciousness wasn't evident. "Tell your mom that I'll be over soon, after I talk with Jared." Emery just smiled and said nothing. I blushed at my totally lame request. *Of course I'd be over later. Duh.*

Not wanting to look more like a moron than I already did, I quickly met Jared at the steps. Chances were, I wasn't the only one who felt self-conscious right now.

"It's cold today," he remarked as we descended the stairs to Spinning Park.

"It feels like it's going to snow," I replied awkwardly.

"Yep," he agreed, and then asked how my day had been.

We carried on these uncomfortable pleasantries until I realized he was leading me to *the* swing. The one that belonged to Emery and me.

"Let's go over there," I suggested, pointing at a picnic table.

Jared shrugged and shifted directions. He sat on top of the table, expecting me to join him. Sheepish, I lingered in front of him.

He watched my feet shuffling in the frozen woodchips for several seconds, then let out a breath. "I want to talk to you about what happened with Chad."

I glanced up at him through my eyelashes. Seeing the painful embarrassment etched across his gorgeous face, I lifted my head and looked at him squarely. I didn't want him to feel embarrassed about protecting me.

"Thank you for looking out for me," I blurted. It was something I should have said a couple days ago. *Why didn't I thank him right after? What is wrong with me?* In regard to Jared, I always seemed to be making the wrong decisions.

"I'm sorry I didn't pound him when he kissed you." His eyes flashed with anger. "You have no idea how much I wanted to. I just didn't think it would be cool to do it at your house." He dropped his gaze to my hands, which dangled at my sides, pondered for a moment, and then grabbed them up.

"Your hands are like ice," he said, and I had no doubt of this, since his hands felt warm and toasty. Cupping my hands in his, he brought them to his mouth and blew into them. His hot breath penetrated my pores, sending a tingling sensation throughout my body like a current of electricity. My head swam.

He lifted dreamy eyes and gave me a smile. "Better?"

"Uh-huh." I nodded, weak in the knees.

His lips curved more.

"Cassy—" He slid his fingers along the outside of my hands, to my palms, so he held a hand in each of his. "I think you know how much I care about you."

I couldn't breathe. "I care about you, too," I managed to say. I wanted to smack myself over how husky my voice sounded. Was it possible for me not to make an idiot of myself?

Jared blinked in surprise. "You do?"

"Isn't it obvious?"

257

"No." He shook his head and let out an amazed laugh. "I thought this was one-sided and you were going to break my heart with the 'I like you as a friend' line."

"My heart's been broken for a long time," I heard escape my mouth. Not that I cared. I was too euphoric to care. "Because I've liked you for a long time."

"Me, too." Jared laughed again. "Okay, let me think. I'm having trouble doing that right now."

I laughed, too. I couldn't think straight, either.

"Okay." He brought my hand to his forehead and tapped my fingers against it. "Now I remember what I was going to say." He looked up into my eyes with a warmth that utterly melted me. "I know you can't date until you're sixteen. Your dad told me when I talked to him yesterday—"

"You talked to my dad—*yesterday*? About me?" I interrupted. *Why would he do that, and*— "Where was I?"

"At Emery's." Jared suddenly looked uncomfortable. He opened his mouth and then shut it, changing his mind about whatever he was going to say. "And, yes, about you," he answered my second question. "I thought your dad should know how I feel, especially since I'm at your house all the time. Plus, it's not what my dad would have done, and I plan to always do the opposite of what he'd do."

"I'm sorry," I said, squeezing his hands. Jared's dad was a total deadbeat.

"Thanks," he replied, and rushed on before his father could become the topic. "So you can't officially be my girlfriend for another 357 days."

I giggled. Jared was counting down the days until we could date. I couldn't have dreamed up a more romantic conversation.

"I know, I'm a dork." He laughed. His laughter faded into earnestness. "Just know until then that you're very special to me."

"And you are to me, too." I chickened out on saying the word *love*, though I suspected my feelings were obvious by the way he smiled. *Someday, I'll tell him I love him. Someday . . .*

A snowflake landed on one of his long, dark eyelashes.

"It's snowing!" I pulled my hands from his and caught snowflakes, lifting my chin to the sky. The sight of ice crystals cascading from the blanket of low-lying clouds mesmerized me, each flake beautiful, complex, and unique. "Why does it become so quiet the moment it starts snowing?" I mused in a hushed voice, not wanting to disturb the stillness that had fallen around us. Closing my eyes, I savored the peace and the cold snowflakes dotting my face. "The noise of everyday life seems to disappear. All I can hear is your breathing, like we're the only two people on the planet."

I opened my eyes and looked at Jared. The expression on his face caused my heart to flutter. No one had ever looked at me so tenderly before.

"You look magical." His gaze brushed over my face with the light strokes of an artist's paintbrush.

*Magical?* My soaring heart took a nosedive into reality.

I looked away as my mind flooded with all the reasons why he and I could never be, ripping apart my naïve daydreams. *Jared is human. I am not. We have no future together. Period.* The fact that I might not age beyond eighteen—ever—ensured that I would live a lonely existence. *Forever young. How can I be with anyone other than another mutant?* The vile abominations created by Arthur King loomed in my thoughts, painting a horrifying picture, not only for myself, but for all of humanity. Monsters were no longer the product of an active imagination. They walked among us.

*And soon the world will know.*

"Cassy, what's wrong?"

*Everything*, I thought, and braved a look at him. "What do you mean by *magical*?" I asked, and braced myself. If he said "your jade-green eyes," I might run.

Relief washed over his face. "I just meant—" He picked up the red curl lying over my shoulder and smiled a smile that made me feel like I was being sucked into a black hole. "I just meant that you are the most beautiful girl I have ever seen." His gaze followed his thumb, gently stroking strands of hair as if they were fine silk.

His soulful eyes lifted to mine, and I swear I saw my future in them. It wasn't so bleak, after all.

And suddenly, just like magic, we were the only two people on the planet again.

*Coming Soon*
*2014*

## Prologue

"There it is again," Patrick Grimm said to himself.

Using his raggedy coat sleeve, he dabbed at the warm blood trickling between his whiskers, but kept his gaze pinned on the glimmer in the water before him. Something had punctured his cheek when he'd rolled down the embankment—a rock or a stick, maybe.

A moment earlier, he had dismissed the twinkle in the dark water as a reflection from the star-studded sky that canopied the lake. On the far end, moonlight exposed shadowy oil rigs ominously lined up like the statues on Easter Island.

*Moai.* That was the name of those giant human figures the Polynesians had carved from stone to warn off invaders.

Patrick hadn't any idea about the name of the lake. It just happened to be the spot where those rednecks that he'd hitched a ride with had shoved him out of their vehicle—a beat-up truck sporting monster tires and a Confederate flag painted on its dented hood. The only thing he knew was that he was somewhere in Montana.

*Or North Dakota?*

Truth be told, Patrick didn't really care where on God's green Earth he was.

"Idiot yokels," he grumbled as he busied himself with lighting a cigarette. Those hicks had dumped him in the middle of nowhere.

They had been getting along just fine until his wee little blunder.

"Who's the heifer?" he had sniggered when he'd glimpsed the snapshot of the ugliest woman he had ever seen clipped to the sun visor, assuming it was a joke. It was then that he had noticed the resemblance between the big boys he'd been sandwiched in between and the woman in the photo.

"That'd be their *momma.*" Patrick shook his head and took a drag from the cigarette. He was always sticking his foot in his mouth, saying and doing the wrong things. If mistakes were dollars, he'd be mighty rich by now.

Patrick had had every opportunity to make something of himself, including an education and a family full of shining examples of success. He'd had doors of opportunity opened for him, welcoming him in. But had he taken his shot? No, not him. Instead, he had traveled down the road of screw-ups, until enough bad choices had caused him to hit the actual road.

Exhaling a stream of smoke, he narrowed his eyes on the glimmer and made out a distinct speck of light. It was moving.

262

"Firefly?" He sopped up some more blood with his sleeve.

As he watched, two more specks of light appeared a dozen or so yards away from the sparkle, each coming from opposite directions.

Patrick dismissed the firefly theory. The sparkles didn't appear to be flying. By their slow movement and the way they faded in and out, he guessed they were underwater.

"Only one way to find out."

He clamped the cigarette between sun-cracked lips, swiped his military backpack off the dirt, and hoisted his worldly belongings onto his back. As he made his way down to the water, he marveled at the fact that the big redneck had thrown the backpack out after him when ejecting him from the truck. It had been pretty generous, considering he had called their mother a cow.

The song "Bad to the Bone" skittered through his mind. He hummed the tune around his cigarette, noting that five more sparkles had joined the ranks. By the time he stumbled onto the rocky beach, he'd counted thirteen specks of light no more than ten feet from shore, swirling through the water as if searching for something. The first sparkle had appeared in the middle of the lake.

He scrutinized the strange phenomenon for a moment before deciding the sparkles were merely some type of water insect and probably posed no danger. At worst, he might get a little bite or sting if he came into contact with one.

"What the . . . ?" Patrick flicked his cigarette onto the rocks. The sparkles had come even closer to shore. "You attracted to my rugged good looks?" Squatting down, he stuck his hand into the cool water and wiggled his fingers. "Well, come on. Let's have a look at you."

Like bees catching the sweet scent of a fragrant rose on the breeze, the sparkles ceased their whirling and moved straightaway to Patrick's hand, bumping up against it.

Patrick laughed, enchanted. A warmth filled him. He couldn't remember the last time he'd felt happy.

"You're beautiful." He gently swished his hand and watched the sparkles dance around his fingertips like miniscule forest fairies. The white shimmer they cast mirrored in his delighted eyes.

"You're . . . luminous."

He scooped up a single sparkle with some water into a cupped palm. The twinkling glow immediately began to fade. Alarmed, Patrick submerged his hand in the lake, and the sparkle regained its luster instantly.

"Guess you need your brothers and sisters to shine," he deduced. After a moment of observation, he recognized a curious pattern in their twinkling, almost like Morse code.

"Do you communicate with those bright flashes?"

All at once, the sparkles swam away, as if summoned by a dinner bell to come home.

"Where are you going?" Patrick felt a strange panic.

He slipped off his backpack and stepped into the lake. Water seeped into his boots.

"Come back!" He trudged after the sparkles that lured him onward, deeper and deeper. "Stop!" When he was waist-deep, he took another step, and the rocky floor beneath him disappeared. He plunged in with a splash.

Opening his eyes in the dark, murky water, he stretched his arms to swim to the surface, but paused when he noticed that the sparkles had stopped moving.

In fact, they were drawing closer.

The unusual happiness swelled in Patrick again.

He watched with amazement as they hovered about two feet from his face, as if observing him, appearing even more luminous underwater. The bright flashes came more quickly, like the beats of a pounding heart.

The darkness underneath him illuminated.

Patrick dropped his gaze and saw a mass of sparkles rising from the depths like an incandescent cloud. The glare from the light they radiated was so intense that he could barely look at them. Panic bloomed in his chest, urging him to escape while he still could. Another part of him overruled the instinct.

His craving for the immense joy grew the closer the cloud came. It was the joy he had ached for his entire, miserable life, a feeling that he had become addicted to the moment the sparkles had touched his calloused hand.

His lungs burned, and his head grew dizzy. Grudgingly, he swam up to the surface, took a gulp of air, and submerged again, right into the cluster of sparkles.

Blinded by their collective brightness, he jerked away in surprise, but before he had time to process what was going on, the sparkles attacked. They rushed into his ears, up his nose, and into the open wound on his cheek, flowing into him like relentless rivers of light.

Terror-stricken, Patrick clawed his way through the water while the invaders continued to swarm into his body. His toe kicked a rock, and he sprung to his feet, screaming. He lifted frantic hands to paw at his ears, when suddenly his fingers dissolved into water.

It's impossible to describe what Patrick felt as he watched his hands fall away into droplets—then his forearms and upper arms, which poured from the empty coat and shirtsleeves, leaving them dangling limply at his sides. Fear, disbelief, denial . . . Yet over top of all the expected emotions, he felt one he would have never expected to feel when his life was coming to an end.

Euphoria.

It was as if an internal choir of angels celebrated in song as his physical core gave way like a ruptured dam. A sweet, cherubic voice caressed his mind with a promise:

*You will be a new man.*

Patrick exploded into water.

# Acknowledgments

Many thanks to:

My family for their encouragement and unwavering support. I love you all!

My sister, Stacey, for helping with revisions. I'm eternally grateful, Stacey, and had a blast!

William Greenleaf for always polishing my work so beautifully.

Kelly Carter for the fantastic cover art.

David C. Cassidy for the ultra-cool cover design and book blurb.

Amy Eye for the fabulous formatting.

My dad, Peter, the historian, for choosing the name Queen Kiya and confirming that her tomb curse was plausible— sort of.

Zach Fortier for the firearm advice. "The zombie killer"— how perfect is that!

My Facebook contest winner, Dion, for furnishing the name Shana Carlos.

Charlotte for providing the name Lucretia Burns, and Anna and McKenna for the name Natalie Fletcher. Please thank your parents for supporting our school in the spring auction.

Last but certainly not least, Cassidy's fans. Thank you for joining me on her journey. I look forward to continuing it with you.

Elise Stokes lives in Washington State with her husband and their four children, where she is at work on Cassidy's next exciting adventure.

Visit www.cassidyjonesadventures.com
www.facebook.com/Cassidy.Jones.Adventures
www.facebook.com/Cassidy.Jones.Adventures.Series
www.twitter.com/CassidyJonesAdv

## Books in the Cassidy Jones Adventures series:

*Cassidy Jones and the Secret Formula*
*Cassidy Jones and Vulcan's Gift*
*Cassidy Jones and the Seventh Attendant*
*Cassidy Jones and the Luminous (Coming 2014)*

Made in the USA
Lexington, KY
23 October 2015